Foods of India

DAL

MONA VERMA

Illustrations
SUHITA MITRA

B&S

Body & Soul Books

ISBN 978-93-81576-14-4
© Mona Verma, 2014

Cover, Illustrations & Artworks Suhita Mitra
Printing Repro India Pvt Ltd

Published in India, 2014
BODY & SOUL BOOKS
An imprint of
LEADSTART PUBLISHING PVT LTD
Trade Centre, Level 1, Bandra Kurla Complex, Bandra (E), Mumbai 400 051, INDIA
T + 91 22 40700804   F +91 22 40700800 E info@leadstartcorp.com W www.leadstartcorp.com

US Office Axis Corp, 7845 E Oakbrook Circle, Madison, WI 53717, USA

To my late Chachaji, Prem & Chachiji, Durupadi ~
who brought me up as their daughter
during my adolescent years

ABOUT THE AUTHOR

Mona Verma (*nee* Pahlajani) was born in 1940, in Sukker, Pakistan, before the fateful events of Partition. Following an Intermediate in Arts from Bhopal University, her interest in cookery took wing after marriage. She learnt the art of cookery by attending classes and experimenting on her own with ingredients and flavours. In 1968, she started her own cookery classes in Calcutta, which became extremely popular, and she was soon appointed cookery teacher for graduate students at St. Loretto's Convent. In 1971, she moved to Mumbai and so did her cookery classes. The fact that, at one time, 13 of her students were running their own cookery classes is a tribute to her skill both as a cook as well as a teacher. For many years she also conducted Finishing Courses for final year students at Vivekanand Education Trust's High School & College. Mona has varied social interests. She has been actively involved with the Lion's Movement; served on the board of *Seva Samiti*, a charitable trust working for needy women; and is an active member of the National Council of Women in India (Nagpur Chapter). She is also a poet and student of Indian classical music. Writing is one of her many passions and her articles have appeared in many newspapers and magazines. She continues to write a Sunday cookery column for *The Hitavada*. Her book, *Fasting Foods Of India* has been published by Leadstart Publishing as part of the *Foods Of India* series. Mona lives in Nagpur with her husband Asoka, a Management Consultant. Mona can be reached at: monaverma@sancharnet.in

ABOUT THE ILLUSTRATOR

Suhita Mitra was born in Kohima, Nagaland – a region of untouched, natural beauty. Wherever the eye travelled, there were hills, trees, flowers and wildlife. Television was still unknown and all that young children had to amuse them was the enchantment offered by the gardens, the playing fields and books… lots of story books. Such an environment was a natural nursery for the imagination. Suhita joined the National Institute Of Design, Ahmedabad, where the untrammeled imagination fostered by her childhood environment suddenly found meaningful channels through art appreciation, photography, freehand drawing, animation and typography. With her love of nature, she feels inspired to give back through her work as an illustrator and designer. Suhita can be reached at: suhita.mitra@gmail.com

CONTENTS

Contents

6

7

8

INTRODUCTION

Welcome to the exotic world of *dal*s. This book presents an imaginative and creative range of recipes to tempt even the most reluctant partaker. *Dal* is a nutrient-rich and essential part of Indian meals. It is served thrice in a *thali* – *dal* with rice, *dal* with *roti* and *dal* with vegetables. In Indian cuisine, *dal* and rice form staple fare and everyone has their own favourite variations.

The art of Indian cooking lies in the careful blending of different spices to yield subtle variations in flavours. The classic tastes of Indian food are characterised by *shata rasas* (7 flavours) – sweet, salty, sour, hot, pungent, bitter and astringent. Indian *dal* preparations are replete with them all. One of the most important characteristics of *dal*s is their ability to blend with any spices, herbs and even non-vegetarian ingredients. They are universally inclusive. Whether one is a good cook or not really depends on one's delicate touch with spices. It is also why Indian mothers begin teaching their children to cook, with *dal*s, as most spices and ingredients can be mixed into *dal*s. Thus novices become well versed with different ingredients and spices and cultivate a sense of smell and colour. This book will be of great help to both teachers and learners.

This collection is a celebration of the best of the numerous varieties of *dal* dishes. It is my desire to introduce to you the amazing nature of *dal*s which can be mixed and matched with any spice or herb and a pinch of imagination, basic knowledge and taste. *Dal* delicacies have always been the 'in' thing in every generation so I have attempted to present age-old *dal* preparations in new, different and unique ways. The recipes are not the usual restaurant fare. While some may be exotic, they are also easy to make, inexpensive, and a gourmet's delight.

Desi ghee/fats have been used to make food rich but the amazing thing about this cuisine is that cooking is only complete when the food oozes out the fat. This can then be drained and reused as it now has the added value of all the spices and flavours. The cuisine presented is a little spicy yet not excessively hot. Health considerations have also been given due importance in writing this book. Every recipe is tried and tested until perfect. Accuracy in measurements is another thing you can count on.

Rich *dal*s are usually made during holidays and festive occasions which makes their appearance at the table more rare. I have provided a range of *dal*s for different occasions as well as for day-to-day cooking. The soups and salads are most uncommon. It a common practice in south India to offer *Sundal* packets with betel nuts and *kum-kum* to guests during *Dassera* or *Navaratri,* as divine food of the gods. The tangy and spicy *chaat*s and *bhel*s are of course, mouthwatering delicacies. The snacks and sandwiches are presented as all-time favourites for morning or late afternoon food. The hot *vada*s, with any local drink, on cold evenings or rainy days, is something to enjoy and relish while sitting in an arm-chair near a window. Every region has its own popular snacks and I have collected and included many of these.

*Dal*s in different forms with different consistencies like curry, *kadhi*, liquid and semi-liquid, etc., have been included keeping in mind diverse eating habits. There are many surprises in the non-vegetarian section as well. Finally the *dal mithai*s are totally new – unheard of, unexpected, never-thought-of, but are very easy to make.

Now all you need to do is invite your family and friends to the table and enjoy meals to remember!

BASIC RECIPES

- Note on Green Chillies
- Bhel Masala
- Chaat Masala
- Nariyal Ka Dudh
- Dhania Jeera Powder
- Curry Powder
- Garam Masala Powder
- Panch Phoran
- Sambar Masala Powder
- Imli Ka Guda
- Thalipeeth Ka Atta
- Ankur Phootna
- Daalia Aur Dhania Ki Chutney
- Tuvar Dal Chutney
- Pudina Aur Imli Ki Chutney
- Khatti Meethi Chutney for Bhel
- Teekhi Chutney for Bhel
- Saunth Chutney for Kabuli Chana Aloo Ring Chaat
- Khatti Meethi Chutney for Papdi Pakodi Aloo Chaat
- Hari Chutney for Papdi Pakodi Aloo Chaat
- Khatti Meethi Chutney for Chana Papdi Sandwich Chaat
- Hari Chutney for Chana Papdi Sandwich Chaat
- Lassan Chutney for Thalipeeth
- Chana Dal Chutney for Chana Dal Kothimbir Vadi
- Hari Chutney for Urad Dal Idli
- Daalia Aur Pudine Ki Chutney for Handwa
- Nariyal ki Chutney for Adai
- Meethi Chutney for Dal Pakwan
- Saunth Chutney for Khasta Kachori
- Teekhi Chutney for Ragda Pattice
- Meethi Chutney for Ragda Pattice
- Dhania Dal Ka Mukhwas

NOTE ON GREEN CHILLIES

Green chillies are one of the ruling herbs and spices in Indian cuisines. There are many varieties of chillies and these are used in numerous ways. This book has used green chillies, mostly in minced form, for the following reasons.

1. Easy to mince in a mincer or with mortar and pestle.
2. Avoids burning of hands while chopping.
3. Makes food tastier.
4. Can be eaten in dishes, unlike larger pieces of green chillies which are often too hot to be consumed.

Note If desired you can use in any other form also

BHEL MASALA

INGREDIENTS
Weight: 75 gms
1 tbsp cumin seeds
1 tbsp coriander seeds
½ tsp black pepper corns, roasted and powdered
1 tsp black salt
25 gms mango powder (*amchur*)
½ tsp ginger powder (*saunth*)

METHOD
1. Combine all the ingredients in a bowl and mix well.
2. Store in an airtight jar and use as required.

CHAAT MASALA

INGREDIENTS
Weight: 150 gms
1¼ tsp red chilli powder
1¼ tsp mango powder (*amchur*)
1½ tsp coriander powder
1½ tsp powdered sugar
1¼ tsp salt
1¼ tsp black salt

METHOD
1. Combine all the ingredients and mix well in bowl.
2. Store in an airtight jar and use as required.

NARIYAL KA DUDH
Coconut Milk

INGREDIENTS
Weight: ½ cup
½ cup grated fresh coconut
1 cup lukewarm water

METHOD
1. Combine the coconut and half the water and blend in a blender to get a liquid mixture. Strain through a muslin cloth, squeezing it to get the 'first milk', which is quite thick.
2. Combine the remaining half quantity of water with the residue and blend in a blender. Strain and squeeze to get the 'second milk', which will be fairly thin.

DHANIA JEERA POWDER
Coriander and Cumin Powder

INGREDIENTS
Weight: 50 gms
2 tbsp coriander seeds
2 tbsp cumin seeds
½ tsp black peppercorns
½ tsp whole asafoetida (*hing*)

METHOD
1.   Roast all the ingredients in a dry pan. Remove and cool for a while.
2.   Grind the cooled ingredients in a grinder to obtain a smooth powder.
3.   Store in an airtight jar and use as required.

14

CURRY POWDER

INGREDIENTS
Weight: 50 gms
3 tbsp coriander seeds, roasted for few minutes
1 tbsp mustard seeds, roasted till they splutter
3 tbsp cumin seeds, roasted till they splutter
1 tsp black peppercorns, roasted till they are hot
1 tsp fenugreek seeds, roasted till reddish brown
20-25 curry leaves, gently fried for few seconds, taking care not to burn them
10 small whole red chillies, roasted in sesame oil

METHOD
1.   Combine all the ingredients and grind in a grinder to make a fine powder.
2.   Store in an airtight jar and use as required.

Garam Masala Powder

Ingredients
Weight: 50 gms
2 tsp oil
4 tbsp cumin seeds
3 tbsp coriander seeds
6 bay leaves
1 tbsp black peppercorns
1 tbsp cloves
5" cinnamon stick
1½ tbsp big cardamoms, pods removed
1 tbsp green cardamoms, pods removed
1 tbsp black cumin seeds
¾ tbsp mace (*javitri*)
¼" nutmeg (*jaiphal*)

Method
1. Heat oil in a pan and separately fry each of the spices for few seconds. Remove.
2. Combine all the fried spices. Grind in a grinder to form a smooth powder.
3. Sieve the powder and store in an airtight jar. Use as required.

PANCH PHORAN

INGREDIENTS
Weight: 75 gms
2 tbsp mustard seeds
2 tbsp cumin seeds
1 tbsp fenugreek seeds
2 tbsp aniseed/fennel seeds (*saunf*)
1 tbsp black onion seeds

METHOD
1. Combine all the ingredients and store in a jar.
2. Shake well before use.

16

SAMBAR MASALA POWDER

INGREDIENTS
Weight: 100 gms
1 tsp oil
¾ cup coriander seeds
¼ cup cumin seeds
1 tsp mustard seeds
1 tsp fenugreek seeds
3 whole red chillies, broken
1 tbsp Bengal gram (*chana dal*)
1 tbsp black beans (*urad dal*)
1 tsp turmeric powder
½ tsp asafoetida (*hing*)

METHOD
1. Heat oil in a pan, and separately fry ingredients (except turmeric and asafoetida) for a few seconds. Remove.
2. Combine all the fried spices and grind to a smooth powder.
3. Add the turmeric and asafoetida and mix well.
4. Sieve the powder and store in an airtight jar. Use as required.

IMLI KA GUDA
Tamarind Pulp

INGREDIENTS
Weight: 150 gms
100 gms / 4 tbsp tamarind
100 ml lukewarm water

METHOD
1. Combine the tamarind and water and set aside for 30 minutes.
2. Mash, squeeze and strain through a muslin cloth to get a thick pulp. Discard the residue.
3. To get a thin pulp, add more water and dilute.

THALIPEETH KA ATTA
Flour for Thalipeeth

INGREDIENTS

To make: 18 *Thalipeeths*

¾ cup mung beans (*moong dal*)

¾ cup black beans (*urad dal*)

¾ cup Bengal gram (*chana dal*)

1¼ cup millet flour (*bajri ka atta*)

1¼ cup milo flour (*jawari ka atta*)

1¼ rice (*chawal*)

4 tbsp coriander seeds

4 tbsp cumin seeds

1 tbsp black peppercorns

4 cloves

METHOD

1. Roast all the spices separately and set aside
2. Combine all the ingredients, mix well and grind to a fine powder
3. Store in an airtight tin and use as required.

Note: It is also possible to get readymade flour

ANKUR PHOOTNA
Sprouting Methods

METHOD I
How to sprout without a sprout maker

1. Soak the lentils/beans/grams to be sprouted in sufficient water overnight.
2. Next morning drain, rinse and place the lentil/beans/gram in a wet muslin cloth. Set aside for 24 hours in a warm place.
   Sprinkle a little water.
3. The sprouting time differs for various grains. After sprouting, wash in warm water and use as required.

METHOD II
How to sprout in a sprout maker

1. Soak the lentils/beans/grams overnight.
2. The lentils/beans/grams should not be dry and should have some moisture when put into a sprout maker.
3. Leave for 24 hours in a sprout maker at room temperature (i.e. 22-26 degrees).
4. Do not keep the sprout maker in a dark place.
5. Place only one type of lentil/bean/gram in each bowl of the sprout maker.
6. Always retain some water in the water container.
7. Remove the lentils/beans/grams as soon as they sprout and do not leave for a long time in order to avoid fungus.
8. Remove and keep the sprouts in the fridge and use within a few days.
9. Clean the sprout maker well before and after use.

DAALIA AUR DHANIA KI CHUTNEY
Roasted Split Bengal Gram & Coriander Chutney

INGREDIENTS
Makes: 1 small bowl
4 tbsp coriander leaves, roughly chopped
3 tbsp roasted Bengal gram *(daalia)*
1 tbsp peanuts
1 capsicum, roughly chopped
1 tsp ginger, roughly chopped
1 tsp green chillies, roughly chopped
1 tbsp mint leaves, roughly chopped
1 pinch turmeric powder
¾ tsp salt
1½ tsp sugar
4 tbsp water

20

METHOD
1. Combine all the ingredients and grind to form a coarse paste.
2. Remove into a serving bowl. Serve with *moong dal cheela* or *kababs*.

TUVAR DAL CHUTNEY
Pigeon Peas Chutney

INGREDIENTS
Weight: 300 gms
125 gms (½ cup) pigeon peas (*tuvar dal*), roasted to a light brown & cooled
4 whole red chillies
1 tsp chopped ginger
6 garlic cloves
½ cup grated dry coconut
25 gms tamarind
15-20 curry leaves
½ tsp salt
1 tsp sugar

METHOD
1. Combine all the ingredients and grind to a smooth paste.
2. Remove into a serving bowl. Serve with *rotis or parathas*.

PUDINA AUR IMLI KI CHUTNEY
Mint & Tamarind Chutney

INGREDIENTS
Makes: ½ cup
25 gms tamarind, pulped
10 tbsp mint leaves, roughly chopped
2 tbsp coriander leaves, roughly chopped
1" piece ginger, roughly chopped
2 garlic cloves, roughly chopped
4 - 6 green chillies, roughly chopped
1 tsp sugar

METHOD
Combine all the ingredients and grind to a smooth chutney. Remove into a serving bowl and serve as desired.

KHATTI MEETHI CHUTNEY for BHEL
Sweet & Sour Chutney for Bhel

INGREDIENTS
Weight: 240 gms
½ cup dates (*khajur*), deseeded
3 tbsp tamarind, pulped
¼ tsp salt
1 tsp sugar
Water as required.

METHOD
Combine all the ingredients and grind to a smooth paste. Remove into a bowl and use as an accompaniment to *bhel*.

Teekhi Chutney for Bhel
Spicy Chutney for Bhel

Ingredients
Weight: 180 gms
1 cup coriander leaves, roughly chopped
½" piece ginger, roughly chopped
1 garlic clove, roughly chopped
3 green chillies, roughly chopped
1 tbsp Bengal gram (*chana dal*), roasted
¼ tsp salt
1 cup water

Method
Combine all the ingredients and grind to a smooth paste. Remove into a bowl and use as an accompaniment to *bhel*.

Teekhi Chutney for Pani Puri
Spicy Chutney for Pani Puri

Ingredients
Weight: 50 gms
4 tbsp coriander leaves, roughly chopped
3 green chillies, roughly chopped
¼ tsp salt
¼ cup water

Method
Combine all the ingredients and grind in a grinder to a coarse chutney. Remove into a bowl and use as an accompaniment with *pani puri*.

SAUNTH CHUTNEY for KABULI CHANA ALOO RING CHAAT
Ginger Powder Chutney for Kabuli Chana Aloo Ring Chaat

INGREDIENTS
Makes: ¾ cup
½ tsp ginger powder (*saunth*)
3 tbsp jaggery
1 tbsp mango powder (*amchur*)
½ tsp cumin powder
½ tsp *garam masala* powder
½ tsp red chilli powder
½ tsp salt
¼ cup water

24

METHOD
Place a pan on the stove and add all the ingredients. Stir for a few minutes till the chutney is slightly thick. Remove into a bowl and use with *kabuli chana chaat*.

KHATTI MEETHI CHUTNEY for PAPDI PAKODI ALOO CHAAT
Sweet & Sour Chutney for Papdi Pakodi Aloo Chaat

INGREDIENTS
Weight: 240 gms
75 gms tamarind, pulped
½ cup jaggery
½ tsp black cumin powder
½ tsp *garam masala* powder
½ tsp red chilli powder
¾ tsp salt
1 drop edible red colour
1¼ cup water

METHOD
Place a pan on the stove and add all the ingredients. Stir till chutney becomes slightly thick. Remove, strain and use with *papdi pakodi aloo chaat.*

HARI CHUTNEY for PAPDI PAKODI ALOO CHAAT
Green Chutney for Papdi Pakodi Aloo Chaat

INGREDIENTS
Makes: ¾ cup
1 tbsp roasted Bengal gram
1 tsp cumin seeds, roasted
3 green chillies, chopped
4 tbsp coriander leaves, chopped
4 tbsp mint leaves, chopped
½ tbsp lime juice
½ tsp salt
½ tbsp sugar
¼ cup water

26

METHOD
Combine all the ingredients and grind to a smooth paste. Remove into a bowl and use with *papdi pakodi aloo chaat*.

KHATTI MEETHI CHUTNEY for CHANA PAPDI SANDWICH CHAAT

Sweet & Sour Chutney for Chana Papdi Sandwich Chaat

INGREDIENTS
Makes: 1 cup

3½ tbsp jaggery
50 gms tamarind, pulped
1 tsp salt
1 tsp *garam masala* powder
1 tbsp cumin seeds, roasted and powdered
½ tsp red chilli powder
1¼ cup water

METHOD
1. Combine all the ingredients and place in a pan. Boil till chutney becomes thick.
2. Remove, strain and use for *chana papdi sandwich chaat*.

HARI CHUTNEY for CHANA PAPDI SANDWICH CHAAT
Green Chutney for Chana Papdi Sandwich Chaat

INGREDIENTS
Makes: ¼ cup
1 cup mint leaves, chopped
1 cup coriander leaves, chopped
3 green chillies, chopped
2 tbsp peanuts
1 tbsp sugar
1 tbsp lime juice
1 tbsp cumin seeds
1 tsp salt
¼ cup water

METHOD
Combine all the ingredients and grind to a very smooth chutney. Remove and use for *chana papdi sandwich chaat*.

LASSAN CHUTNEY for THALIPEETH
Garlic Chutney for Thalipeeth

INGREDIENTS
Weight: 100 gms
15-20 garlic cloves
2 tbsp desiccated coconut
2 tbsp peanuts, roasted
1 tsp red chilli powder
1 tsp salt

METHOD
Combine all the ingredients and grind to a smooth chutney. Remove and serve with *thalipeeth*.

CHANA DAL CHUTNEY for CHANA DAL KOTHIMBIR VADI
Bengal Gram Chutney for Chana Dal Kothimbir Vadi

INGREDIENTS
Makes: ½ cup.
2 tbsp fried Bengal gram (*chana dal*)
2 tbsp chopped coriander leaves
2 tbsp grated dry coconut
1 tsp chopped ginger
1 garlic clove, chopped
¼ tsp chopped green chillies
2 whole red chillies
3 tsp lime juice
10-15 curry leaves
½ tsp sugar
½ tsp salt

METHOD
Combine all the ingredients and grind to a fine paste. Remove into a serving bowl and serve with *chana dal kothimbir vadi*.

HARI CHUTNEY for URAD DAL IDLI
Green Chutney for Urad Dal Idli

INGREDIENTS
Makes: ½ cup.
½ cup coriander leaves, finely chopped
1 tsp ginger, finely chopped
2 green chillies, finely chopped
¼ tbsp grated fresh coconut
¼ tsp salt
1/8 cup water
2 tsp lime juice
1 tbsp oil
½ tsp mustard seeds
1/8 tsp asafoetida *(hing)*

METHOD
1. Combine the coriander leaves, ginger, green chillies, coconut, salt, water and lime juice and grind to form a smooth paste.
2. Heat oil in a frying pan and the add mustard seeds and asafoetida. Fry till seeds pop. Pour this over the chutney and mix well. Remove into a serving bowl and serve with *urad dal idli*.

DAALIA AUR PUDINE KI CHUTNEY for HANDWA
Roasted Split Bengal Gram & Mint Leaves Chutney for Handwa

INGREDIENTS
Weight: 200 gms
25 gms split husked roasted Bengal gram (*daalia*), roasted again
3 tbsp mint leaves, finely chopped
3 tbsp coriander leaves, finely chopped
25 gms peanuts, roasted
25 gms grated fresh coconut
2 tbsp tamarind pulp
1" piece ginger, chopped
4 garlic cloves, chopped
4 green chillies, chopped
½ tsp salt
1 tsp sugar

32

METHOD
Combine all the ingredients and grind to form a coarse thick chutney.
Remove into a serving bowl and use as an accompaniment with *handwa*.

NARIYAL KI CHUTNEY for ADAI
Coconut Chutney for Adai

INGREDIENTS

Makes: 200 gms

150 gms (1 small) fresh coconut, grated
50 gms raw mango, grated
6 green chillies, roughly chopped
2½ tbsp fried Bengal gram *(chana dal)*
2 tbsp coriander leaves, finely chopped
1 tsp salt
2 tbsp oil
½ tsp mustard seeds
½ tsp cumin seeds
2 whole red chillies, broken
8 curry leaves

METHOD

1. Combine the coconut, mango, chillies, Bengal gram, coriander leaves and salt. Grind to form a coarse paste. Set aside.
2. Heat oil in a frying pan and add the mustard and cumin seeds, whole red chillies and curry leaves. Stir and fry for few minutes.
3. Pour this over the chutney and mix well. Remove into a bowl and serve with *adai*.

MEETHI CHUTNEY for DAL PAKWAN
Sweet Chutney for Dal Pakwan

INGREDIENTS
Makes: ½ cup
50 gms jaggery
2 tbsp tamarind pulp
½ tsp red chilli powder
¼ tsp *garam masala* powder
¼ cup water
½ tsp salt

METHOD
1. Place a pan on the stove and add the jaggery and tamarind pulp. Mix and stir well.
2. Add the salt, red chilli and *garam masala* powders, and water. Stir till slightly thick. Remove into a bowl and serve with *dal pakwan*.

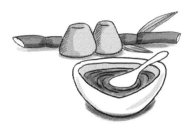

SAUNTH CHUTNEY for KHASTA KACHORI
Ginger Chutney for Khasta Kachori

INGREDIENTS
Makes: ½ cup
50 gms jaggery, grated
5 tsp mango powder (*amchur*)
½ tsp cumin powder
½ tsp red chilli powder
1½ tsp ginger powder (*saunth*)
½ tsp *garam masala* powder
¾ tsp salt
1 cup water

METHOD
Place pan on the stove and add in all the ingredients. Stir and cook for 1-2 minutes till the chutney changes colour and becomes slightly thick. Remove into a bowl and serve with *khasta kachori*.

TEEKHI CHUTNEY for RAGDA PATTICE
Hot Chutney for Ragda Pattice

INGREDIENTS
Weight: 200 gms

7 whole red chillies, soaked in ¼ cup hot water, for 30 minutes
1" piece ginger, roughly chopped
15 garlic cloves, roughly chopped
½ tsp turmeric powder
1 tbsp lime juice
¾ tsp salt
4 tbsp water

METHOD

36

Combine all the ingredients and grind to form a coarse chutney. Remove into a bowl and serve with *ragda pattice*.

MEETHI CHUTNEY for RAGDA PATTICE
Sweet Chutney for Ragda Pattice

INGREDIENTS
Weight: 200 gms
25 gms tamarind, pulped
½ cup jaggery, grated and soaked in ½ cup water
¾ tsp salt
1 tsp ginger powder (*saunth*)
1 tsp cumin powder
½ tsp *garam masala* powder
½ tsp red chilli powder

METHOD
1. Place a pan on the stove and add in all the ingredients. Stir and cook till the chutney becomes slightly thick.
2. Remove, cool and serve with *ragda pattice*.

DHANIA DAL KA MUKHWAS
Coriander Seed Lentil Mouth Freshner

INGREDIENTS
Makes: 400 gms

100 gms (10 tbsp) coriander seed lentil (*dhania dal*), roasted till crisp

100 gms (10 tbsp) aniseed/fennel seeds (*saunf*), stems removed by rubbing between the palms

4 tsp lime juice

½ tsp black salt

30 gms (4 tbsp) carum seeds (*ajwain*)

2 tsp lime juice

¼ tsp black salt

50 gms (5 tbsp) sweet aniseed (*churi varially*)

100 gms dry coconut, cut into thin flakes and roasted

30 gms (3 tbsp) sesame seeds (*til*), roasted

25 gms (2 tbsp) kernel seeds (*char magaz)*, roasted

½ tsp salt

METHOD
1. Mix the aniseed, lime juice and black salt. Rub well and leave overnight. Next morning, dry in the sun for 2 days or roast in a microwave for a few minutes or roast in a dry pan. Set aside.
2. Mix the carum seeds, lime juice and black salt. Rub well and leave overnight. Next morning dry in the sun for 2 days or roast in a microwave for few minutes or roast in a dry pan. Set aside.
3. Combine all the ingredients in a big bowl. Add the sweet aniseed and ½ tsp of salt. Mix lightly with your hands.
4. Store in an airtight jar and use after meals as a digestive / mouth freshner.

38

SOUPS & APPETISERS

- Ankurit Channe Aur Phalli Shorba
- Bhuni Moong Dal Ka Shorba
- Dal Aur Sabji Ka Shorba
- Masoor Dal Shorba
- Nariyal Aur Dal Shorba
- Tuvar Dal Shorba
- Masoor Dal Rasam
- Tuvar Dal Amti
- Tuvar Dal aur Tamater Rasam
- Tuvar Dal Rasam

ANKURIT CHANNE AUR PHALLI SHORBA
Sprouted Grams & Beans Soup

INGREDIENTS
Serves: 6
For the Soup
1 cup mixed *dal*s & beans, comprising:
  sprouted white chickpeas (*kabuli chana*)
  sprouted black chickpeas (*kala chana*)
  sprouted whole mung beans (*sabut moong*)
  sprouted moth beans (*matki*)
  sprouted cow peas (*chavli*)
2 tbsp butter
1 big onion, finely chopped
3 cloves garlic, minced
1 medium-sized tomato
1 tsp salt
½ tsp black pepper powder
6 cups water
¼ tsp mint powder
10-12 mint leaves, finely chopped

For the Garnish
50 gms (2 cubes) cheese, grated

40

METHOD
1. Heat butter in a pressure cooker.
2. Add the onion and fry till light brown.
3. Add the sprouted grams and beans. Stir and fry for a few minutes.
4. Add the garlic, tomato, salt and black pepper powder. Fry for a few seconds.
5. Add water and close the pressure cooker. Cook under pressure for 10-15 minutes. Allow the pressure to fall on its own before opening the cooker.
6. Remove and strain the mixture. Set aside as the soup stock.
7. Blend the residue in a blender and squeeze through a muslin cloth.
8. Discard the residue and mix the squeezed liquid with the ready soup stock.
9. Pour the soup mixture into the saucepan and place on the stove. Allow the soup to simmer for a few minutes.
10. Add the mint powder and mint leaves. If desired, add 1 tbsp butter.
11. Serve hot in a soup bowl garnished with grated cheese.

BHUNI MOONG DAL KA SHORBA
Mung Beans Soup

INGREDIENTS
Serves: 6
For the Soup
250 gms (1 cup) mung beans (*moong dal*)
2 cups water
1 tsp cumin powder
1½ tsp coriander powder
¼ tsp turmeric powder
½ tsp red chilli powder
1 tsp salt
1 tsp sugar

For the Tempering
50 gms (2 tbsp) butter
2 tsp cumin seeds
4 bay leaves
2 tbsp finely chopped coriander leaves

For the Garnish
50 gms (2 cubes) cheese, grated

METHOD
1. Heat a dry pan and add the moong *dal* and roast till light brown.
2. Remove and cool for 8 to 10 minutes. Wash in water.
3. Place the *dal* and water in a saucepan and boil for a few minutes.
4. Add the powdered spices, then cover and cook on low heat for 15 minutes.
5. Add salt and sugar. Stir and cook for about 15 minutes till *dal* is tender.
6. Heat butter in a saucepan.
7. Add the cumin seeds. When they splutter, add the bay leaves and fry for a few seconds. Pour in the cooked *dal* mixture and stir.
8. Serve hot in a soup bowl, garnished with cheese.

42

Dal aur Sabji ka Shorba
Lentil & Vegetable Soup

INGREDIENTS
Serves: 6
For the Stock
150 gms bottle gourd (*lauki*), roughly chopped
150 gms white pumpkin (*bhopla*), roughly chopped
150 gms tomato, roughly chopped
150 gms onion, roughly chopped
6 cups water

For the Soup
1 cup mixed lentils comprising:
 Pigeon peas (*tuvar dal*)
 Bengal gram (*chana dal*)
 Mung beans (*moong dal*)
 Red lentil (*masoor dal*)
2 tbsp rice, picked, washed & strained
3 tbsp butter, salted
2 large onions, finely chopped
1½ tsp salt
1½ tsp black pepper powder

For the Garnish
8 – 10 mint leaves
4 slices of bread, cubed & fried to make croutons
OR
50 gms cottage cheese (*paneer*) cubed & fried

METHOD

1. Put the vegetables and water in a pressure cooker and cook under pressure for 30 minutes. Allow pressure to fall on its own before opening the cooker. Remove.
2. Strain the stock through a fine sieve and discard the residue or squeeze the stock through a muslin cloth and discard the residue. Set aside.
3. Heat butter in a saucepan and add the onion. Fry till golden brown.
4. Add the *dals* and rice. Stir and fry for 2-3 minutes.
5. Add the vegetable stock. Add salt & black pepper and simmer for two minutes.
6. Put the entire mixture into a pressure cooker. Cook under pressure for 30 minutes. Allow pressure to fall on its own before opening the cooker.
7. Remove, cool and blend in a blender. Pass through a sieve.
8. Pour the soup into a saucepan and allow it to come to a boil twice. Remove.
9. Serve hot in a soup bowl, garnished with mint leaves and croutons/*paneer* cubes.

44

MASOOR DAL SHORBA
Red Lentil Soup

INGREDIENTS
Serves: 6
For the Soup
1 tbsp butter
1 medium-sized onion, finely chopped
125 gms (½ cup) red lentil (*masoor dal*), cleaned & washed
50 gms (2 tbsp) rice, picked & washed
1 medium-sized carrot, grated

1 small tomato, cut into 4
1 tsp salt
½ tsp black pepper powder
1½ tsp curry powder
5 cups water
1 tbsp lime juice

For the Garnish
½ tsp finely chopped coriander leaves

METHOD
1. Heat butter in a saucepan and add the onion. Stir and fry till the onion is translucent.
2. Add the *dal* and rice. Stir for a few minutes.
3. Add the carrot, tomato, salt, black pepper powder and curry powder. Stir till well mixed.
4. Add water. Transfer into a pressure cooker and cook under pressure for 20-25 minutes. Allow the pressure to fall on its own before opening the cooker.
5. Remove the soup into a bowl and allow it to cool for 8-10 minutes. Blend in a blender.
6. Pass through a strainer and discard the residue, if any.
7. Pour the soup into a saucepan and place the pan on the stove and stir and simmer for a few minutes.
8. Remove into a soup bowl and add the lime juice. Mix well.
9. Serve hot, garnished with coriander leaves.

NARYIAL AUR DAL SHORBA
Coconut & Lentil Soup

INGREDIENTS
Serves: 6
For the Soup
125 gms (½ cup) pigeon peas (*tuvar dal*), cleaned, washed
  & soaked for 15 minutes & drained
¼ tsp turmeric powder
1 tsp salt
1 tsp jaggery (*gur*) or demarara sugar
8 cups water for the soup
1 cup vegetable stock
1 cup hot water, for soaking the tamarind
25 gms tamarind, pulped

For the Tempering
2 tbsp oil
½ tsp mustard seeds (*rai*)
8 curry leaves
4 green chillies, finely minced
1 tsp garlic paste
1 cup coconut milk
½ tsp salt
¼ tsp black pepper powder

For the Garnish
1 tbsp finely chopped coriander leaves

NARIYAL AUR DAL SHORBA

METHOD

1. Put all the soup ingredients into a pressure cooker and cook under pressure for 10–15 minutes. Allow pressure to fall on its own before opening the cooker.
2. Remove, cool, mash and then strain through a muslin cloth. Discard the residue.
3. Add the tamarind pulp and mix well. Set aside.
4. Heat oil in a frying pan and add the mustard seeds. When they splutter, add the curry leaves, green chillies and garlic paste. Stir for 2 minutes.
5. Add the soup, coconut milk, salt and black pepper powder. Simmer for a few minutes and then remove.
6. Serve hot in a soup bowl, garnished with coriander leaves.

48

Tuvar Dal Shorba
Pigeon Peas Soup

Ingredients
Serves: 6
For the Soup
125 gms (½ cup) pigeon peas (*tuvar dal*), cleaned & washed
4 cups water
1 tsp coriander powder
1 tsp cumin powder
1 tsp black pepper powder
300 gms. tomatoes, puréed
1 tsp salt
1 tsp butter

For the Garnish
1 tbsp finely chopped coriander leaves
25 gms (1 cube) cheese, grated

Method
1. Cook *tuvar dal* in 4 cups water, under pressure for 8-10 minutes. Allow pressure to fall on its own before opening the cooker.
2. Blend the mixture in a blender to obtain a purée.
3. Put the *dal* purée into a saucepan and place the pan on the stove.
4. Add in all the other ingredients except the butter. Stir and simmer for a few minutes.
5. Add the butter and stir, mixing well.
6. Remove into a soup bowl and serve hot, garnished with coriander leaves and grated cheese.

MASOOR DAL RASAM
Red Lentil Appetiser

INGREDIENTS

Serves: 6

For the *Rasam*

125 gms (½ cup) red lentil (*masoor dal*), cleaned, washed
  & soaked for 15 minutes & drained
2½ cups water
1 green chilli, finely chopped
1 tsp salt
A pinch of turmeric powder

For the Tempering

1 tbsp oil
½ tsp mustard seeds
1 tsp cumin seeds
1 red chilli, broken
6 curry leaves
1 tsp black peppercorns
½ tsp ginger, crushed
½ tsp garlic, crushed
A pinch of asafoetida (*hing*)
3 medium-sized tomatoes, puréed
½ tsp salt
1½ cups water
2 tbsp tamarind pulp
½ tsp shredded jaggery

For the Garnish

1 tbsp finely chopped coriander leaves

METHOD

1. Place all the ingredients for the *masoor dal* into a pressure cooker and cook under pressure for 10 minutes. Allow pressure to fall on its own before opening the pressure cooker.
2. Remove and mash the *dal* to form a purée and set aside.
3. Heat oil in a pan and add the mustard seeds. When they splutter, add the cumin seeds, chilli, curry leaves, black peppercorns, ginger, garlic and asafoetida. Stir for a minute.
4. Add the tomato purée, salt, water, tamarind pulp and jaggery. Stir and cook for a few minutes.
5. Pour the *dal* over the tempering and mix well. Cook covering the pan for a few minutes, on reduced heat.
6. Remove, strain through a muslin cloth and discard the residue.
7. Serve hot, garnished with coriander leaves.

TUVAR DAL AMTI
Pigeon Peas Appetiser

INGREDIENTS
Serves: 6
For the *Amti*
125 gms (½ cup) pigeon peas (*tuvar dal*), cleaned & washed
5 cups water
¼ tsp turmeric powder
1½ tsp salt
2 tbsp tamarind pulp
2 tbsp desiccated coconut
1 tbsp jaggery

For the Tempering

1 tbsp clarified butter (*ghee*)

1 tsp mustard seeds

4 garlic cloves, minced

6 green chillies, minced

8-10 curry leaves

½ tbsp finely chopped coriander leaves.

METHOD

1. Place the *tuvar dal*, water, turmeric powder and salt in a pressure cooker and cook under pressure for 8-10 minutes. Allow the pressure to fall on its own before opening the lid.
2. Add the tamarind pulp, desiccated coconut and jaggery. Cook, stirring occasionally for 2-3 minutes. Set aside.
3. Heat oil in heavy-bottomed pan and add the mustard seeds. When they splutter, add the garlic, green chillies and curry leaves and stir for a few seconds.
4. Pour the *dal* mixture over the tempering and simmer on low heat for about 5-6 minutes.
5. Sprinkle the coriander leaves and stir.
6. Remove into a serving bowl and serve hot.
7. If desired, *amti* can be served with boiled rice.

TUVAR DAL AUR TAMATER RASAM
Pigeon Peas & Tomato Appetiser

INGREDIENTS
Serves: 6
For the *Rasam*
125 gms (½ cup) pigeon peas (*tuvar dal*), clean, washed
 & soaked for 10 minutes & drained
½ tsp clarified butter (*ghee*)
1/8 tsp turmeric
1 tsp salt
2 medium-sized tomatoes, finely chopped
4 cups of water
½ tsp cumin seeds, crushed
½ tsp black peppercorns, crushed
4 cloves garlic, finely minced
½" piece ginger, finely minced
2 tbsp finely chopped coriander leaves
1 tbsp tamarind extract
5-6 curry leaves

For the Tempering
1 tbsp clarified butter (*ghee*)
½ tsp mustard seed
A pinch of asafoetida (*hing*)
One red chilli, broken

METHOD

1. Place the *ghee, tuvar dal*, turmeric, salt, tomato and water into a pressure cooker. Cook under pressure of 6-8 minutes. Allow the pressure to fall on its own before opening the cooker.
2. Remove and strain the mixture. Mash the residual *dal* and tomatoes and strain through a sieve. Discard the final residue.
3. Put the strained *dal* and tomato liquid into a saucepan and add all the other ingredients. Mix well.
4. Heat the *ghee* in a frying pan and add the tempering spices. Fry till they splutter.
5. Pour the tempering over the *dal* and tomato liquid in the saucepan.
6. Put the sauce pan on the stove, stir and cover. Simmer the *rasam* over low heat for a few minutes. Serve hot with boiled rice.

54

TUVAR DAL RASAM
Pigeon Peas Appetiser

INGREDIENTS
Serves: 6
For the *Rasam*
250 gms (1 cup) pigeon peas (*tuvar dal*), cleaned & washed
6 cups water
¾ tsp salt
1/8 tsp turmeric
½ tsp black peppercorns, crushed coarsely
½ tsp cumin seeds, crushed coarsely
4 cloves garlic, crushed coarsely
15 curry leaves, washed
2-3 sprigs of coriander leaves, washed
25 gms tamarind, pulped

For the Tempering

1½ tbsp clarified butter (*ghee*)

½ tsp mustard seeds (*rai*)

3 dried red chillies, broken

METHOD

1. Boil the *dal* with 8 cups of water, in a saucepan.
2. Cook over medium heat for 15 minutes and then on low heat for another 15 minutes, till the *dal* is tender.
3. Remove the clear *dal* liquid on top into a separate bowl and set aside.
4. Add 2 cups of water to the residual thick *dal* in the saucepan. Mix and boil again for a few minutes.
5. Squeeze the mixture to extract the remaining *dal* liquid and mix this with the clear *dal* liquid set aside in the bowl.
6. This process can be repeated until there is finally 4 cups of *dal* liquid, by adding more water to the residual *dal* if necessary. Finally, discard the residue.
7. Season the *dal* liquid by adding all the other ingredients for the *rasam*, including the tamarind extract. Mix well.
8. Heat the *ghee* in a saucepan and add the mustard seeds. When they splutter, add the red chillies. Stir till the red chillies turn brown.
9. Pour the seasoned *dal* mixture into the saucepan for tempering and boil just once.
10. Remove into a serving bowl. *Rasam* has a fresh fragrant tang, if served immediately.

SALADS & ACCOMPANIMENTS

- Baby Corn, Beans Sprouts & Mushroom Salad
- Capsicums, Cottage Cheese, Sprouted Whole Mung Beans & Moth Salad
- Corn Salad
- Koshumbir
- Prawn & Sprouts Salad
- Moong Dal Salad
- Sprouts Salad With Mango & Honey
- Sprouts Salad With Mustard Dressings
- Sprouted Whole Mung Beans, Radish & Curd Salad
- White Chickpeas Salad
- Bhura Chana Sundal I
- Bhura Chana Sundal II
- Chana Dal Sundal
- Moong Dal Sundal
- Ambyachi Dal

BABY CORN, BEAN SPROUTS & MUSHROOM SALAD

This pleasing combination of baby corn & bean sprouts with mushroom,
is a perfect salad for calorie conscious individuals

INGREDIENTS
Serves: 6
2 tbsp olive oil
2 spring onions, sliced into rings
½ tsp grated ginger
2 garlic cloves, grated
8 baby corns, slantingly cut, boiled, rinsed & drained
1 cup bean sprouts, steamed
75 gms raw mushrooms, sliced, boiled & rinsed
½ tsp salt
½ tsp white pepper powder

METHOD
1. Heat olive oil in pan and add the onion rings. Fry till light brown.
2. Add the ginger and garlic and stir for 1 – 2 minutes.
3. Add all other ingredients and mix and stir for 2 minutes.
4. Remove and serve.

Capsicum, Cottage Cheese, Sprouted Whole Mung Beans & Moth Salad

Ingredients
Serves: 6

¼ cup whole mung beans *(sabut moong)*, sprouted
¼ cup moth beans (*matki*), sprouted
4 tbsp water
1 medium-sized capsicum (*Simla mirch*), cut into strips
100 gms cabbage, shredded
50 gms carrot, shredded
100 gms cottage cheese (*paneer)*, cut into big pieces
Butter, for sautéing vegetables & frying *paneer*
A pinch of black pepper powder
2 green chillies, slit into two
2 spring onions, cut into wedges
½ tsp sugar
2 tsp salad oil
½ tsp whole grain French mustard
1 tsp white pepper powder
¼ tsp salt

58

Method
1. Place the sprouts and water in a pan and steam for 2 minutes. Remove.
2. Sauté all the vegetables in butter for 2-3 minutes. Remove.
3. Fry the *cottage cheese* in butter, sprinkling black pepper powder while frying. Remove & cut into small pieces.
4. Mix all the boiled, sautéed and fried ingredients with the remaining ingredients in a bowl and mix well by tossing. Remove into a serving bowl/dish and serve.

CORN SALAD

This is an unusual salad using corn, bean sprouts & mushrooms
with vegetables and pickle oil

INGREDIENTS
Serves: 6
1 corn cobb, cooked in a pressure cooker till tender & kernels removed
½ cup bean sprouts
1 medium-sized potato, boiled, peeled & cubed
5 raw mushrooms, sliced, boiled in salted water & rinsed
1 medium-sized capsicum, cored & cubed
3 spring onions, sliced & severed in rings
1 tbsp finely chopped celery
1 tbsp pickle oil
1 tsp grated ginger
1 tbsp lime juice
½ tsp salt
½ tsp black pepper powder

METHOD
1. Combine the corn, bean sprouts, potato, mushrooms, capsicum and onions. Mix well.
2. Add the remaining ingredients and toss, mixing well.
3. Remove onto a serving bowl/dish and serve.

KOSHUMBIR

A spoonful of this refreshing salad makes a meal complete

INGREDIENTS
Serves: 6

175 gms (¾ cup) Bengal gram (*chana dal*) or split mung beans
  (*moong dal chilka*) cleaned, washed, soaked for 4-6 hours, then drained
1 small carrot, grated
2 small cucumber, finely chopped
½ cup finely chopped cabbage
1 tsp finely chopped green chillies
1 tbsp finely chopped raw mango or 4 tbsp lime juice
1 cup grated fresh coconut
½ tsp salt

60

For the Tempering
2 tbsp oil
1 tsp mustard seeds
A few curry leaves

For the Garnish
3 tbsp finely chopped coriander leaves

METHOD
1. Combine all the salad ingredients together and toss, mixing lightly. Place the *koshumbir* in a salad bowl.
2. Heat oil in pan and add the mustard seeds. When they splutter, add the curry leaves. Remove from heat.
3. Pour the tempering over the *koshumbir*, mixing lightly. Serve garnished with coriander leaves.

Prawn & Sprouts Salad

Ingredients
Serves: 6

2 tbsp mustard oil
1 cup shelled prawns
2¼ cups bean sprouts, boiled
1 medium-sized tomato, finely chopped
6 spring onions, finely chopped
10 whole dried red chillies, fried in mustard oil
¾ cup grated fresh coconut
5 garlic cloves, chopped
2 tbsp finely chopped coriander leaves
½ tsp lime juice
1½ tsp *garam masala* powder
1½ tsp red chilli powder
½ tsp salt
½ head lettuce leaves (*salad patta*)

Method
1. Heat the mustard oil in a pan and add the prawns. Fry quickly till cooked.
2. Add the bean sprouts, tomato, spring onions and saute for a few minutes. Remove.
3. Combine the whole red chillies, mustard oil, coconut, garlic and coriander leaves and grind in a grinder to form a fine coconut mixture.
4. Combine the prawn sprout and coconut mixtures, lime juice, *garam masala* powder, red chilli powder and salt, in a bowl. Mix lightly.
5. Arrange lettuce leaves in a salad bowl. Place the salad in it and serve.

MOONG DAL SALAD

INGREDIENTS
Serves: 6

250 gms (1 cup) mung beans (*moong dal*), picked clean, washed
  & soaked for 2 hours & then drained

½ cup freshly grated coconut

A pinch of asafoetida (*hing*)

2 tbsp finely chopped raw mango

1 tsp finely chopped green chillies

1 tsp salt

1 tbsp finely chopped coriander leaves

2 tsp lime juice

62

METHOD
1. Mix all the ingredients, tossing lightly, in a bowl.
2. Serve as a standalone dish or as an accompaniment.

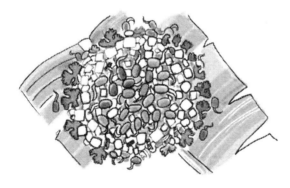

SPROUTS SALAD WITH MANGO & HONEY

INGREDIENTS
Serves: 6
50 gms each of:
  Whole roasted Bengal gram (*bhura chana*), sprouted
  Whole white chickpeas (*kabuli chana*), sprouted
  Whole mung beans (*sabut moong*), sprouted
  Cow peas (*chavli*), sprouted
  Moth beans (*matki*), sprouted
1 medium-sized raw mango, cubed
½ cup freshly grated coconut
1 tbsp finely chopped coriander leaves
½ tsp finely chopped green chillies
1 medium-sized potato, boiled, peeled & cubed
½ tsp salt
1 tbsp honey

For the Garnish
25 gms cheese, grated

METHOD
1. Place the *bhura chana* and *kabuli chana* sprouts in a pressure cooker along with ¾ cup water and cook under pressure for 5-8 minutes. Allow the pressure to fall on its own before opening the cooker. Remove and set aside.
2. Place the *moong*, *chavli* and *matki* sprouts in a pan with ¼ cup water. Place pan on the stove and cook till tender but grains separate. Remove and set aside.
3. Put all the sprouts together in a bowl and add the other ingredients. Mix lightly.
4. Garnish with cheese and serve.

SPROUTS SALAD WITH MUSTARD DRESSING

INGREDIENTS

Serves: 6

50 gms each of:

Whole roasted Bengal gram (*bhura chana*), sprouted

Whole white chickpeas (*kabuli chana*), sprouted

Whole mung beans (*sabut moong*), sprouted

Cow peas (*chavli*), sprouted

Moth beans (*matki*), sprouted

1 medium-sized potato, boiled, peeled & cubed

1 medium-sized tomato, blanched & finely chopped

1 medium-sized cucumber, peeled & cubed

¾ tsp salt

1 tsp salad oil

3 tsp whole grain French mustard salad dressing

To Arrange for Serving

1 head lettuce leaves, washed, thick stems removed & chopped

½ tbsp powdered sugar

9 tbsp thick curd, whisked together with powdered sugar

For the Garnish

1 medium-sized carrot, peeled & grated

½ head lettuce leaves, washed, stem removed & finely chopped

METHOD

1. Place the *bhura chana* and *kabuli chana* sprouts in a pressure cooker along with ¾ cup water. Cook under pressure for 5-8 minutes. Allow the pressure to fall on its own before opening the cooker. Remove and set aside.
2. Place the *moong*, *chavli* and *matki* sprouts in a pan with ¼ cup water. Place pan on the stove and cook till sprouts are tender but separate. Remove and set aside.
3. Put all the sprouts together in a dish.
4. Add the potato, tomato, cucumber and salt and mix lightly.
5. Add the salad oil and rub well.
6. Add the mustard dressing and mix well. Set aside.
7. Take a plate or a big bowl and arrange the lettuce leaves first. Then put the prepared salad on top of the lettuce leaves.
8. Pour the curd over the salad.
9. Garnish with finely chopped lettuce leaves and the grated carrot and serve.

SPROUTED WHOLE MUNG BEANS, RADISH & CURD SALAD

INGREDIENTS
Serves: 6
¼ cup whole mung beans (*sabut moong*), sprouted
4 tbsp water
1 medium-sized radish, grated & leaves chopped off
1 tsp minced ginger
¾ tsp minces green chillies
1 small onion, finely chopped
½ tsp mustard seeds, roasted & pounded
½ tsp cumin powder
1 tbsp powdered sugar
½ tsp salt
1 cup curd, whisked

METHOD
1. Place a thick heavy-bottomed pan on the stove and cook the sprouted beans and water, with a lid on, stirring occasionally for 5-6 minutes, on low heat, till the sprouts are slightly soft.
2. In a bowl, mix the cooked sprouts lightly with all the ingredients except the curd.
3. Pour the curd over the mixture and mix gently.
4. Serve in a serving bowl / dish.

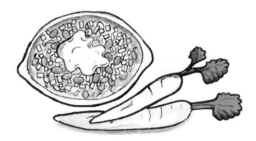

WHITE CHICKPEAS SALAD

INGREDIENTS
Serves: 6

175 gms (¾ cup) whole white chickpeas (*kabuli chana*), cleaned, washed
  & soaked in water with ¼ tsp soda-bi-carb, then drained and rewashed
¾ cup water
1 large-sized potato, boiled, peeled & cubed
1 large-sized tomato, blanched & finely chopped
1 small raw mango, grated
¾ tsp black salt
¾ tsp red chilli powder
¾ tsp dry mint (*pudina*) powder
¾ tsp cumin powder
1 tsp salad oil

For the Garnish
½ tbsp finely chopped coriander leaves

METHOD
1. Place the *kabuli chana* and water in a pressure cooker and cook under pressure for 6-8 minutes. Allow the pressure to fall on its own before opening the cooker. Remove, strain and set aside.
2. Combine the cooked *kabuli chana*, tomato, potato and mango in a bowl.
3. Add all the remaining ingredients and mix lightly.
4. Garnish with coriander leaves and serve.

BHURA CHANA SUNDAL – I
Black Chickpeas Accompaniment

INGREDIENTS
Serves: 6
For the *Dal*
175 gms (¾ cup) black chickpeas (*bhura chana*), washed
  & soaked overnight, then drained
1½ cups water
¾ tsp salt
¼ tsp turmeric powder

For the Tempering
¾ tsp clarified butter (*ghee*)
1½ tsp black beans (*urad dal*)
¾ tsp mustard seeds
¼ tsp asafoetida (*hing)*
½ cup grated fresh coconut
¾ tsp salt

METHOD
1. Place the *bhura chana* along with the water, salt and turmeric powder into a pressure cooker. Cook under pressure for about 5-8 minutes. Allow the pressure to fall on its own before opening the lid. Remove and set aside.
2. Heat the *ghee* in a frying pan and add the mustard seeds. When they splutter, add the *urad dal* and fry till it turns light brown.
3. Add the asafoetida, coconut and salt. Stir, mixing well and fry for 2 mins.
4. Add the cooked *chana*. Stir & mix well.
5. Remove into a serving bowl and serve as an accompaniment.

BHURA CHANA SUNDAL II
Black Chickpeas Accompaniment

INGREDIENTS
Serves: 6
For the *Dal*
175 gms (¾ cup) black chickpeas (*bhura chana*), sprouted
  & boiled in 2½ cups of water
100 gms fresh coconut, finely minced
4 dried whole red chillies, boiled in ¼ cup water (till water dries up)
  & coarsely pounded
1½ tbsp oil
1 tsp salt
½ tsp lime juice
½ tbsp finely chopped coriander leaves (optional)

METHOD
1. Heat the oil in a pan and add the red chillies. Stir for a few seconds on reduced heat.
2. Add the coconut, stir and fry for 2-3 minutes on reduced heat till light brown.
3. Add the *bhura chana*, salt, lime juice and stir for 2-3 minutes.
4. Sprinkle the coriander leaves (optional) and mix lightly.
5. Remove into a serving bowl and serve hot as an accompaniment.

CHANA DAL SUNDAL
Bengal Gram Accompaniment

INGREDIENTS

Serves: 6

For the *Dal*

250 gms (1 cup) Bengal gram (*chana dal*), picked clean, washed
  & soaked for 2 hours & then drained

2 cups water

1 tsp salt

For the Tempering

4 tsp oil

1 tsp mustard seeds

2 pinches of asafoetida (*hing*)

10-15 curry leaves

1½ tsp minced green chillies

2 tsp minced ginger

2 tsp sugar

2 cups grated fresh coconut

2 tsp lime juice

For the Garnish

1 tbsp finely chopped coriander leaves

METHOD

1. Boil the *chana dal*, water and salt in a saucepan till the *dal* is tender. Remove and set aside.
2. Heat the oil in a pan and add the mustard seeds. When they splutter, add the curry leaves and fry for a minute or so till crisp.
3. Add the asafoetida, green chillies and ginger. Fry for 1-2 minutes.

70

4. Add the coconut and sugar. Stir for a few minutes.
5. Add the *dal*. Stir and mix well for a few minutes.
6. Remove into a serving bowl. Add the lime juice and mix well.
7. Garnish with coriander leaves and serve as an accompaniment.

MOONG DAL SUNDAL
Mung Beans Accompaniment

INGREDIENTS
Serves: 6
For the *Dal*
250 gms (1 cup) mung beans (*moong dal*), cleaned, washed & strained
2 tbsp oil
1½ tsp salt
¼ tsp turmeric powder
2 cups water

For the Tempering
4 tbsp oil
1½ tsp mustard seeds
1½ tsp minced green chillies
2 tsp minced ginger
½ cup grated fresh coconut
2 tsp sugar
2 tsp lime juice

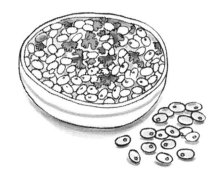

For the Garnish
2 tbsp finely chopped coriander leaves

METHOD
1. Heat the oil in saucepan. Add the *dal*, salt and turmeric powder. Stir and fry for a few minutes.
2. Add the water, cover the pan and cook till the *dal* is tender, the grains separated and the water has evaporated. Remove and set aside.
3. Heat the oil in a pan and add the mustard seeds. When they splutter, add the chillies, ginger, coconut and sugar. Stir and fry for a few minutes.
4. Add the *dal.* Stir for a few minutes.
5. Remove into a serving bowl and add the lime juice. Mix well.
6. Garnish with coriander leaves and serve as an accompaniment.

AMBYACHI DAL
Bengal Gram with Mango

72

INGREDIENTS
Serves: 6
For the *Dal*
250 gms (1 cup) Bengal gram (*chana dal*), cleaned, washed & soaked for 5-6 hrs, then drained
1 small raw mango, peeled & grated
2 tsp sugar
1 tsp salt
½ tsp minced green chillies

For the Tempering
1 tbsp oil
5-6 curry leaves
1 tsp mustard seeds
A pinch of turmeric powder
A pinch of asafoetida (*hing*)
¼ tsp red chilli powder

For the Garnish
1 tbsp finely chopped coriander leaves

METHOD
1. Grind the *dal* coarsely in a grinder.
2. Combine all the other ingredients for the *dal* with the ground *dal*, and mix well. Remove into a serving bowl and set aside.
3. Heat the oil in a frying pan and add the curry leaves and mustard seeds. When they splutter add the other ingredients for tempering and mix well.
4. Pour the tempering over the *dal* mixture.
5. Garnish with the coriander leaves and serve as an accompaniment.

SNACKS & SANDWICHES

- Ankurit Chana Cutlets
- Ankurit Kabab
- Chakli
- Chana Dal aur Arvi ki Patrail
- Chana Dal aur Kamal Kakdi Kabab
- Chana Dal Bada
- Chana Dal Bhajia
- Chana Dal Kothimbir Vadi
- Chana Dal Muthia Kabab
- Dahi Vada
- Dal aur Gobi Ke Patton Ke Patike
- Dal aur Palak ki Vadi
- Dal Lagi Masala Bhindi
- Dal Mix Vada
- Dal Sikka

- Khasta Kachori
- Handwa
- Medu Vada
- Moong Aur Chana Dal Pattice
- Moong Aur Chana Dal Samosa
- Moong Dal Aur Gehun Ka Dalia
- Moong Dal Aur Chawal Ka Bonda
- Moong Dal Upma
- Ragda Pattice
- Tali Hui Channe Ki Dal
- Urad Aur Moong Dal Idli
- Dal Sandwich
- Parutwali Sandwich
- Rajma Toast
- Sabut Moong Sandwich

ANKURIT CHANA CUTLETS
Sprouted Black Chickpeas Cutlets

INGREDIENTS
Makes: 12

100 gms black chickpeas (*bhura chana*), sprouted
100 gms potatoes (*aloo*), boiled, peeled & mashed
2 tsp cornflour
1 medium-sized onion, finely chopped
½ tsp finely chopped green chillies
1 tsp salt
1 tsp finely chopped coriander leaves
1 tsp pomegranate seeds (*anardana*), pounded
1 tsp lime juice
Oil for shallow frying

METHOD
1. Grind the sprouted *bhura chana* to form a coarse paste. Remove into a bowl.
2. Add all the other ingredients, except the oil. Mix and mash well.
3. Divide the mixture into 12 portions.
4. Shape each portion into a round or square shaped cutlet. Set aside.
5. Heat oil on a griddle and flat fry 2-4 cutlets at a time till golden brown.
6. Repeat the process for the remaining cutlets and remove the cutlets onto kitchen paper to soak up any excess oil.
7. Serve hot with any chutney of your choice.

ANKURIT KABAB
Mixed Sprouted Kababs

INGREDIENTS
Makes: 20
¼ cup each of:
   Black chickpeas (*bhura chana*), sprouted
   White chickpeas (*kabuli chana*), sprouted
   Whole mung beans (*sabut moong*), sprouted
   Cow peas (*lobia/chavli*), sprouted
1 medium-sized potato (*aloo*), boiled, peeled, & mashed
2 tbsp finely chopped onions
1 tsp minced ginger
¾ tsp minced green chillies
6 garlic cloves, minced
½ tbsp finely chopped mint leaves
2 tbsp finely chopped coriander leaves
½ tsp pomegranate seeds (*anardana*), pounded
  slices of bread, soaked in water for a few minutes &
  tightly squeezed in a napkin
3 tbsp thick curd, whisked
3 tbsp breadcrumbs
1 tsp salt
Oil for deep frying

METHOD

1. Place the *bhura chana* and *kabuli chana*, with ½ cup water, into a pressure cooker and cook under pressure for 6 to 8 minutes. Allow the pressure to fall on its own before opening the cooker. Remove and set aside.
2. Place the *sabut moong* and *chavli,* along with ½ cup water, into a saucepan. Place the saucepan on the stove and cook covered till the *moong* and *chavli* are tender. Remove and set aside.
3. Combine all the beans and peas in a *thali* (platter).
4. Add the potatoes, coriander leaves, onion, bread, salt, ginger, garlic, green chillies, mint leaves and *anardana*.
5. Mash well and divide the mixture into 20 portions.
6. Take a portion, form into an oval roll of 3"to 4" length. Smear with curd and coat with breadcrumbs.
7. Repeat the process for the remaining portions.
8. Heat oil in a frying pan and fry 3-4 rolls at a time till light brown and crisp.
9. Remove the *kababs* onto kitchen paper to soak up any excess oil.
10. Serve hot with the chutney of your choice.

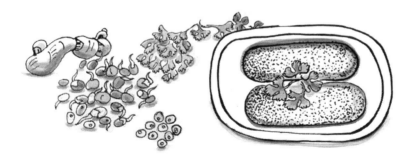

CHAKLI
Rice & Gram Flour Savoury

INGREDIENTS
Makes: 30

cleaned & ground separately into a coarse powder
    300 gms (1¼ cups) rice
    125 gms (½ cup) black beans (*urad dal*)
    125 gms (½ cup) bengal gram (*chana dal*)
2 tsp sesame seeds
½ tsp red chilli powder
½ tsp soda
2 tbsp clarified butter (*ghee*)
1 tsp salt
¾ cup water
Oil for deep frying

78

METHOD
1. Combine the rice and *dal* flours, red chilli powder, sesame seeds, salt, soda and mix well. Rub well with *ghee*. Gradually add water and knead to form a stiff, smooth dough. Divide the dough into 4 portions.
2. Put the first portion of *chakli* dough into a piston/ *chakli*-maker mould / *sancha* (attached to a disc with a star-shaped hole of about ¼ " diameter). Press in a circular motion onto clean paper, making medium-sized concentric circles of 3" diameter OR press into straight lines and shape into circles with your hand.
3. Repeat the process with the remaining 3 portions of dough.
4. Heat *oil* in frying pan and slide a few *chakli*s at a time using a spatula. Fry till crisp and light brown.
5. Remove the *chakli*s onto kitchen paper to soak up any excess oil.
6. Store in an airtight jar/tin and use as required.

CHANA DAL AUR ARBI KI PATRAIL
Bengal Gram & Colocasia Leaf Rolls

INGREDIENTS
Makes: 20
For the *Patrail*
6 colocasia leaves (*arbi patta*), washed & thick stems and veins removed
250 gms (1 cup) Bengal gram (*chana dal*), cleaned, roasted, cooled
  & ground into a coarse powder
50 gms grated fresh coconut, roasted in a dry pan for a minute
 25 gms tamarind, pulped
1 tsp minced ginger
2 garlic cloves, minced
1 tsp minced green chillies
¼ tsp asafoetida (*hing*)
1 tsp red chilli powder
½ tsp turmeric powder
1 tsp coriander powder
2 tsp sugar
¼ tsp soda
1½ tsp salt
2 tbsp finely chopped coriander leaves
2 tbsp hot oil

For the Seasoning

1 tsp minced green chillies

½ tsp turmeric powder

2 tsp mustard seeds

3 tsp lime juice

2 tsp sugar

1 tsp salt

3 tbsp oil

For the Garnish

50 gms grated fresh coconut

2 tbsp finely chopped coriander leaves

METHOD

80

1. Combine all the *patrail* ingredients except the *arbi patta*s and mix well to form a thick batter/paste.
2. Place 1 colocasia leaf inverted on a board and apply the paste all over the surface.
3. Place another leaf inverted on top of the first and apply paste on this also.
4. Place a third leaf inverted on the first two and then roll tightly from the tapering end to the opposite end.
5. Repeat the process for the remaining leaves and paste.
6. Steam the two rolls for 15 minutes. Allow them to cool completely.
7. Cut each roll into 10 medium-sized slices (*patrail*).
8. Heat the oil in a pan and add the mustard seeds. When they splutter, add the green chillies, turmeric, lime juice, salt, sugar, and the *patrail*. Mix gently for 2-3 minutes.
9. Remove into a serving bowl, garnish with fresh coconut, coriander leaves and serve hot.

CHANA DAL AUR KAMAL KAKDI KABAB
Bengal Gram & Lotus Stem Kababs

INGREDIENTS
Makes: 25-30

125 gms (½ cup) Bengal gram (*chana dal)*, cleaned, washed
 & soaked for 3-4 hrs., then drained & ground into a coarse paste. Set aside.
150 gms lotus stem (*kamal kakdi*), washed, mud & stem removed, scraped/
 peeled, washed again & grated
1 tsp minced ginger
4 garlic cloves, minced
1 tsp minced green chillies
1 tbsp finely chopped coriander leaves
1 tbsp finely chopped mint leaves
½ tsp pomegranate seeds (*anardana*)
½ tsp carum seeds (*ajwain*)
½ tsp asafoetida (*hing*)
1½ tsp salt
Oil for deep frying

METHOD
1. Combine all the ingredients except the oil, in a bowl or *thali*. Mix well using your hands.
2. Roughly divide into 25-30 portions. Moisten your palms, take a small portion and make a rough irregular oval roll, pressing lightly and binding it well with your fingers and palm.
3. Heat oil in a deep frying pan and slide 2-3 rolls in at a time. Baste, turning over, till golden brown.
4. Remove the *kababs* onto kitchen paper. Repeat the process for the other portions.
5. Serve hot with ketchup or chutney.

CHANA DAL BADA
Bengal gram Fritters

INGREDIENTS
Makes: 25-30
250 gms (1 cup) Bengal gram (*chana dal*), cleaned, washed,
  soaked for 2-3 hrs. & drained. Set aside ¼ cup *dal.*
1 large onion, finely chopped
2 tsp grated ginger
4 whole red chillies
1 tsp cumin seeds, roasted
A pinch of asafoetida (*hing*)
1 tsp salt
Oil for deep frying

82

METHOD
1. Combine the *dal* (apart from the ¼ cup set aside) and whole red chillies
    and grind to form a coarse paste.
2. Add all the remaining ingredients except the oil and mix well.
3. Divide the batter into 25-30 portions. Moisten your palms and take a
    portion and flatten by patting it to the thickness of a biscuit.
4. Press the soaked *dal* grains onto both sides.
5. Heat the oil in a deep frying pan and slide 3-4 rolls in at a time. Baste and
    turn over medium heat first and then on low heat, till slightly crisp and
    golden brown.
6. Remove the *bada*s onto kitchen paper to soak up any excess oil.
7. Repeat the process for the remaining portions.
8. Serve hot with any chutney or chilli sauce.

CHANA DAL BHAJIA
Bengal gram Fritters

INGREDIENTS
Serves: 6

250 gms (1 cup) split Bengal gram (*chana dal*), cleaned, washed
& soaked overnight, then drained & wiped dry with a napkin
A pinch of turmeric powder
½ tsp salt
3 medium-sized onions (cut into wedges)
1 tsp minced ginger
3 garlic cloves, minced
1 tsp minced green chillies
1 tbsp finely chopped coriander leaves
1 tsp carum seeds (*ajwain*)
½ tsp salt
Mustard oil for deep frying

METHOD
1. Combine the *dal*, turmeric powder and salt and grind into a smooth paste. Remove into a bowl.
2. Add all the remaining ingredients except the mustard oil and mix well.
3. Heat oil in a frying pan till a wisp of blue smoke rises from the surface.
4. Make small dumplings with your hand and slide 4-5 of them at a time into the oil. Baste and turn till crisp and light brown.
5. Remove the *bhajia*s onto kitchen paper to soak up any excess oil
6. Repeat the process with the remaining batter.
7. Serve hot with a chutney of your choice.

CHANA DAL KOTHIMBIR VADI
Bengal gram Coriander Cutlets

INGREDIENTS
Serves: 6

250 gms (1 cup) Bengal gram (*chana dal*), cleaned, washed,
  & soaked for 2 hrs., then drained & ground to a fine paste
125 gms split Bengal gram flour (*besan*)
2 cups finely chopped coriander leaves
2 tsp minced ginger
4 garlic cloves, minced
1 tsp minced green chillies
1 tsp red chilli powder
1 tsp cumin powder
1/8 tsp turmeric powder
2 tsp salt
½ tbsp oil
Oil for deep frying

84

METHOD
1. Combine the *dal* paste with the other ingredients except the oil (for deep frying), in a bowl or *thali*. Mix well to form a soft dough. Divide into 5 portions.
2. Grease your hands well, then take each portion and make cylindrical rolls by rolling on a board to a length of 5".
3. Place the rolls on a greased *thali* and steam for about 20 minutes. Cool and cut into thick slices.
4. Heat oil in a frying pan and slide 5-6 *vadis* in at a time. Fry basting with oil, till light brown
5. Remove the *vadis* onto kitchen paper and repeat the process for the rest.
6. Serve hot with *chana dal chutney* or any chutney of your choice.

CHANA DAL MUTHIA KABAB
Bengal gram Kababs

INGREDIENTS
Makes: 20

125 gms (½ cup) Bengal gram (*chana dal*), cleaned, washed
& soaked for 5 hrs., then drained & ground into a coarse paste
1 medium-sized potato (boiled, peeled & mashed)
1 medium-sized onion (finely chopped)
2 tsp minced ginger
8 garlic cloves, minced
1 tsp minced green chillies
¼ cup washed & finely chopped spinach leaves
¼ cup washed & finely chopped fenugreek leaves
1 tbsp finely chopped coriander leaves
1 tsp salt
2 tbsp oil
Oil for deep frying

METHOD
1. Heat oil in a frying pan and add the ginger, garlic and green chillies. Stir and fry for a minute or two.
2. Add the onions and stir, frying till light brown.
3. Add the spinach and fenugreek leaves. Stir and cook for a minute.
4. Add the *dal* and salt and stir constantly, scraping the sides and bottom of the pan to prevent sticking and scorching.
5. Remove from the stove and cool. Add the coriander leaves and potato. Mix and mash well.
6. Divide the mixture into 20 portions.

7. Heat oil in a deep frying pan and take portions of the mixture in your palm and lightly, with your fingers, form oval -haped *muthia*s. Slide 2-3 *muthia*s into the oil at a time. Fry, basting with the oil, till light brown.
8. Remove the *muthia*s onto a kitchen paper and repeat the process for the rest.
9. Serve hot with a chutney or sauce as desired.

DAHI VADA
Lentil Pattice in Curd

INGREDIENTS
Makes: 30

86

For the *Vada*s
300 gms (1¼ cups) Bengal gram (*chana dal*), cleaned, washed
  & soaked for 8 hrs., then drained
2 tsp minced ginger
2 tsp minced green chillies
1 tsp salt
1 cup water
Oil for deep frying

For the Curd Mixture
5 cups thick fresh curd, whisked
1 cup water
4 tbsp powdered sugar

For Sprinkling
2 tsp cumin seeds, roasted and powdered
½ tsp black pepper powder

½ tsp red chilli powder
1 tsp salt
½ tsp black salt
½ cup finely chopped coriander leaves

METHOD

1. Mix all the ingredients for *vada* except oil and grind together to a rough batter and set aside.
2. Combine and mix all the ingredients for Curd mixture, beat and set aside.
3. Heat the oil in a frying pan, moisten your palms and take small portions of the batter, slightly flatten and slide a few at a time into the oil. Fry, basting with the oil till light brown.
4. Remove the *vada*s onto kitchen paper to remove any excess oil.
5. Soak the *vada*s in water for 10 minutes. Remove and press gently between your palms to squeeze out excess water.
6. Place the *vada*s on a serving dish and pour the curd mixture over them.
7. Sprinkle all the spices in lines to form squares.
8. Garnish with coriander leaves between the squares and serve.

DAL AUR GOBI KE PATTON KE PATIKE
Lentil & Cabbage Slices

INGREDIENTS

Serves: 6

For the Batter

125 gms (½ cup) mung beans (*moong dal*)

¼ cup pigeon peas (*tuvar dal*)

¼ cup rice

For the *Masala* Paste

2 tsp coriander seeds

25 gms tamarind

3 whole red chillies

1 tsp cumin powder

2 tbsp grated dry coconut

1 tsp chopped ginger

4 garlic cloves, chopped

1½ tsp salt

3 tbsp water,

1½ tbsp finely chopped coriander leaves

200 gms tender cabbage, outer leaves & midrib removed, washed, wiped and halved

For the Tempering

2 tbsp oil

1 tsp mustard seeds

For the Garnish

2 tbsp grated fresh coconut

2 tbsp grated raw mango (preferably Rajapuri)

OR

2 tsp lime juice

1 tbsp finely chopped coriander leaves
¼ tsp red chilli powder
¼ tsp black pepper powder

METHOD

1. Wash, soak for 2 hours, drain and grind to a fine paste *moong dal, tuvar dal and* rice separately. Set aside.
2. Mix all the ingredients for *masala* paste except coriander leaves and cabbage and grind to a fine *masala* paste. Set aside.
3. Combine the *dal*, rice and *masala* pastes, coriander leaves and mix well.
4. Divide the batter into 20 portions.
5. Place half a cabbage leaf on a board, apply the batter all over the surface and roll tightly from one end to the other and tie lightly with a thread.
6. Repeat the same process for the remaining leaves and batter.
7. Place the rolls on a greased *thali* and steam for 15 minutes.
8. Remove, cool, cut the threads and discard them.
9. Cut each roll into 3 pieces.
10. Heat oil in a frying pan and add the mustard seeds. When they splutter, add the rolls, stir and fry gently for a minute or two.
11. Remove onto a serving dish, garnish with all the garnishing ingredients and serve hot.

DAL AUR PALAK KI WATI
Lentil & Spinach Canapés

INGREDIENTS
Makes: 12

2 tbsp mung beans (*moong dal*)
2 tbsp Bengal gram (*chana dal*)
(Cleaned, washed & soaked for 2 hrs. Then drained & ground into
a very smooth paste. If required, add 1 tbsp water to ease churning.)
½ tbsp white butter (for the *dal*)
4 tbsp cleaned, washed and finely chopped spinach (*palak*)
1 tbsp white butter (for the *palak*)
1 medium-sized onion, finely chopped
½ tsp minced ginger
2 garlic cloves, minced
½ tsp minced green chillies
1 tbsp flour (*maida*)
1 tbsp water
½ tsp salt
25 gms (1 cube) cheese, grated
12 canapés (any available in the market)
3 tsp tomato ketchup (¼ tsp for each)

For the Garnish
75 gms (3 cubes) cheese, grated
A few finely chopped coriander leaves

90

METHOD

1. Clean, wash and soak in sufficient water for 2 hours *moong dal* and *chana dal* together. Drain and grind in grinder to a smooth paste. Add 1 tsp water for easy churning, if required.
2. Place a heavy-bottomed pan on the stove and heat butter. Add the *dal* paste. Stir constantly for 3-4 minutes scraping the sides and bottom of the pan to prevent sticking and scorching. Remove *dal* paste and set aside.
3. Place the same pan on the stove, add butter and the onions. Stir till light brown.
4. Add the ginger, garlic and green chillies. Stir till the raw aroma disappears.
5. Add the flour and water and stir for 1-2 minutes.
6. Add the spinach for and stir for 3-4 minutes.
7. Add the salt and *dal* and mix well.
8. Remove from the stove and add the cheese. Mix well and divide into 12 portions.
9. Roast a canapé on a dry, thick griddle for a minute or two to make it crisp.
10. Remove canapé and place a portion of the filling into the canapé.
11. Top with cheese, tomato ketchup and coriander leaves.
12. Place canapé on a griddle again for 1-2 minutes on medium heat, till crisp.

OR

13. Place in the oven for a few minutes after filling and topping, till crisp.
14. Repeat the process with the remaining canapés and filling.
15. Arrange in a serving dish and serve immediately.

DAL LAGI MASALA BHINDI
Lentil Coated Spicy Lady Fingers

INGREDIENTS

Serves: 6 (30-40 pieces)

250 gms ladies fingers (*bhindi*), wiped with a wet cloth, head & tail removed
  & slit vertically
½ tsp salt
1/8 tsp turmeric powder
Oil for deep frying

For the Filling
2½ tbsp oil
2 tbsp rice flour
1½ tsp minced ginger
4 garlic cloves, minced
1 tsp minced green chillies
2 tsp coriander powder
½ tsp mango powder
¼ tsp turmeric powder 1 tsp salt

For the Coating
125 gms Bengal gram (*chana dal*), cleaned, washed
  & soaked for 2-3 hrs., then drained & ground into a smooth paste
3 tbsp flour (*maida*)
1 tbsp milo flour (*jawari atta*)
4 garlic cloves, minced
½ tsp red chilli powder
1¼ tsp salt
¼ cup water

92

METHOD

1. Sprinkle the salt and turmeric powder on the *bhindi* and set aside for a while.
2. Heat oil in a frying pan and fry 5-6 *bhindi*s at a time, till greenish-brown.
3. Remove the *bhindi*s onto kitchen paper and set aside.
4. Heat oil in a pan and add the rice flour and stir for 1-2 minutes.
5. Add the ginger, garlic and green chillies. Stir for 1-2 minutes till the raw aroma disappears.
6. Add the coriander, turmeric and mango powders, and salt. Stir well for 2-3 minutes.
7. Remove and fill a sufficient amount of filling into each *bhindi*. If the *bhindi*s are long enough, cut into two.
8. Combine all the coating ingredients in a bowl and mix well with your hands to form a smooth batter.
9. Heat the same oil used for frying the *bhindi*s.
10. Dip one *bhindi* into the batter at a time and coat with the batter.
11. Slide 5-6 coated pieces into the oil and fry till crisp and golden brown.
12. Remove the *bhindi*s onto the kitchen paper to remove any excess oil.
13. Repeat the process for the remaining *bhindi*s.
14. Serve hot with chutney or a sauce of your choice.

DAL MIX VADA
Mixed Lentil Savoury Pattice

INGREDIENTS
Makes: 25
¼ cup each of:
   Mung beans (*moong dal*)
   Pigeon peas (*tuvar dal*)
   Bengal gram (*chana dal*)
   Black beans (*urad dal*)
(Cleaned, washed & soaked separately for 2 hrs, then drained)
2 tsp minced ginger
15 garlic cloves, minced
1 tsp minced green chillies
6 whole red chillies
½ tbsp coriander seeds
20 curry leaves, chopped
1 tbsp chopped coriander leaves
(Roast all the herbs and spices in oil and set aside)
1 tsp red chilli powder
1 tsp salt
Oil for deep frying

METHOD
1. Combine all the *dals* and roasted spices and herbs. Grind into a coarse batter.
2. Add the red chilli powder and salt. Mix well.
3. Divide the batter into 25 portions.
4. Heat the oil in a frying pan.
5. Moisten hands and take a portion of the batter and flatten *vada* on your palm.

94

6. Gently slide 3-4 *vada*s into the oil at a time. Fry over medium heat, basting them with the oil, till golden brown.
7. Remove the *vada*s onto kitchen paper to remove any excess oil.
8. Repeat the same process for the remaining portions.
9. Serve hot with a chutney of your choice.

DAL SIKKA
Lentil Coins

INGREDIENTS
Makes: 16
2 tbsp each of:
   Pigeon peas (*tuvar dal*)
   Bengal gram (*chana dal*)
   Mung beans (*moong dal*)
(Cleaned, washed & soaked together in sufficient water for 2 hrs., then drained & ground into a smooth paste)
1 tbsp whole mung beans (*sabut moong*), sprouted and boiled
1½ tsp clarified butter (*ghee*)
1 small onion, chopped
1 tsp minced ginger
4 garlic cloves, minced
1 tsp minced green chillies
1 small piece cabbage (*patta gobi*), shredded
1 small potato (*aloo*), boiled, peeled & mashed
1 small carrot, grated
½ tbsp finely chopped coriander leaves
1 tsp salt
4 slices of bread

For the Coating
2 tbsp flour (*maida*)
2 tbsp corn flour
½ tsp salt
6 tbsp water
Breadcrumbs for coating
Oil for deep frying

METHOD

1. Place a heavy-bottomed pan on the stove and heat the *ghee*. Add the onion and stir for a minute. Add the ginger, garlic and green chillies. Stir for a while.
2. Add the *dal* paste and stir constantly for 3-4 minutes, scraping the sides and bottom of the pan to prevent sticking and scorching.
3. Add all the vegetables, sprouts, coriander leaves and salt. Stir, mixing well, for 2-3 minutes. Remove and cool the mixture. Set aside.
4. Cut each slice of bread into 4 round coins of 1½" diameter. Set aside.
5. Soak the crust left after cutting the coins in water. Then squeeze in a muslin cloth. Add this to the *dal* mixture and mix well. Divide the mixture in 16 equal portions.
6. Combine all the coating ingredients and mix well to get a smooth, sticky paste.
7. Take a bread-round, smear a little paste on one side and around the edges. Take a portion of the *dal* mixture and roll into a ball. Place it on the bread-round and stick by pressing gently. Make another coat of the sticky paste over the *dal* mixture and dredge breadcrumbs over it. Dust off excess crumbs. Prepare all the coins likewise.
8. Heat oil in a deep frying pan and slide 2-3 coins in at a time into the oil. Fry the coins, basting with the oil till golden brown.
9. Remove the coins onto kitchen paper to remove any excess oil.
10. Repeat the process with the remaining rounds/*dal* mixture/batter.
11. Serve hot, topped with tomato ketchup and 1-2 coriander leaves.

KHASTA KACHORI
Lentil Filled & Fried Savoury Pastry

INGREDIENTS

Makes: 24

For the Dough

400 gms (3 cups) flour (*maida*)

3 tbsp clarified butter (*ghee*)

¼ tsp soda

¾ tsp salt

¾ cup water

For the Filling

175 gms (¾ cup) black beans (*urad dal*), cleaned, washed
  & soaked for 6hrs., then drained & ground with ¼ cup water,
  into a smooth paste

6 tbsp oil

½ tsp asafoetida(*hing)*

½ cup Bengal gram flour (*besan*)

1½ tbsp cumin seeds, roasted & powdered

3 tbsp coriander powder

1 tsp red chilli powder

1 tsp dry mango powder

1 tsp dry ginger powder (*saunth*)

½ tsp turmeric powder

4 whole black cardamoms, powdered

½ tsp caromom seeds (*ajwain*), lightly roasted

½ tsp salt

1 tsp black salt

Oil for deep frying

1 tsp saunth chutney (refer Contents)

To Assemble
250 gms (1 cup) thick curd, whisked
½ tsp cumin powder
¼ tsp salt
½ tsp castor sugar
¼ tsp red chilli powder

For the Garnish
1 cup fine fried gram flour strings (*sev*)

METHOD

1. Combine the flour, *ghee*, salt and soda. Rub thoroughly. Gradually add water and knead to form a smooth dough.
2. Divide the *kachori* dough into 30 portions. Place a heavy-bottomed pan on the stove and heat oil. Add the asafoetida and ground *dal*. Stir constantly, scraping the sides and bottom of the pan to prevent sticking and scorching.
3. Add the gram flour and stir for 1-2 minutes.
4. Add the cumin, coriander, red chilli, dry mango, dry ginger, turmeric, salt, black salt, black cardamom powders and *ajwain*. Stir and cook till light brown.
5. Remove, cool and divide the filling into 24 portions.
6. Roll each portion (with a rolling pin), into ¼" thick, small round *rotis*. Place a portion of filling on each *roti*. Gather all the edges towards the centre and seal well. Gently press the edges with your fingers and lightly flatten the *kachoris*. Heat oil in a frying pan and put in a few *kachoris* at a time. Fry on reduced heat, pressing the *kachoris* with a perforated spoon till cooked, puffed up and golden.
7. Combine the curd, cumin and red chilli powders, salt and sugar. Mix well.
8. Place the *khasta kachoris* on a serving dish. Make a hole in the centre of each *kachori* and pour in the curd mixture and *saunth chutney*.
9. Serve garnished with *sev*.

98

HANDWA
Lentil Cake

INGREDIENTS
Serves: 6
For the Batter
125 gms (½ cup) rice
125 gms (½ cup) Bengal gram (*chana dal*)
¼ cup pigeon peas (*tuvar dal*)
¼ cup black beans (*urad dal*)
¼ cup mung beans (*moong dal*)
2 tbsp curd
½ cup hot water

For the Vegetables
50 gms peas, coarsely pounded
50 gms cauliflower, minced
1 medium-sized tomato, chopped
50 gms red pumpkin/bottle gourd (*bhopla/lauki*), grated & water squeezed out
1 small onion, chopped
2 tsp minced ginger
4 garlic cloves, minced
1 tsp minced green chillies
2 tbsp oil
2 tbsp finely chopped coriander leaves

To Add
3 tbsp oil
3 tbsp water
¼ tsp soda
2 tsp sugar

½ tsp red chilli powder
1½ tsp salt
A small pinch of turmeric powder

For the Tempering
2 tbsp oil
1/8 tsp asafoetida (*hing*)
1 tsp mustard seeds
1 tsp cumin seeds
8-10 curry leaves

For the Garnish
2 tbsp sesame seeds
1 cup grated fresh coconut
1 tbsp finely chopped coriander leaves

100

METHOD
1. Clean, wash and soak rice and lentils separately in sufficient water for 6 hrs. Drain and grind to a smooth paste separately.
2. Combine in a wide mouth saucepan the *dal* and rice pastes, curd and hot water. Mix well and allow the batter to ferment for 10-12 hours.
3. Heat oil in a pan, add the onions and stir till onions transluscent. Add the ginger, garlic, green chillies. Stir fry for 2-3 minutes. Add all the vegetables, coriander leaves and mix lightly. Stir fry and cook for few minutes and then add the mixture to batter.
4. Heat oil, water and soda in a pan till it slightly changes colour and boils. Add the red chilli and turmeric powders, sugar, salt and mix for a minute or so. Pour the mixture over batter.
5. Heat oil in a pan and add the asafoetida, mustard and cumin seeds. When they splutter, add the curry leaves, stir fry for few seconds and then pour over the batter.

6. Now mix the batter well.
7. Grease a heavy griddle and pour 2 ladlefuls of the batter into it. Spread gently to a diameter of 6-7" and ¼ " thickness, on low heat.
8. Sprinkle sesame seeds on the round. Cover with a dome-shaped lid and bake for 10 minutes till the top turns a biscuit colour.
9. Turn and bake covered for another 5-6 minutes.
10. Remove onto a serving dish.

OR

Grease a tin (preferably an aluminium tin of 6" diameter and 2" thickness), with *ghee* and dust well with flour. Pour half the quantity of batter into it and sprinkle with sesame seeds. Bake covered on a thick heavy griddle on very low heat or on medium hot charcoal, for 20 minutes. When it turns a biscuit colour, remove, cool, unmould and place on a serving dish. Repeat the process with the remaining half quantity of batter.

OR

Grease small aluminium *wati*s (moulds) with *ghee* and dust well with flour. Pour 2 tbsp batter into each, sprinkle with sesame seeds and place on a heavy griddle. Bake covered on low heat for about 6-8 minutes. (You can also place the griddle on medium hot charcoal and bake over it.) Invert (it won't fall on turning) and bake for 4-5 minutes till the top is biscuit brown. Remove, cool, unmould and place on a serving dish.

OR

Bake it in a pre-heated oven at 200 degrees Fahrenheit.

11. Cut into even pieces if it is big enough, sprinkle with fresh coconut, coriander leaves and serve hot with *dalia* & *pudina chutney* (see index) or any pickle oil.

MEDU VADA
South Indian Savoury Doughnuts

INGREDIENTS

Makes: 30

250 gms (1 cup) Bengal gram (*chana dal*), cleaned, washed
  & soaked for 6-7 hrs., then drained & ground, with ¾ cup water,
  into a smooth paste
2 tsp ginger paste
1½ tsp green chilli paste
125 gms (½ cup) rice (optional), ground to a smooth powder
1 tsp salt
Oil for deep frying

102

METHOD
1. Combine the *dal* paste, rice flour, ginger, green chilli paste and salt. Mix well.
2. Heat oil in pan, moisten your palms and take a small portion of the *vada* batter and slightly flatten on your palm, making a hole in the centre with your thumb.

    OR

    Put a small portion of batter on moistened plastic paper, slightly flattening it and making a hole in the centre with your finger. Turn over onto your palm.

    OR

    You can use a *vada* maker (available in the market).
3. Slide a few *vada*s at a time into the oil and fry, basting with the oil till light brown.
4. Remove onto a serving dish and serve hot with coconut chutney and *sambar*.

MOONG AUR CHANA DAL PATTICE
Mung Beans & Bengal Gram Patties

INGREDIENTS
Makes: 15

125 gms (½ cup) mung beans (*moong dal*)

125 gms (½ cup) Bengal gram (*chana dal*)

(Cleaned, washed & soaked separately for 6 hrs., then drained & wiped dry
  with a napkin & ground separately into coarse pastes.)

4 tbsp clarified butter (*ghee*)

2 tsp minced ginger

6 garlic cloves, minced

1 tsp minced green chillies

½ tsp salt

2 tbsp finely chopped coriander leaves

5 medium-sized potatoes (*aloo*), boiled, peeled & mashed

1 tsp salt

1 tbsp butter

50 gms cottage cheese (*paneer*), grated

½ tsp black pepper powder

3 slices of bread, soaked in water for a few seconds &
  squeezed in a muslin cloth

Butter or *ghee* for shallow frying

METHOD

1. Place a heavy-bottomed pan on the stove and heat *ghee*. Add the ginger, garlic and green chillies. Stir fry for a minute or two.
2. Add the *dal* pastes and salt. Cook for 3-4 minutes on medium heat, stirring constantly and scraping the sides and bottom of the pan to prevent sticking and scorching.
3. Remove into a bowl, add the coriander leaves and mix well. Divide the mixture into 15 portions.

4. Combine the potatoes, salt, butter, *paneer*, black pepper powder and bread, in a *thali*. Mash and mix well to form a soft dough. Divide into 15 portions.
5. Take a portion of the dough in your palm and form a *katori* or hollow shape with your fingers. Stuff a portion of the *dal* filling into it and close from all sides. Seal well and flatten lightly between your palms.
6. Heat *ghee* or butter on a griddle and shallow fry a few *pattice* at a time, pressing with the ladle and turning once and adding *ghee*/butter again. Cook till all sides are light brown.
7. Remove the *pattice* onto kitchen paper to dry off any extra oil.
8. Repeat the process with the remaining portions of *dal* filling and potato dough.
9. Serve hot with a chutney of your choice.

104

MOONG AUR CHANA DAL SAMOSAS
Mung Beans & Bengal Gram Savouries

INGREDIENTS
Makes: 12

¼ cup mung beans (*moong dal*)
¼ cup Bengal gram (*chana dal*)
(Cleaned, washed & soaked for 1 hr., then drained)
1¼ cups water
¾ tbsp clarified butter (*ghee*)
½ tsp black cumin seeds (*shahjeera*)
1 medium-sized onion, finely chopped
2 tsp minced ginger
½ tsp minced green chillies
1/8 tsp turmeric powder
½ tsp cumin powder
½ tsp mango powder
½ tsp *garam masala* powder
½ tsp curry powder (refer Contents)
½ tsp dry fenugreek leaves (*kasuri methi*)
1 tsp salt
1 tbsp finely chopped coriander leaves
½ cup flour (*maida*)
½ tsp salt
½ tbsp *ghee*
1/8 cup water
Clarified butter (*ghee*) for deep frying

METHOD

1. Place the *dal*s and water in a saucepan. Place the pan on the stove and boil till the *dal* is tender but the grains separate.
2. Heat the *ghee* in a frying pan and add the black cumin seeds. When they splutter, add the onions. Stir fry till light brown.
3. Add the ginger and green chillies. Stir fry for a minute or two.
4. Add the *dal*s, turmeric, cumin, mango, *garam masala* and curry powders. Stir fry till well mixed. Add the *kasuri methi* and salt. Stir fry for few minutes.
5. Remove into a bowl and add the coriander leaves. Mix lightly and divide into 12 portions.
6. Combine the flour, salt and *ghee*. Rub together well. Gradually add water and knead into a stiff dough. Divide into 6 portions.
7. Roll out a round *chapati* of 5-6" diameter with each portion and pile the *chapatis*, dredging flour between them. Cut each *chapati* into half and turn each half into a cone.
8. Fill the cone with one portion of the filling, moisten the edges with water and press down the open edges to seal.
9. Heat *ghee* in a frying pan and fry 1-2 *samosa*s at a time on medium heat, basting with the oil till they turn crisp and light brown.
10. Remove the *samosa*s onto kitchen paper to remove any excess oil.
11. Repeat the process with the remaining dough and filling.
12. Serve hot with tomato sauce or a chutney of your choice.

MOONG DAL AUR GEHUN KA DALIA
Mung Beans & Broken Wheat Snack

INGREDIENTS
Serves: 6
125 gms (½ cup) mung beans (*moong dal*), washed
 & soaked for 2 hrs. & drained
½ tsp salt
½ cup water
125 gms (½ cup) broken wheat (*dalia*)
1 tbsp clarified butter (*ghee*)
¼ tsp salt
1½ cups water

For the Tempering
½ tbsp clarified butter (*ghee*)
½ tsp minced green chillies
½ tsp cumin seeds
10-15 curry leaves

For the Garnish
1 tbsp finely chopped coriander leaves

METHOD
1. Boil the *dal*, salt and water in a saucepan for 5-6 minutes till *dal* is tender but grains separate. While boiling, remove any scum. Remove from fire, drain and set aside the *dal*.
2. Heat *ghee* in a frying pan and add the *dalia*. Stir fry on medium heat till the unique aroma of the *dalia* is released and it becomes light brown.
3. Add water and salt, mix well and cook covered on reduced heat till ¾ done. Remove from fire and set aside the *dalia*.

4. Heat *ghee* in a saucepan and add the green chillies and cumin seeds. When they splutter, add the curry leaves. Stir fry for few seconds.
5. Add the *dalia* and stir fry for few minutes.
6. Add the *dal*. Mix and cook covered till tender.
7. Remove into a serving bowl, garnish with coriander leaves and serve hot.

MOONG DAL AUR CHAWAL KA BONDA
Mung Beans & Rice Balls

INGREDIENTS
Makes: 25
¼ cup rice

125 gms (½ cup) mung beans (*moong dal*), cleaned, washed & drained
1 cup water
1 tbsp black beans (*urad dal*)
1 tbsp Bengal gram (*chana dal*)
(Both *dals* roasted)
1 small onion, finely chopped
2 tsp minced ginger
6 garlic cloves, minced
2½ tsp minced green chillies
2 tbsp finely chopped coriander leaves
½ tsp salt
1½ tbsp clarified butter (*ghee*)
1¼ cups Bengal gram flour (*besan*)
1 tbsp rice flour
¼ tsp carum seeds (*ajwain*)
A pinch of turmeric powder
¼ tsp baking powder

½ tsp salt
½ - ¾ cup water
Oil for deep frying

METHOD
1. Place a heavy-bottomed pan on the stove and add the *moong dal*, rice and water. Cook till the *dal* and rice are dry and tender.
2. Remove into a bowl. Add the onion, ginger, garlic, green chillies, salt coriander *ghee*, *urad* and *chana dals* and mix well. Divide the mixture into 25 portions.
3. Combine the *besan*, rice flour, salt, turmeric powder, *ajwain*, and baking powder in a bowl. Gradually add water and mix well to form a smooth batter.
4. Heat oil in a deep frying pan. Take one portion of the mixture and make a small round ball/*bonda*. Coat it with the batter.
5. Fry 2-3 *bonda*s at a time, basting with the oil till light brown. Remove the *bonda*s onto kitchen paper.
6. Repeat the process with the remaining batter and mixture.
7. Serve hot.

MOONG DAL UPMA
Ground Mung Beans Snack

INGREDIENTS
Serves: 6
250 gms (1 cup) mung beans (*moong dal*), cleaned, washed
  & soaked for 3 hrs., then drained & ground into a coarse batter/paste.

For the Tempering
8 tbsp oil
1 tsp mustard seeds
1 tsp cumin seeds
2 medium-sized onions, finely chopped
15-20 curry leaves
2 tsp minced green chillies
2 tsp salt
4 tbsp grated fresh coconut

For the Garnish
2 tbsp finely chopped coriander leaves

METHOD
1. Grease a *thali* and spread the *dal* paste on it. Steam for 1-2 minutes.
2. Remove, cool and crumble with your hands.
3. Heat oil in a saucepan and add the mustard and cumin seeds. When they splutter, add the onions. Stir fry for a few seconds.
4. Add the curry leaves and green chillies. Stir fry for a minute or two.
5. Add the *dal*, salt and fresh coconut. Mix well and fry for few minutes.
6. Remove into a serving bowl. Garnish with coriander leaves and serve hot.

110

RAGDA PATTICE
Potato Patties with Spiced Chickpeas

INGREDIENTS
Serves: 6
For the *Pattice*
10 medium-sized potatoes (*aloo*), boiled, peeled and mashed
4 small bread roll (*pav*), soaked in water and squeezed in a muslin cloth
1 tsp *garam masala* powder
2 tsp salt
Oil for shallow frying

For the *Ragda*
500 gms (2 cups) white chickpeas (*kabuli chana*), cleaned, washed & soaked
   with ¾ tsp salt, ½ tsp soda and 6 cups water, overnight & drained. Retain
   the water. 250 gms (1 cup) dried peas (*vatana*), cleaned, washed & soaked
   with ½ tsp salt and 2½ cups water overnight & drained. Retain the water.
4 tbsp oil
3 tsp red chilli powder
1 tsp *garam masala* powder
1 tsp turmeric powder
2 tbsp cumin powder
1 tsp dry mango powder
1½ tsp salt
1 tsp black salt

To Sprinkle
1 tsp pomegranate (*anardana*) powder
½ tsp *garam masala* powder
1 tsp red chilli powder
2 tsp cumin powder

1 tsp salt
½ tsp black salt
(Combine all the ingredients and mix well)

For the Onion Mixture
4 medium-sized onions, finely chopped
1 tsp minced green chillies
¾ cup raw mango, finely chopped
½ cup finely chopped coriander leaves
(Combine all the ingredients and mix well)

Teekhi Chutney (refer Contents)
Meethi Chutney (refer Contents)

112

METHOD
1. Combine the potatoes, *pav*, salt and *garam masala* powder. Mash and mix to form a smooth potato mixture.
2. Shape the potato mixture into round balls.
3. Roll the balls into round ½"thick discs with a rolling pin.
4. Cut each *pattice* with a heart-shaped cutter.
5. Repeat the process with the rest of the potato mixture.
6. Heat oil in a griddle and place a few *pattice* at a time, turning and pressing with ladle. Shallow fry till brown.
7. Remove the pattice onto kitchen paper to remove any excess oil.
8. Place the *chana* in a pressure cooker and cook under pressure for 6-8 minutes in the same *chana* water. Allow the pressure to fall on its own before opening the cooker. Remove the *chana* and drain. Set aside the *chana* water again.
9. Take 3 tbsp of the boiled *chana* and coarsely mash it.
10. Place the *vatana* in a pressure cooker and cook under pressure for 5-6 minutes in the same *vatana* water. Allow the pressure to fall on its own

before opening the cooker. Remove the *vatana* and drain. Set aside the *vatana* water again.

11. Take 3 tbsp of the boiled *vatana* and coarsely mash it.
12. Heat oil in pan and add the boiled and also coarsely mashed *chana* and *vatana*. Stir for a few minutes.
13. Add the salt, black salt, red chilli, *garam masala*, turmeric, cumin and dry mango powders. Mix and stir well.
14. Pour the preserved *chana* and *vatana* water. Keep stirring till a semi-liquid consistency is achieved.
15. Arrange 2 pattice on a serving plate and pour 2 ladlefuls of the *ragda* over them.
16. Spread ½ tsp *teekhi chutney* and 2 tsp *meethi chutney* on top.
17. Sprinkle a pinch of *masala* and garnish with 3 tsp of onion mixture and serve hot.

TALI HUI CHANNE KI DAL
Fried Bengal Gram

INGREDIENTS
Weight: 250 gms
250 gms (1 cup) Bengal gram (*chana dal*), cleaned, washed
  & soaked overnight with 1 tsp soda & drained
1 tsp red chilli powder
¼ tsp turmeric powder
1 tsp *garam masala* powder
1 tsp salt
Oil for deep frying

METHOD

114

1. Wash the *dal* again 2-3 times, then drain and spread on a towel to dry for 30 minutes. Wipe dry with a cloth.
2. Heat oil in a deep frying pan and fry a little of the *dal* a time, over medium heat, till light brown.
3. Repeat the process for the remaining *dal*.
4. Combine all the spices. Mix well and sprinkle on the fried *dal*. Toss the *dal*.
5. Cool and store in an airtight jar/tin and use as required.

Urad & Moong Dal Idli
Black Beans & Mung Beans Steamed Cakes

Ingredients
Makes: 18
¾ cup mung beans (*moong dal*)
¼ cup black beans (*urad dal*), cleaned, washed
  & soaked for 2 hrs. & drained
2 garlic cloves, minced
½ tsp minced green chillies
2 tbsp finely chopped coriander leaves ¾ tsp salt
(Ground all together to form a smooth batter)

For the Tempering
1 tbsp oil
½ tsp mustard seeds
½ tsp cumin seeds
8-10 curry leaves, broken

Method
1. Heat oil in a frying pan and add the mustard and cumin seeds. When
    they splutter, add the curry leaves and fry for a minute.
2. Pour this tempering over the batter and mix well.
3. Grease the *idli* moulds with oil and pour a ladleful of batter into each.
4. Steam for 10 minutes.
5. Repeat the process for the remaining batter.
6. Remove onto a serving dish and serve hot with green chutney (see index)
    or any coconut chutney.

DAL SANDWICH
Lentil Sandwiches

INGREDIENTS
Makes: 6 x 4
125 gms (½ cup) mixed *dals*, eg. 2 tbsp each of:
   Mung beans (*moong dal*)
   Pigeon peas (*tuvar dal*)
   Bengal gram (*chana dal*)
(Cleaned, washed & soaked for 2 hrs., then drained &
  ground together into a coarse paste.)
6 spring onions, chopped
2 medium-sized tomatoes, blanched, peeled and chopped
1 small carrot, grated
1 medium-sized cucumber, grated
1 tsp minced ginger
2 garlic cloves, minced
1 tsp minced green chillies
2 tbsp butter
75 gms (3 cubes) cheese, grated
1 tbsp finely chopped coriander leaves
½ tsp black pepper powder
½ tsp white pepper powder
1 tsp salt
12 slices of brown bread
12 lettuce leaves/tender cabbage leaves, stem removed,
  washed and broken roughly
3 tbsp butter (¼ tsp for each slice)
6 tsp tomato ketchup (1 tsp for each sandwich)
75 gms (3 cubes) cheese, grated

116

METHOD

1. Place a heavy-bottomed pan on the stove and add 1½ tbsp butter.
2. When it melts, add the onions and stir till they turn a light brown.
3. Add the ginger, garlic and green chillies. Stir for a minute.
4. Add the *dal* paste and stir constantly, scraping the sides and bottom of the pan to prevent sticking and scorching.
5. Add the salt, white and black pepper powders, ½ tbsp butter and mix well.
6. Add the carrots, coriander leaves and stir for a minute.
7. Remove into a bowl and add the cucumber, tomatoes and cheese. Mix gently.
8. Divide the filling into 6 portions.
9. Butter all the bread slices. Place one lettuce/cabbage leaf on each of 6 slices.
10. Place one portion of the filling on each of the 6 slices and spread lightly.
11. Apply sauce on top of the filling.
12. Sprinkle cheese over this and place another lettuce/cabbage leaf over it all.
13. Cover with the remaining 6 buttered slices of bread.
14. Press lightly and cut diagonally into 4 triangles. Wrap in wax paper and place in a ziplock bag and serve as required.
15. If desired you can also grill the sandwiches and serve hot.

PARUTWALI SANDWICH
Layered Sandwiches

INGREDIENTS
Makes: 8

125 gms (½ cup) each of:
  Rice
  Mung beans (*moong dal*)
  Bengal gram (*chana dal*)
  Black beans (*urad dal*)
(Cleaned, washed & soaked separately for 3 hrs. & drained)
1 tsp salt
¼ tsp soda
1 cup grated fresh coconut
1 tsp chopped green chillies
1 tbsp tamarind pulp
½ tsp salt
1/8 tsp turmeric powder
50 gms cottage cheese (*paneer*), grated
2 tbsp finely chopped coriander leaves
1 cup grated fresh coconut
Butter for shallow frying

METHOD
1. Mix the *dal*s and rice. Grind to form a coarse batter and remove into a bowl. Add soda and salt and mix well. Divide into 2 portions.
2. Combine the coconut, green chillies, tamarind, salt, turmeric powder and grind to form a smooth paste. Remove into a bowl and add the *paneer*. Mix well.
3. Grease a *thali* and spread one portion of the batter on it. Spread the filling on top of the batter, pressing lightly.

4. Cover the filling with another portion of batter and steam for 15-20 minutes.
5. Remove and cool for 10-12 minutes. Then cut into triangles.
6. Heat the butter in a non-stick pan and shallow fry a few sandwiches at a time, turning once or twice, till light brown on both sides.
7. Remove the sandwiches onto kitchen paper and repeat the process.
8. Place on a platter, garnish with coconut and coriander leaves and serve hot.

RAJMA TOAST
Kidney Beans Toast

INGREDIENTS

Makes: 12

100 gms red kidney beans, (*rajma*), washed & soaked overnight & drained

1½ cups water

4 tbsp butter

2 tbsp cream

2 medium-sized onions, made into paste

4 small tomatoes, blanched, peeled & puréed

1 tsp ginger paste

1 tsp garlic paste

2½ tbsp hot and sweet sauce/any tomato sauce

1 tsp soya sauce

1 tsp sugar

1 tsp salt

A pinch of edible dry red/orange colour (optional)

12 slices of bread

A few coriander leaves

100 gms (4 cubes) cheese, grated

METHOD

1. Place the *rajma* and water in a pressure cooker and cook under pressure for about 8-10 minutes. Allow the pressure to fall on its own before opening the cooker.
2. Remove the *rajma*, drain and reserve the *rajma* water.
3. Place a heavy-bottomed pan on the stove and add 3 tbsp butter and the onions and stir till the onion turn slightly brown.
4. Add the ginger and garlic and stir for 1-2 minutes.
5. Add the tomato purée, *rajma*, salt, **sugar,** red chilli powder and cook, stirring occasionally, till the mixture is slightly thick.
6. Add the soya sauce, hot and sweet sauce, red/orange colouring, cream and 1 tbsp butter (if desired). Stir and mix well.
7. Add the leftover *rajma* water and simmer on reduced heat, stirring occasionally till slightly thick.
8. Toast the bread slices and apply a little butter onto each (if desired).
9. Place a ladleful of *rajma* on this and sprinkle grated cheese. Top with coriander leaves and serve hot.

120

SABUT MOONG SANDWICH
Whole Mung Beans Sandwiches

INGREDIENTS

Makes: 6

125 gms (½ cup) whole mung beans (*sabut moong*), washed
 & soaked overnight & drained
A small pinch of turmeric powder
½ tsp salt
1 cup water
½ tbsp butter

1 small onion, finely chopped
2 eggs, boiled, cubed or grated
2 minced green chillies
2 small tomatoes, finely chopped
1/8 tsp black pepper powder
¼ tsp aniseed, powdered
1 tbsp thick curd, whisked
25 gms (1 cube) cheese, grated
1 tbsp finely chopped coriander leaves
3 tbsp butter
12 slices of bread

METHOD

1. Place the *moong*, turmeric powder, salt and water in a saucepan on the stove. Boil for 8-10 minutes till the *moong* is tender. Remove and lightly mash.
2. Heat butter in a frying pan and add the onions. Stir fry till light brown.
3. Add the eggs and green chillies. Stir fry for a few minutes.
4. Add the tomatoes, *moong*, curd, black pepper and aniseed powders. Stir and cook for a few minutes.
5. Remove from the stove and add the coriander leaves and cheese. Mix well and divide into 6 portions.
6. Butter all the slices of bread, placing a portion of filling on one slice and covering with another slice.
7. Toast in a greased toaster on medium heat till light brown on both sides.
8. Repeat the process with the remaining bread slices and filling. (If desired spread ¼ to ½ tsp butter on the top and bottom of the bread slices while toasting.)
9. Remove onto a serving dish and serve hot with tomato chilli sauce.

CHAATS & BHELS

- Ankurit Chana Chaat
- Chana Papdi Sandwich Chaat
- Kabuli Chana Aloo Ring Chaat
- Mangalorian Chaat
- Papdi Pakodi Aloo Chaat
- Sanke Chaat
- Bhel Puri & Pani Puri
- Chana Chor Garam Bhel
- Chana Dal Aur Tamater Ki Bhel

ANKURIT CHANA CHAAT
Tangy Sprouted Black Chickpeas

INGREDIENTS
Serves: 6

250 gms (1 cup) black chickpeas (*bhura chana*), sprouted
1 cup water
A pinch of turmeric powder
½ tsp salt
2 small onions, finely chopped
2 small tomatoes, finely chopped
2 small potatoes (*aloo*), boiled and cubed
100 gms/1 medium-sized cabbage, shredded
2 medium-sized cucumbers, finely chopped
1 tsp minced green chillies
4 whole red chillies, roasted and powdered
2 tbsp finely chopped coriander leaves
4 tsp lime juice
1 tsp salt
2 small carrots, finely chopped (optional)

METHOD

1. Place the *bhura chana*, water, turmeric powder and salt into a pressure cooker. Cook under pressure for about 6-8 minutes. Allow the pressure to fall on its own before opening the cooker. Remove into a serving bowl.
2. Add the onions, tomatoes, potatoes, cabbage, cucumber, green chillies, red chilli powder, coriander leaves, lime juice and salt. (If desired add the carrots.)
3. Mix well with a fork and serve.

CHANA PAPDI SANDWICH CHAAT
White Chickpeas & Thin Bread Sandwiches

INGREDIENTS
Serves: 6
For the *Papdi*
1 cup flour (*maida*), sifted
1 tsp carum seeds (*ajwain*)
1½ tbsp oil
½ tsp salt
¾ cup water
Oil for deep frying

For the *Chana*
125 gms (½ cup) white chickpeas (*kabuli chana*), cleaned,
    washed & soaked overnight, then drained
1¾ cups water
1/8 tsp soda
½ tsp salt
2 tbsp oil
3 green chillies, ground to paste
½ tsp *garam masala* powder
½ tsp turmeric powder
1 tsp salt
1 tbsp finely chopped coriander leaves
2 big potatoes (*aloo*), boiled, peeled and mashed

For the Curd Mixture
300 gms (1¼ cups) curd, whisked
1 tbsp powdered sugar

For the Chutney
½ cup *Meethi chutney* (see Contents)
1/8 cup *Teekhi chutney* (see Contents)

To Sprinkle
1 tsp cumin seeds, roasted and powdered
¼ tsp black pepper powder
1¼ tsp black salt
¼ tsp carum seeds (*ajwain*)
½ tbsp mango powder (*amchur*)
¼ tsp salt
2 tsp dry ginger powder (*saunth*)
½ tsp dry mint leaves
1 tsp red chilli powder
½ cup semolina (*sev*)
1 tbsp finely chopped coriander leaves

METHOD
1. Combine all the *papdi* ingredients and knead, gradually adding water, to form a semi-stiff dough.
2. Divide the dough into 2 big portions and roll each portion into a round disc. Using a round cutter, cut into 12 small round *papdi*s. For each portion.
3. Lightly and evenly prick the round *papdi*s with a fork.
4. Heat oil in a frying pan and fry 5-6 *papdi*s at a time, till crisp. Drain and remove to cool. Then store in an airtight jar.
5. Place the *chana*, soda, water and salt in a pressure cooker. Cook under pressure for about 8-10 minutes. Allow the pressure to fall on its own before opening the cooker. Remove.
6. Heat oil in a pan and add the *chana*, turmeric and *garam masala* powders, salt, green chillies paste, coriander leaves and potatoes. Stir and cook for 1-2 minutes. Mix well.
7. Remove and cool. Then divide the filling into 12 portions.

8. Arrange 12 *papdi*s on a serving dish and place a portion of filling on each. Cover each with the remaining 12 *papdi*s.
9. Pour the curd mixture evenly over the *papdi* sandwich.
10. Pour both the chutneys evenly over the curd mixture.
11. Sprinkle the *masala, sev* and coriander leaves and serve.

KABULI CHANA ALOO RING CHAAT
Tangy White Chickpeas & Potato Rings

INGREDIENTS
Serves: 6
125 gms (½ cup) white chickpeas (*kabuli chana),* picked, washed, soaked with ¼ tsp soda overnight, then washed & drained
A pinch of turmeric powder
¼ tsp salt
1 cup water
½ tsp cumin powder
½ tsp *garam masala* powder
½ tsp black salt
1/8 tsp turmeric powder
¼ tsp black pepper powder
1 tsp dry fenugreek leaves (*kasuri methi*)
4 medium-sized potatoes (*aloo*), boiled and peeled
¼ cup green chutney (refer Contents)
1/8 cup saunth chutney (refer Contents)
375 gms (1½ cups) curd, whisked & beaten well with 1 tbsp powdered sugar

For Sprinkling
Chaat masala (refer Contents to make your own/ or available packeted)

126

METHOD

1. Place the *kabuli chana*, turmeric powder, salt and water in a pressure cooker. Cook under pressure for about 6-8 minutes. Allow the pressure to fall on its own before opening the cooker. Remove into a bowl.
2. Add the cumin, *garam masala*, turmeric, black pepper powders, black salt, dry fenugreek leaves and mix well. Divide the mixture into 12 portions.
3. Cut the potatoes into 3 thick slices. Make a hole in the centre of each slice, giving them a ring-like shape.
4. Stuff the filling into the ring, pressing lightly with your palms (if the ring breaks, still stuff the filling in and the join the severed parts of the ring)
5. Repeat the process with the remaining potatoes and filling.
6. Arrange the rings on a serving dish and pour the curd over each ring, followed by the green Chutney. Spread the saunth chutney around the green chutney.
7. Sprinkle the *chaat masala* over the top.
8. Put into the refrigerator for a few minutes and serve.

Note The pieces which you remove from the potato slices while making rings, can also be added to the filling if desired

MANGALORIAN CHAAT
Tangy Mangalorian Dish

INGREDIENTS
Serves: 6

250 gms (1 cup) white chickpeas (*kabuli chana*), cleaned, washed
  & soaked with ¼ tsp soda overnight, then washed & drained
4 tea bags
2 pinches turmeric powder
½ tsp salt
2½ cups water
125 gms (½ cup) Bengal gram (*chana dal*), cleaned, washed & for 2 hrs. &
drained
6 tbsp oil
2 tsp minced ginger
12 garlic cloves, minced
1 tsp minced green chillies
2 tsp dry fenugreek leaves (*kasuri methi*)
½ tsp *garam masala* powder
1 tsp mango powder (*amchur*)
1 tsp black pepper powder
½ tsp red chilli powder
2 medium-sized onions, finely chopped
4 small potatoes (*aloo*), boiled, peeled and cubed
1 tsp *bhel masala* (refer Contents)
1 tsp *chaat masala* (refer Contents)
½ tsp black salt
500 gms (2 cups) curd, whisked & beaten well with 4 tbsp powdered sugar
200 gms mixed *farsan*/thick *sev*
2 tbsp finely chopped coriander leaves

128

METHOD

1. Place the *kabuli chana*, tea bags, half the turmeric powder, salt and water, into a pressure cooker. Cook under pressure for about 6-8 minutes. Allow the pressure to fall on its own before opening the cooker. Remove into a bowl and discard the tea bags.
2. Place the *chana dal*, and the remaining turmeric powder, salt and water, into a saucepan. Place the pan on the stove and cook the *chana dal* till tender but grains still separate. Remove.
3. Heat oil in a frying pan and add the ginger, garlic, green chillies and dry fenugreek leaves. Stir fry for a minute or two.
4. Add the *garam masala*, *amchur*, black pepper and red chilli powders. Stir fry for a few minutes.
5. Add the *kabuli chana*, *chana dal* and salt. Mix well and cook for 2-3 minutes.
6. Remove into a bowl and add the onions, potatoes, *bhel* and *chaat masala*s and black salt.
7. Add the curd, sugar, *farsan* and coriander leaves. Mix well and serve.

PAPDI PAKODI ALOO CHAAT
Thin Bread & Lentil Savoury with Potatoes & Curd

INGREDIENTS
Serves: 6
¼ cup flour (*maida*), sifted
1/8 cup wheat flour, sifted
¼ cup semolina (*rawa*)
½ tsp onion seeds
½ tsp salt
1 tbsp oil
¼ cup water

250 gms (1 cup) mung beans (*moong dal*), cleaned,
  washed & soaked for 2-3 hrs., then drained
2 green chillies, roughly chopped
1 tsp black cumin seeds
½ tsp *garam masala* powder
A pinch of baking powder
½ tsp salt
1 tbsp roughly chopped coriander leaves
medium-sized potatoes (*aloo*), boiled, peeled and mashed
Oil for deep frying

For the Curd Mixture
750 gms (3 cups) curd, whisked
1 tsp red chilli powder
1 tsp cumin seeds, roasted & powdered
½ tsp *garam masala* powder
1 tsp salt
1 tsp powdered sugar
A few finely chopped coriander leaves
A few finely chopped mint leaves
(Combine all & beat well to form a smooth mixture)

For the Chutney
1/8 cup *Teekhi chutney* (refer Contents)
½ cup *Meethi chutney* (refer Contents)

130

For the *Masala* & Garnish
1 tsp black cumin powder
1 tsp red chilli powder
1 tsp *garam masala* powder
½ tsp salt
2½ black salt
(Combine all of the above & mix well.)
2 tbsp finely chopped coriander leaves

METHOD
1. Combine all the flours, onion seeds, salt and oil. Mix well and gradually adding water and knead well to form a semi-stiff dough.
2. Divide the dough into 4 large round portions and roll each portion into a disc. Cut each disc with a zig-zag cutter, into 6 square *papdi*s. Lightly prick each *papdi* with a fork.
3. Heat oil in a pan and fry a few *papdi*s at a time till crisp.
4. Drain, remove and cool. Store in an airtight jar.
5. Combine the *dal*, green chillies, cumin seeds, *garam masala* and baking powders, salt, and coriander leaves. Grind into a smooth *pakodi* batter and remove.
6. Heat oil in a frying pan. Take a small portion of *pakodi* batter and slide in.
7. Put in a few *pakodi*s at a time and fry, basting with oil, till golden yellow.
8. Drain, cool and then soak in hot water for 10-15 minutes. Remove and gently squeeze. Set aside.
9. Arrange the *papdi*s on a serving dish and place the *pakodi*s on the arranged *papdi*s. Spread the potatoes over this and pour the curd mixture evenly. Pour both the chutneys evenly on the curd. Sprinkle the *masala* and coriander leaves and serve.

SANKE CHAAT

Bengal gram Squares with Curd & Potato

INGREDIENTS

Serves: 6

250 gms (1 cup) Bengal gram (*chana dal*), cleaned, washed
  & soaked overnight, then drained, washed again 2-3 times & drained
1 tsp red chilli powder
1 tsp salt
½ tsp baking powder
½ tbsp finely chopped coriander leaves
4 tbsp oil for shallow frying
500 gms (2 cups) curd, whisked & beaten well with 1 tbsp powdered sugar
6 tbsp *saunth chutney* (refer Contents)
100 gms potato *sali* (available readymade)
1 tbsp finely chopped coriander leaves

METHOD

1. Combine the *chana dal*, salt, red chilli powder and grind into a smooth batter. Remove into a bowl.
2. Add the baking powder, coriander leaves and mix well.
3. Pour the batter onto a greased *thali* and steam for 8-10 minutes.
4. Remove and cool. Then cut into small pieces (approx. 25).
5. Heat oil in a frying pan and add the *sanke* pieces. Stir fry for a few minutes and then remove onto kitchen paper to get rid of any excess oil.
6. Arrange the *sanke* pieces on a serving dish and pour the curd evenly over them.
7. Pour the *saunth chutney* in lines or circles.
8. Garnish with the potato *sali* and coriander leaves. Put into the refrigerator for a few minutes to cool and then serve.

SANKE CHAAT

BHEL PURI

INGREDIENTS

Serves: 6

1 cup flour (*maida*), sifted
1½ tbsp oil
½ tsp salt
¼ cup water
Oil for deep frying
6 cups puffed rice (*kurmura,* – available in the market)
½ cup fried Bengal gram (*chana dal* - available in the market)
2 medium-sized potatoes (*aloo*), boiled, peeled & cubed
1 cup finely chopped onions
½ cup finely chopped raw mango
180 gms *Teekhi chutney* (refer Contents)
240 gms *Khatti Meethi chutney* (refer Contents)
1¼ cups thin *bhel puri sev* (available in the market)
½ tsp salt
1½ tbsp lime juice
¾ cup finely chopped coriander leaves

METHOD
1. Combine the flour, oil, salt, water and knead to a smooth dough. Divide into two.
2. Roll portions into discs and with a round cutter of 1½ inch diameter, cut 12 small *puris* from each disc.
3. Heat oil in a frying pan and fry a few *puris* at a time till crisp.
4. Drain, remove, cool and crush 12 *puris* into pieces and set aside the remaining 12.
5. Combine the puffed rice, fried *dal*, potaotes, onions, mango, salt, lime juice, broken *puris*, both chutneys, in a serving bowl and mix well.
6. Sprinkle the *sev* and coriander leaves and serve with the remaining 12 *puris*.

Note These *puris* are also known as *papdi*. In Mumbai, the origin of this dish, the road side vendor serves, once the *bhel* has been eaten, a small mixed portion of puffed rice, *sev* and salt to wrap up the taste and clean the mouth

CHANA CHOR GARAM BHEL
Pressed Bengal Gram Spicy Snack

INGREDIENTS
Serves: 4

50 gms (5 tbsp) pressed Bengal gram (*chana chor garam*)
50 gms (5 tbsp) pressed black chickpeas (*kala chana chor garam*)
10 gms (1 tbsp) fried spicy Bengal gram (refer Contents for recipie/ also available in the market)
50 gms (5 tbsp) potato *sali* (available in the market)
100 gms ½ cup white chickpeas (*kabuli chana*), boiled
1 small potato (*aloo*), boiled, peeled & cubed
¼ tsp *chaat masala* (refer Contents)
¼ tsp red chilli powder
50 gms (1 small piece) raw mango (preferably Rajapuri), cubed
1 small onion, finely chopped
2 tbsp finely chopped coriander leaves
1 tbsp lime juice
½ tsp salt
¼ tsp black salt

METHOD
Combine all the ingredients in a serving bowl. Mix well by tossing lightly and then serve immediately.

CHANA DAL AUR TAMATER KI BHEL
Bengal Gram & Tomato Bhel

INGREDIENTS
Serves: 4
50 gms (¼ cup) Bengal gram (*chana dal*), cleaned, washed
  & soaked for 2 hrs., then parboiled & drained
1 small potato, boiled, peeled & cubed
50 gms (1 small piece) raw mango (preferably Rajapuri), cubed
2 small tomatoes, cubed
1 small onion, finely chopped
4 tbsp finely chopped coriander leaves
4 tbsp finely chopped mint leaves
2 green chillies, finely chopped
½ tsp *bhel masala*
½ tsp mango powder (*amchur*)
¼ tsp black salt
¼ tsp salt

METHOD
Combine all the contents in a serving bowl. Mix well by tossing lightly and
serve.

PANI PURI

INGREDIENTS
Serves: 4
1½ cup flour (*maida*), sifted
1 cup semolina (*rawa*)
2 tbsp split gram *dal* powder
¾ tsp salt
¾ cup water
Oil for deep frying

For the *Jaljeera*
25 gms tamarind, pulped
½ tsp red chilli powder
1 tbsp cumin seeds, roasted & powdered
1 tsp ginger powder (*saunth*)
½ tsp salt
¾ tsp black salt
3 tbsp powdered sugar
½ tbsp lime juice
2 tbsp chopped coriander leaves
1" ginger, chopped
4 green chillies, chopped
1 tbsp finely chopped mint leaves
(Ginger, green chillies, coriander and mint leaves to be ground to a fine paste.)
6 mint leaves
1 cup water
(Combine all the ingredients above & set aside for 1 hour. Then sieve through a muslin cloth and add a few ice cubes if desired.)

For the Filling

4 tbsp black chickpeas (*bhura chana*), cleaned, washed & overnight, then
  drained & boiled in ¼ cup water till tender

4 tbsp whole mung beans (*moong*), cleaned, washed & soaked overnight, then
  drained, sprouted and boiled in ½ - ¾ cup water till tender

½ tsp salt

(Mix the *chana*, *moong* and salt well)

For the Chutney

50 gms *Teekhi chutney* (refer Contents)

400 gms *Meethi chutney* (refer Contents)

METHOD

138

1. Combine the flour, semolina, *dal* powder and salt. Gradually add water
    and knead well to form a slightly stiff dough.
2. Divide the dough into 5 portions. Roll each portion into a thin big circle,
    dredging a little flour in-between.
3. Cut the rolled dough with a 2" round cutter dusted with flour.
4. Pile up 10 discs on top of each other, dredging flour on it and then cover
    with a moist muslin cloth. Set aside for 8-10 minutes.
5. Heat oil in a frying pan and fry a few *puris* at a time, pressing them lightly
    with a perforated spoon till they puff up and turn crisp and slightly brown.
6. Remove, drain, cool and store in an airtight jar.
7. Combine ¾ cup of *meethi chutney* and the *jaljeera* and mix well. Pour into 6
    serving bowls.
8. Make a hole in the centre of each *puri* by pressing with your thumb. Place
    the puris on a serving tray. Fill the *puris* with 1 tsp of the *chana* and *moong*
    mixture, followed by ¼ tsp *teekhi chutney* and ½ tsp *meethi chutney*.
9. Arrange the puris on a serving dish and serve with the *jaljeera*. Pour *jaljeera*
    inside a cracked *puri*, filling it completely, and then eat it whole.

SPROUTS, BEANS & LENTILS

- Ankurit Matki
- Ankurit Matki Aur Tamater
- Ankurit Matki Misal
- Ankurit Sabut Masoor Ki Amti
- Ankurit Bhura Chana Masala Tari
- Rasedar Lobia Tari
- Rajma Masala
- Val Tari Channe Ke Tukde Ke Sath
- Vatana Usal

ANKURIT MATKI
Sprouted Moth

INGREDIENTS

Serves: 6

250 gms (1 cup) moth beans (*matki*), sprouted

6 tbsp oil

2 small onions, finely chopped

¼ tsp turmeric powder

2 tsp salt

50 gms (1 medium-sized piece) raw mango (preferably Rajapuri), grated

1 tbsp grated fresh coconut

1 tbsp finely chopped coriander leaves

140

For the *Masala* (ground into a smooth paste)

8-10 black peppercorns

2 tsp chopped ginger

6 garlic cloves, chopped

4 whole red chillies

1 tsp coriander seeds

1 tsp cumin seeds

2 tbsp grated dry coconut,

METHOD

1. Heat oil in a saucepan and add the onions. Stir fry till light brown.
2. Add the *masala* and stir fry till the onions and *masala* are well mixed.
3. Add the *matki*, salt, turmeric powder and mix well. Cook covered for 5 minutes on reduced heat till the *moth* is tender.
4. Add the mango and coconut. Stir and cook for few minutes. Mix well.
5. Serve hot, garnished with coriander leaves, along with rice or *rotis*.

ANKURIT MATKI AUR TAMATER
Sprouted Moth & Tomatoes

INGREDIENTS
Serves: 6

250 gms (1 cup) moth beans (*matki*), sprouted
2 tbsp clarified butter (*ghee*)
2 small onions, finely chopped
4 medium-sized tomatoes, blanched & finely chopped
2 tsp minced ginger
4 garlic cloves, minced
1½ minced green chillies
½ cup coconut milk (refer Contents)
¼ tsp turmeric powder
1½ tsp salt
2 tbsp finely chopped coriander leaves

METHOD
1. Heat the *ghee* in a saucepan and add the onions. Stir fry till light brown.
2. Add the ginger, garlic and green chillies. Stir fry for a minute or two.
3. Add the *matki*, stir and cook for a few minutes.
4. Add the tomatoes, salt, turmeric powder, coconut milk and mix well. Cook covered for 5 minutes till the *matki* is tender.
5. Remove into a serving bowl, garnish with coriander leaves and serve hot with *roti*s or rice.

ANKURIT MATKI MISAL
Savoury Sprouted Moth Mix

INGREDIENTS
Serves: 6

250 gms (1 cup) moth beans (*matki*), sprouted

4 tbsp oil

2 small onions, finely chopped

2 tsp minced ginger

4 garlic cloves, minced

1 tsp red chilli powder

A pinch of turmeric powder

1 tsp salt

2 medium-sized tomatoes, cubed

2 small onions, finely chopped

2 tbsp finely chopped coriander leaves

2 cups mixed *farsan* (salted, dry Gujarati snacks mix, available in the market)

3 tsp lime juice

OR

50 gms (1 small piece) raw mango (preferably Rajapuri), grated

12 tbsp curd, beaten well with 1 tbsp sugar (optional)

METHOD
1. Heat oil in a saucepan and add the onions. Stir fry till transparent.
2. Add the ginger, garlic and green chillies. Stir fry for a minute or two.
3. Add the *matki*, red chilli and turmeric powders, and salt. Stir till well mixed. Cook covered for 5 minutes till ¾ done.
4. Remove into a serving bowl and add the tomatoes, onions, coriander leaves, *farsan*, lime juice/mango and mix well. Serve as it is or with sweet curd.

142

ANKURIT SABUT MASOOR KI AMTI
Sprouted Whole Red Lentil Curry

INGREDIENTS
Serves: 6
250 gms (1 cup) whole red lentil (*sabut masoor*), sprouted

For the *Masala*
4 tbsp oil
2 small onions, finely chopped
8 tbsp grated dry coconut
8 garlic cloves, chopped
2 tsp grated jaggery
10 pieces tamarind
4 tbsp water

For the *Curry*
4 tbsp oil
4 small onions, finely chopped
A pinch of asafoetida (*hing*)
3 tsp red chilli powder
1 tsp *garam masala* powder
2 tsp coriander powder
¼ tsp turmeric powder
2 tsp salt
2 cups coconut milk (refer Contents)
2 cups hot water
2 tbsp finely chopped coriander leaves

METHOD

1. For making *masala*, heat oil in a frying pan and add onions, coconut, and garlic. Stir fry till light brown. Remove.
2. Add the tamarind and jaggery. Grind into a smooth paste, gradually adding water to ease churning. Set aside the *masala*.
3. For curry, heat oil in a saucepan and add onions and the asafoetida. Stir fry till light brown.
4. Add the *masoor*, red chilli, *garam masala*, coriander and turmeric. Stir and cook for a few minutes.
5. Add hot water, stir well and cook covered on reduced heat till the *masoor* is tender.
6. Add the cooked *masala*, salt and coconut milk. Simmer for a few minutes.
7. Remove into a serving bowl and garnish with coriander leaves. Serve hot with *rotis* or rice.

ANKURIT BHURA CHANA MASALA TARI
Sprouted Black Chickpeas Spicy Gravy

INGREDIENTS
Serves: 6

250 gms (1 cup) black chickpeas (*bhura chana*), cleaned, washed
  & soaked overnight, then drained and & sprouted
6 tbsp oil
2 tsp ginger paste
2 tsp garlic paste
2 tsp green chilli paste
2 tsp coriander leaves paste
½ tsp red chilli powder
¼ tsp turmeric powder
1 tsp cumin powder
1 tsp *garam masala* powder
4 medium-sized tomatoes, finely chopped
4 tamarind flowers, broken into pieces
1½ tsp salt
3 cups water
1 tbsp finely chopped coriander leaves

METHOD
1. Heat oil in a saucepan and add the ginger, garlic, green chillies and
    coriander pastes. Stir fry for 1-2 minutes.
2. Add the red chilli, turmeric, cumin and *garam masala* powders. Stir
    quickly and add the tomatoes, tamarind flowers and salt.
3. Add the *bhura chana* and water. Mix well. Transfer into a pressure cooker.
    Cook under pressure for about 6-8 minutes. Allow the pressure to fall
    on its own before opening the cooker. Remove into a bowl and serve hot
    with *paratha*s or rice.

RASEDAR LOBIA TARI
Cow Peas Curry

INGREDIENTS
Serves: 6

250 gms (1 cup) *lobia/chavli* (cow peas), picked, washed,
  soaked in sufficient water for 2 hrs. & drained
6 tbsp oil
2 medium-sized onions, made into a paste
2 tsp ginger paste
1½ tsp garlic paste
1 tsp cumin powder
½ tsp red chilli powder
½ tsp *garam masala* powder
1/8 tsp turmeric powder
¼ tsp black pepper powder
3 medium tomatoes, puréed
 1 tbsp finely chopped coriander leaves
1½ cups water

METHOD
1. Heat oil in a saucepan and add the onion paste. Stir fry till onions are half done. Add the ginger and garlic pastes. Stir fry till light brown.
2. Add the cumin, red chilli, *garam masala* and turmeric. Stir fry for a few minutes and add the tomato purée. Stir and cook for a few minutes.
3. Add the *lobia* and mix well. Add the black pepper powder and coriander leaves. Add water, stir and mix well. Transfer the contents into a pressure cooker. Cook under pressure for about 5-6 minutes. Allow the pressure to fall on its own before opening the cooker.
4. Remove into a serving bowl and serve hot with *rotis* or *jeera* rice.

RAJMA MASALA
Spicy Red Kidney Beans

INGREDIENTS

Serves: 4

200 gms (1 cup) red kidney beans (*rajma*), cleaned, washed
& soaked overnight, then drained

1¼ cups water

3 medium-sized onions, paste

5 medium-sized tomatoes, blanched & puréed

4 tbsp curd, whisked

2 tsp ginger paste

1 tsp garlic paste

3 tbsp clarified butter (*ghee*)

¼ tsp turmeric powder

3 tsp coriander-cumin powder (*dhania-jeera* powder)

1 tsp *garam masala* powder

½ tsp red chilli powder

1½ tsp salt

1 tbsp finely chopped coriander leaves

For the *Masala*

4 whole red chillies

2 tsp poppy seeds (*khus-khus*)

4 cloves

2" cinnamon stick

2 big cardamoms

2 tbsp grated dry coconut

(Ground into a smooth lump of *masala*)

METHOD

1. Place the *rajma* in a pressure cooker. Cook under pressure for about 10-12 minutes till ¾ done. Allow the pressure to fall on its own before opening the cooker. Remove and drain but preserve the stock water.
2. Heat the *ghee* in a heavy-bottomed pan and add the onion paste. Fry till half done.
3. Add the ginger and garlic pastes and stir till light brown.
4. Add the ground lump of *masala* and stir well till mixed.
5. Add the *rajma* and stir. Mix well till half done.
6. Add the curd and tomato purée. Stir and mix well.
7. Add the turmeric, red chilli, coriander-cumin and *garam masala* to the stock water and mix well.
8. Stir for 4-5 minutes, simmering on low heat.
9. Sprinkle the coriander leaves and mix well for 2-3 minutes.
10. Remove into a serving bowl and serve hot with *roti*s or rice.

VAL TARI CHANNE KE TUKDE KE SATH
Field Beans Gravy with Split Bengal Gram Pancakes

INGREDIENTS
Serves: 6
125 gms (½ cup) husked field beans (*val*), cleaned, washed &
 soaked overnight & drained
½ cup water

For the Pancakes
125 gms (½ cup) Bengal gram (*chana dal*), cleaned, washed & soaked
overnight, then drained, washed again in running water, drained & ground
 into a fine paste
1 tbsp finely chopped onions
½ tsp minced green chillies
1 tsp minced ginger
2 garlic cloves, minced
A small pinch of turmeric powder
2 tbsp finely chopped coriander leaves
1 tbsp grated fresh coconut

For the Curry
3 tbsp oil
12 curry leaves
1 medium-sized onion, finely chopped
2 tsp minced green chillies
1 tsp minced ginger
4 garlic cloves, minced
½ tsp cumin powder
1½ red chilli powder
½ tsp *garam masala* powder

1 tsp salt
½ cup tamarind pulp
25 gms jaggery
2 tbsp finely chopped coriander leaves, ground to paste
1¼ cup coconut milk (refer Contents)
½ cup luke warm water, if required

For the Garnish
1 tbsp finely chopped coriander leaves

METHOD

1. Place the *val* and water in a saucepan and cook till tender. Remove & set aside.
2. Combine the *dal*, onion, chillies, ginger, garlic, turmeric powder, coriander leaves and coconut. Mix well.
3. Spread the mixture over a greased *thali* and steam for 5 minutes.
4. Remove, cool, and cut into squares.
5. Heat oil in a frying pan and fry 5-6 squares at a time till light brown.
6. Remove the squares onto kitchen paper to remove any excess oil.
7. Heat oil in a saucepan and add the curry leaves and onions. Stir fry till the onion turns light brown.
8. Add the chillies, ginger and garlic. Stir fry for a minute or two.
9. Add the cumin, red chilli and *garam masala* powders and salt. Stir fry quickly.
10. Add the tamarind pulp, jaggery, coriander paste and coconut milk. Stir till well mixed.
11. Add the *val* and simmer covered, for a few minutes (if the gravy is thick add the ½ cup lukewarm water).
12. Add the *dal* squares and bring to the boil till the squares are slightly tender.
13. Remove into a serving bowl. Garnish with coriander leaves and serve hot with *roti*s or rice.

150

VATANA USAL
Dry Peas Savoury Mix

INGREDIENTS
Serves: 4
250 gms (1 cup) dry peas (*vatana*), cleaned, washed
  & soaked overnight & drained
¾ cup water
4 tbsp oil
½ tsp mustard seeds
8-10 curry leaves, broken
1 large-sized onion, minced
2 tsp ginger paste
2-2½ tsp garlic paste
1½ tsp green chillies paste
¼ tsp turmeric powder
1 tsp red chilli powder
½ tsp *garam masala* powder
1 tsp coriander-cumin powder (*dhania jeera* powder)
1½ tsp salt
2 small tomatoes, puréed
2 tbsp finely grated fresh coconut
25 gms tamarind, pulped
2 tbsp jaggery
3 cups water
2 tbsp finely chopped coriander leaves

METHOD
1. Place the *vatana* and water in a pressure cooker. Cook under pressure for about 5-6 minutes. Allow the pressure to fall on its own before opening the cooker. Remove and drain but preserve the stock water.
2. Heat oil in a heavy-bottomed pan and add the mustard seeds. When they splutter, add the curry leaves and stir for a few minutes.
3. Add the onions and stir till they turn light brown.
4. Add the ginger, garlic, green chillies and stir till the raw aroma disappears.
5. Add the red chilli, turmeric, coriander-cumin and *garam masala* powders, and salt. Stir and mix well for 1-2 minutes.
6. Add the tomatoes, coconut, tamarind pulp and jaggery. Stir and cook for 2-3 minutes.
7. Add the *vatana*. Stir and cook for 2-3 minutes.
8. Add water, stir and cook covered, for 6-8 minutes. Stir occasionally.
9. Sprinkle the coriander leaves and mix well.
10. Remove into a serving bowl and serve hot with plain boiled rice or *chapati*s or *pav*s. (If you like, you can also pour this gravy onto *Misal*).

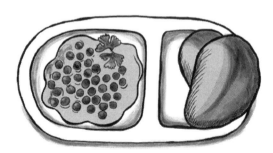

DAL WITH KADHI

- Ankurit Moong Kadhi
- Chana Dal Vadi Tamater Ke Sauce Mein
- Moong Dal Dahi Mein
- Moong Dal Ke Tukde Dahi Kadhi Mein
- Moong Dal Vadi Dahi Mein

ANKURIT MOONG KADHI
Sprouted Whole Mung Beans Curry

INGREDIENTS
Serves: 4
125 gms (½ cup) whole mung beans (*sabut moong*), sprouted
7 tbsp curd, whisked
A small pinch of citric acid
2½ cups water
1½ tbsp Bengal gram flour (*besan*)
1 tbsp clarified butter (*ghee*)
1/8 tsp asafoetida (*hing)*
1 tsp minced ginger
½ tsp minced green chillies
8-10 curry leaves
¼ tsp turmeric powder
½ tsp red chilli powder
2½ tsp sugar
1 tsp salt
1 tbsp finely chopped coriander leaves

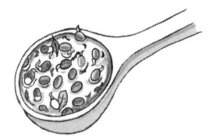

For the Tempering
2 tbsp clarified butter (*ghee*)
1 tsp cumin seeds
4 garlic cloves, minced
1 tbsp grated dry coconut

154

METHOD

1. Heat the *ghee* in a heavy-bottomed saucepan and add the asafoetida, curry leaves, green chillies and ginger. Fry for 1-2 minutes.
2. Add the sprouted *moong* and stir for 1-2 minutes.
3. Add the turmeric and red chilli powders, and the salt and sugar. Stir and mix well but gently, for 2-3 minutes.
4. In a pan, heat the curd, water, flour and citric acid. Mix well and bring to a boil and pour it over the sprouts.
5. Heat the *ghee* in a pan and add the cumin seeds, garlic and coconut. Stir for 1-2 minutes and pour over the *kadhi*. Add the coriander leaves and stir.
6. Simmer on reduced heat for 3-4 minutes, stirring occasionally and gently.
7. Remove into a serving bowl and serve hot with plain boiled rice.

CHANA DAL VADI TAMATER KE SAUCE MEIN
Bengal Gram Savories in Tomato Sauce

INGREDIENTS
Serves: 6
250 gms (1 cup) Bengal gram (*chana dal*), cleaned, washed
 & soaked for 2 hrs. & drained
6 whole red chillies
1 tsp aniseed
2 tsp minced ginger
2 tbsp finely chopped coriander leaves
1½ tsp salt
(Grind together to form a coarse batter and divide into 15-20 portions)
Oil for deep frying
125 gms (½ cup) pigeon peas (*tuvar dal*), cleaned, washed
 & soaked 8-10 minutes & drained
2 cups water
8 medium-sized tomatoes, blanched and puréed

For the Tempering
4 tbsp oil
½ tsp asafoetida (*hing*)
1 tsp mustard seeds
1 tsp cumin seeds
½ tsp fenugreek seeds
10-15 curry leaves
2 tsp minced ginger
8 garlic cloves, minced
2 tbsp dry fenugreek leaves (*kasuri methi*)
1 tbsp finely chopped coriander leaves

METHOD

1. Place a portion of *dal* batter on your moist palms and lightly pat and press into a roughly round shape.
2. Heat oil in a frying pan and slide 6-8 *vadi*s in at a time and cook on medium heat. Fry till light brown. Remove the *vadi*s onto kitchen paper and cool. Set aside.
3. Place the *tuvar dal* and water in a pressure cooker. Cook under pressure for about 6-8 minutes. Allow the pressure to fall on its own before opening the cooker.
4. Remove into a bowl. Add the tomato purée and mash well till smooth.
5. Heat oil in a pan and add the mustard and cumin seeds. When they splutter, add the asafoetida, curry leaves, ginger, garlic and dry fenugreek leaves. Fry quickly.
6. Pour the prepared *dal* over the tempering and cook briefly. Transfer the *dal* into a saucepan and simmer a little before adding the *vadi*s. Cook for a few minutes.
7. Remove into a serving bowl and serve hot with *roti*s or rice.

MOONG DAL DAHI MEIN
Mung Beans in Curd

INGREDIENTS
Serves: 4
125 gms (½ cup) mung beans (*moong dal*), cleaned & washed
2½ cups water
A pinch of turmeric powder
½ tsp salt

For the Tempering
1½ tbsp clarified butter (*ghee*)
1/8 tsp asafoetida (*hing*)
1 tsp mustard seeds
1 tsp cumin seeds
½ tsp fenugreek seeds
4-5 curry leaves, broken
1 tsp minced ginger
1 tsp minced green chillies
1 tsp dry fenugreek leaves
¼ tsp salt
3 tbsp curd, whisked
½ cup water
A pinch of turmeric powder
½ tsp black pepper powder
1 tbsp finely chopped coriander leaves

METHOD

1. Place the *moong dal*, water, turmeric powder and salt into a saucepan. Cook till the *dal* is tender and thick. While cooking, remove any scum. Remove from fire.
2. Heat the *ghee* in a pan and add the asafoetida, mustard seeds, cumin seeds and fenugreek seeds. When they splutter, add the curry leaves, ginger, green chillies and fenugreek leaves. Stir fry for a few seconds.
3. Add the *dal* and water. Stir and cook for a few minutes.
4. Add the salt, curd and turmeric powder. Stir and cook till well mixed.
5. Add the black pepper powder and coriander leaves. Mix well.
6. Remove into a serving bowl and serve hot with assorted *rotis* or rice.

MOONG DAL KE TUKDE DAHI KADHI MEIN
Mung Beans Pancakes in Curd Curry

158

INGREDIENTS

Serves: 4

125 gms (½ cup) mung beans (*moong dal*), cleaned, washed
  & soaked for 5-6 hrs. & drained
1½ tsp chopped ginger
2 garlic cloves
2 green chillies
1/8 tsp turmeric powder
¾ tsp salt
(Ground together to form a smooth paste)
2 tbsp oil
½ - ¾ cup water
Clarified butter (*ghee*) for deep frying
3 tbsp clarified butter (*ghee*)
½ tsp mustard seeds

Moong Dal ke Tukde Dahi Kadhi Mein

½ tsp cumin seeds
1/8 tsp asafoetida (*hing)*
3 whole red chillies
1 tsp dry fenugreek leaves (*kasuri methi*)
10-15 curry leaves
250 gms (1 cup) curd (slightly sour)
3 cups water
A pinch of turmeric powder
1 tsp salt
1-2 tsp sugar

METHOD

1. Heat oil in a pan and add the *dal* paste. Stir and cook for 1-2 minutes.
2. Add water and stir. Cook on low heat till the *dal* forms a smooth lump.
3. Grease a *thali* and spread the cooked *dal* on it. Smoothen with your hands.
4. Steam for 5-6 minutes. Remove, cool and cut into medium-sized squares.
5. Heat *ghee* in a frying pan and fry a few squares at a time till very light brown.
6. Heat *ghee* in a pan and add the mustard and cumin seeds. When they splutter, add the asafoetida, red chillies, dry fenugreek leaves and curry leaves. Stir for a few minutes.
7. Place the curd, water, turmeric powder and salt in a bowl and beat well.
8. Add it to the tempered spices and stir for few minutes. Mix well, adding the sugar. Cook the curry on low heat till it simmers. Break 4-5 pieces of fried *dal* squares to make crumbs and add to the curry for thickness. While simmering, smoothen the squares so that they are thoroughly mixed in with the curd curry.
9. Add the fried squares to the curry. Cook till the squares are slightly soft.
10. Remove into a serving bowl and serve hot with *rotis* or rice.

160

MOONG DAL VADI DAHI MEIN
Mung Beans Savoury in Curd

INGREDIENTS
Serves: 6
125 gms/12-13 *moong dal vadi*s
2 tbsp oil
375 gms (1½ cups) curd
3 tbsp Bengal gram flour *(besan)*
(Beat the curd & *besan* well with a wooden churner)
3 tbsp oil
1/8 tsp asafoetida *(hing)*
½ tsp mustard seeds
½ tsp cumin seeds
2 medium-sized onion, finely chopped
1 tsp minced ginger
½ tsp minced green chillies
1 whole red chilli, broken
½ tsp turmeric powder
1 tsp coriander seeds, crushed
1 tsp aniseeds, crushed
3 cups water
1½ tsp salt
2 tbsp dry fenugreek leaves *(kasuri methi)*
1 tsp red chilli powder
2 tbsp hot oil
1 tbsp finely chopped coriander leaves

METHOD

1. Heat oil in a frying pan and add the *vadis*. Stir fry till golden brown.
2. Heat oil in a saucepan and add the asafoetida, mustard and cumin seeds. When they splutter, add the onions and fry till light brown.
3. Add the ginger and green chillies. Stir fry for a few minutes.
4. Add the red chilli, coriander, turmeric and aniseeds powders. Stir fry for a minute or two.
5. Add the *vadis* and mix well. Add water and cook covered for 10 minutes on medium heat.
6. Add the salt and dry fenugreek leaves.
7. Add the curd and *besan* mixture and mix well.
8. When the *vadis* become soft and the curry becomes thick, add the red chilli powder and hot oil. Mix well. Cook for a few minutes.
9. Remove into a serving bowl. Garnish with coriander leaves and serve hot with rice.

MAIN COURSES

- Ankurit Channe Ki Parutwali Biryani
- Ankurit Sabut Moong Dosa
- Bharahua Moong Dal Cheela
- Bhune Moong Dal Ki Roti
- Bhura Chana Cheela
- Chawal Aur Pili Moong Dal Ka Uttapam
- Chole Bhature
- Dahi Misal
- Dal Adai
- Dal Bati

- Dal Burgers
- Dal Dhokli
- Dal Pakwan
- Dal Roti Rolls
- Dal Thepla
- Malvani Vade
- Masoor Dal Khichdi
- Moong Dal Khichdi
- Moong Dal Paratha
- Moong Dal Puris
- Thalipeeth

ANKURIT CHANNE KI PARUTWALI BIRYANI
Sprouted Chickpeas & Beans Layered Biryani

INGREDIENTS
Serves: 6

1 cup mixed beans and peas (eg. Black chickpeas (*bhura chana*), white
  chickpeas (*kabuli chana*), whole mung beans (sabut *moong*), cow peas (*lobia/
  chavli*), moth beans (*matki*), sprouted

4 whole red chillies

12 garlic cloves, minced

2 tbsp finely chopped coriander leaves

15 sprigs finely chopped mint leaves

5 cloves

8 black peppercorns

1 tsp poppy seeds (*khus-khus*)

2 cinnamon sticks of 2"each

1 tsp cumin seeds

2 tbsp grated fresh coconut

1 tsp salt

4 tbsp clarified butter (*ghee*)

2 tbsp millet flour (*bajri ka atta*)

3 medium-sized tomatoes, blanched & finely chopped

1 big cardamom

2 bay leaves

1½ cups rice

½ tsp salt

1¾ cups water

Ankurit Channe ki Parutwali Biryani

METHOD

1. Place the sprouted *bhura chana* and *kabuli chana* with ½ cup water into a pressure cooker. Cook under pressure for about 6-8 minutes. Allow the pressure to fall on its own before opening the cooker. Remove into a bowl and set aside.
2. Place the *moong, lobia* and *matki*, with ¾ cup water, into a saucepan and boil for 8-10 minutes till the beans are tender. Remove into a bowl and set aside.
3. Combine the whole red chillies, garlic, coriander and mint leaves, cloves, 4 black peppercorns, poppy and cumin seeds, 1 cinnamon stick, coconut and salt. Grind to a smooth lump of *masala*.
4. Heat *ghee* in a saucepan, add the *masala* lump and stir till the raw aroma disappears.
5. Add the cooked sprouts and *bajri ka atta*. Stir fry till well mixed.
6. Add the tomatoes, stir and cook for a few minutes adding ¼ water to ease the stirring process. Remove and set aside the gravy.
7. Heat *ghee* in a saucepan and add the cardamom, 4 black peppercorns, 1 cinnamon stick and the bay leaves. Stir fry for a few minutes.
8. Add the rice and salt. Stir fry for 2-3 minutes.
9. Add water and cook for 5-8 minutes till the rice is tender. Remove and set aside. (If desired, spread 1 tbsp *ghee* over the rice and mix.)
10. Heat *ghee* in a heavy-bottomed saucepan.
11. First place a layer of rice, followed by a layer of gravy – till the final rice layer.
12. Cover tightly and cook on very low heat for 5-8 minutes.
13. Place the *biryani* on a serving dish and serve hot with curd or *papad*.

ANKURIT SABUT MOONG DOSA
Sprouted Whole Mung Beans Pancakes

Dosa originates from South India but immensely popular all over India as a snack food, with or without filling in it. This recipe is the variation using beans.

INGREDIENTS
Serves: 6
For the Batter
½ cup sprouted whole mung beans (*sabut moong*)
1 tsp minced ginger
2 garlic cloves, minced
½ tsp minced green chillies
1 red chilli, broken
1 tsp cumin powder
½ salt
(Blend all the above in a blender, adding water to make a smooth batter of pouring consistency)

For the Filling
1 tsp butter
1 medium-sized onion, finely chopped
¼ tsp minced ginger
2 garlic cloves, minced
¼ tsp salt
1 tbsp finely chopped coriander leaves
Oil for frying

METHOD

1. Heat butter in a pan and add the onions, ginger, garlic green chillies, salt and coriander leaves. Sauté for 2-3 minutes. Remove and divide into 6 portions.
2. Heat a griddle and smear it with a little oil. Pour a ladleful of batter in the centre and quickly spread with a circular motion, with the back of the ladle, to a thin 5" diameter. Turn over the *dosa* and cook the other side also.
3. Spread the filling on one half of the *dosa* and fold over and press lightly.
4. Remove onto a serving dish and repeat the process.
5. Serve hot with a chutney of your choice.

168

BHARAHUA MOONG DAL CHEELA
Mung Beans Stuffed Pancakes

Cheela is thin pancake and is popular food from Central India. Original *cheela* is made from *besan* (Bengal gram flour). This recipe is a variation.

INGREDIENTS
Makes: 12
For the Batter
250 gms (1 cup) mung beans (*moong dal*), cleaned, washed
  & soaked for 1hr. & drained
1 tsp salt
1 cup water
(Ground into a medium-coarse batter & set aside)

For the Filling
12 tsp clarified butter (*ghee*), 1 tsp for each *cheela*
3 big onions, finely chopped

2 tsp minced ginger
1 tsp minced green chillies
4 tbsp finely chopped coriander leaves
1 firm medium-sized tomato, finely chopped
1 tsp salt
1 tbsp oil

METHOD
1. Heat oil in a pan and sauté the ginger, green chillies, coriander leaves, onions and tomato, for a minute or two.
2. Add salt and mix well. Remove and divide into 12 portions.
3. Place a thick non-stick griddle/pan on medium heat and grease it all over with a thin and oily muslin cloth.
4. Pour 1½ ladlefuls of batter onto the griddle and spread it in a circular motion with the back of the ladle to form a fairly thin disc of 5" diameter.
5. When the base is slightly brown, pour ½ tsp *ghee* all around the edges and onto the surface. Turn over to the other side and pour the remaining ½ tsp *ghee* onto the surface.
6. Place one portion of the filling slightly towards one edge of the pancake (*cheela*), and fold the rest over the filling and roll.
7. Press lightly and cook on reduced heat for 1-2 minutes till done. Repeat with all.
8. Remove onto a serving dish and serve hot with green coriander chutney.

BHUNE MOONG DAL KI ROTI
Roasted Mung Beans Indian Breads

INGREDIENTS
Makes: 24

250 gms (1 cup) mung beans (*moong dal*), roasted to a light brown
  & soaked for 2 hrs. Then drained & ground into a smooth paste
3 tbsp clarified butter (*ghee*)
1 tsp cumin powder
1 tsp red chilli powder
½ tsp *garam masala* powder
1 tbsp pomegranate seeds (*anardana*), lightly roasted & pounded
1 tbsp dry fenugreek leaves (*kasuri methi*)
½ tbsp finely chopped coriander leaves
1½ tsp salt
Butter for shallow frying
2 cups flour (*maida*)
1 tsp black cumin seeds
½ cup water

METHOD
1. Heat *ghee* in a pan and add the cumin, red chilli and *garam masala* powders and salt. Stir for a few minutes.
2. Add the *dal* and stir. Cook till all the spices are well mixed.
3. Remove and add the *anardana*, dry fenugreek and coriander leaves. Mix well.
4. Divide the mixture into 24 portions.
5. Combine the flour and some *ghee* and rub well.
6. Add in some salt and the black cumin seeds.
7. Gradually add in the water and knead to form a smooth dough.
8. Cover the dough with a wet muslin cloth and set aside for ½ an hour.

9. Divide the dough into 24 portions and make round balls with a depression in the centre.
10. Stuff one portion of the filling into each depression. Gather all the edges together and seal. Shape into balls.
11. Roll the balls on a rolling board dusted with a little flour to make small, flat *roti*s of 4" diameter.
12. Heat a griddle and grease it with butter. Place a *roti* on it and smear a little butter all around the edges and on the surface. Fry both sides till light brown. Repeat with the remaining *roti*s.
13. Place the *roti*s on a serving dish and serve hot with vegetables, curd or a chutney of your choice.

BHURA CHANA CHEELA
Black Chickpeas Pancakes

INGREDIENTS

Makes: 6

125 gms (½ cup) black chickpeas (*bhura chana*), cleaned, washed
 & soaked overnight, then drained, washed again & ground into a fine batter.
1 small onion, finely chopped
1 medium-sized tomato, blanched and finely chopped
1 tsp minced green chillies
2 tbsp finely chopped coriander leaves
1 tsp salt
Butter for shallow frying

METHOD
1. Combine all the ingredients and mix well.
2. Heat a non-stick griddle and grease it with butter. Pour in one ladleful of batter and spread in a circular motion with the back of the ladle to form a disc of 4-5" diameter and 1/4 " thickness.

3. Smear butter on both sides of the *cheela* and cook first over medium heat and then on reduced heat, till light brown. Turn once and cook till crisp.
4. Remove the *cheela* onto kitchen paper to remove any excess butter and then repeat the process with the remaining batter.
5. Place the *cheela*s on a serving platter and serve hot with chutney.

CHAWAL AUR PILI MOONG DAL KA UTTAPAM
Rice & Mung Beans Pancakes

INGREDIENTS
Makes: 6
125 gms (½ cup) rice
125 gms (½ cup) mung beans (*moong dal*)
(Washed & soaked separately for 2 hrs. & drained)
¾ cup water
2 tsp roughly chopped ginger
¾ tsp roughly chopped green chillies
2 tbsp grated fresh coconut
1 tbsp fresh curd, whisked
½ tsp sugar
1 tsp salt
(Ground to a very smooth batter & set aside for 2 hrs.)
1 tbsp finely chopped coriander leaves
4 tsp butter (½ tsp for each *uttapam*)

For the Topping (optional)
2 medium-sized onions, finely chopped
½ tsp salt
1 tbsp finely chopped coriander leaves
(Mixed together)

172

METHOD
1. Combine the batter and coriander leaves. Mix well. Pour a ladleful of batter into a greased, hot griddle. Spread thinly in a circular motion with the back of the ladle to a diameter of 6". Smear ¼ tsp of butter all around the edges. Turn when the base is slightly cooked and light brown and smear ¼ tsp butter around the edges.
2. Remove onto a serving platter and serve hot; if using topping, then with any chutney of your choice.

CHOLE BHATURE
White Chickpeas with Leavened Deep-Fried Breads

This is the original delicacy the north of India but is now very popular all over India and is one of the best known dishes in restaurants and street food alike.

INGREDIENTS
Makes: 6
For the *Chole*
500 gms (2 cups) white chickpeas (*kabuli chana*), cleaned, washed & soaked overnight in 8 cups water and 1½ tsp soda,
2 tsp red chilli powder
4 tsp pomegranate seeds (*anardana*), roasted & ground
1 tsp *garam masala* powder
1 tsp black pepper powder
½ tsp turmeric powder
2 tsp cumin powder
1 tsp salt
1 tsp black salt
4 tbsp oil
½ cup hot oil

For the Onion Mixture

4 medium-sized onions, well washed, cut into wedges &
  soaked for 25-30 mins
1 medium-sized tomato, cut into wedges
1 tbsp lime juice
½ tsp salt
¼ tsp edible dry orange colouring
2 tbsp finely chopped coriander leaves
(Combine all the ingredients & mix well. Remove into a serving bowl.)

For the Garnish

3" piece ginger, shredded & shallow fried
6 green chillies, slit & shallow fried
2 tbsp finely chopped coriander leaves

174

METHOD

1. Place the *kabuli chana* and the same water in a pressure cooker. Cook under pressure for about 8-10 minutes. Allow the pressure to fall on its own before opening the cooker. Remove and drain but preserve the water.
2. Heat oil in a pan and add the *chana*, black salt, salt, red chilli, pomegranate seeds, and *garam masala*, turmeric and cumin powders. Stir till *the chana* turns black.
3. Add the preserved *chana* water gradually and stir constantly till the *chana* is thoroughly coated with the *masala*.
4. Pour hot oil over the *chole* and mix lightly.
5. Remove into a serving bowl and garnish with green chillies, ginger and coriander leaves. Serve hot with the *bhatura* and onion mixture.

INGREDIENTS

For the *Bhature*

Makes: 12 *Bhaturas*

2¼ cups flour (*maida*), sifted

½ cup semolina (*rawa*)

¼ tsp soda

1 tsp sugar

½ cup curd

¼ tsp salt

3 tbsp water

1 tsp melted *ghee*

Oil for deep frying

METHOD

1. Combine all the ingredients except the water and *ghee* and mix well.
2. Gradually add the water and knead into a dough.
3. Grease your palms with *ghee* and knead the dough till smooth.
4. Cover the dough with a wet cloth and set aside for 4 hours to ferment.
5. Divide the dough into 12 portions and shape into balls.
6. Roll each ball with a rolling pin, to a diameter of 4" and ¼" thickness.
7. Place the rolled *bhatura*s on a tray and cover with a wet cloth.
8. Heat oil in a frying pan to smoking point and fry one *bhatura* at a time, basting and turning till slightly brown and puffed.
9. Remove the *bhatura*s onto kitchen paper to get rid of any excess oil.
10. Place the *bhatura*s on a serving platter and serve hot with the *chole*.

DAHI MISAL
Curd Savoury Mix

INGREDIENTS
Serves: 6

125 gms (½ cup) whole mung beans (*sabut moong*), sprouted
¼ cup moth beans (*matki*), sprouted
¼ cup black chickpeas (*bhura chana*), sprouted
¼ cup white chickpeas (*kabuli chana*), sprouted
1 tbsp oil
1 tsp red chilli powder
¼ tsp turmeric powder
1 tsp mango powder
1 tsp salt

For the Gravy

2 tsp grated ginger
6 garlic cloves
½ tsp chopped green chillies
1 tbsp chopped coriander leaves,
(All ground into a fine paste)
50 gms dried peas (*vatana*), boiled
1 medium-sized onion, finely chopped
1 medium-sized tomato, puréed
1½ tsp coconut milk
2 tbsp tamarind pulp
1 tsp curry *masala* (refer Contents)
½ tsp turmeric powder
½ tsp *garam masala* powder
1 tsp sugar
1 tsp salt
4 tbsp oil

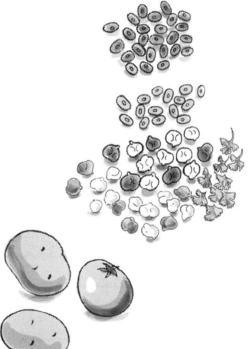

For Tempering the Gravy

1 tbsp oil
½ tsp mustard seeds
1 tsp cumin seeds
5-6 curry leaves
1 tsp red chilli powder

For the *Chivda*

200 gms thick pressed rice (*poha*), cleaned
100 gms peanuts, roasted in a few drops of oil
10-15 curry leaves, roasted in a dry pan
25 gms roasted split Bengal gram (*dalia* – available in the market)
½ tsp red chilli powder
1/8 tsp turmeric powder
1 tsp sugar
½ tsp salt
Oil for deep frying

For the *Aloo Bhaji*

1 tbsp oil
2 medium-sized potatoes (*aloo*), boiled, peeled & cubed
1/8 tsp turmeric powder
½ tsp salt

To Arrange

200 gms mixed *farsan*
400 gms curd, whisked & well mixed with 2 tbsp powdered sugar
6 tbsp onions, finely chopped
3 tbsp finely chopped coriander leaves
6 bread rolls (*pavs*), slit

METHOD

1. Boil the moong in ¾ cup water till tender and drain out excess water
2. Boil the matki in ½ - ¾ cup water till tender and drain out excess water
3. Pressure cook *bhura chana* and *kabuli chana* together, in ¾ cup water till tender, then drain out excess water.
4. Heat oil in a pan and add all the sprouts, salt, red chilli, turmeric and mango powders. Stir well for a few minutes. Remove and set aside.
5. Heat oil in a heavy-bottomed pan and add the onions and fry till light brown.
6. Add the *masala paste* and stir till the raw aroma disappears. Add the boiled vatana, tomato purée, coconut milk, tamarind pulp, *curry masala*, the turmeric and *garam masala* powders, sugar and salt. Stir, mixing well and simmer on reduced heat for a few minutes before tempering.
7. Heat oil in a griddle and add the mustard and cumin seeds. When they splutter, add the curry leaves and stir for a few seconds.
8. Add the red chilli powder and pour it over the gravy. Stir, mixing well. Remove from fire and set aside the gravy.
9. Heat a deep frying pan and add sufficient oil to fry the *chivda*. When the oil is very hot, place the poha in a colander and dip into the oil.
10. When the *poha* puffs up and becomes crisp, lift the colander and strain the excess oil by tossing the crisp *poha* lightly.
11. Combine the fried *poha*, peanuts, curry leaves, *dalia*, turmeric and red chilli powders, sugar and salt, in a deep vessel and mix well by tossing lightly. Set aside the *chivda*.
12. Heat oil in a pan and add the potatoes, salt and turmeric powder. Stir for a few minutes.
13. Add a ladleful of the prepared gravy and stir for few minutes. Remove the *aloo bhaji*.
14. In a serving dish, place the first layer of *aloo bhaji* followed by a layer of *chivda* and then a layer of the sprouts.
15. Now place a layer of mixed *farsan* and cover with the gravy.
16. Pour the curd over it all and sprinkle the onions and coriander leaves over it. Serve hot with slit *pavs*.

DAL ADAI
Lentil, Rice & Vegetable Savoury Pancakes

INGREDIENTS
Makes: 15
125 gms (½ cup) boiled rice (*ukhada chawal*), cleaned, washed
 & soaked for 5 hrs. & drained
125 gms (½ cup) Bengal gram (*chana dal*)
¼ cup pigeon peas (*tuvar dal*)
¼ cup black beans (*urad dal*)
¼ cup mung beans (*moong dal*)
(Cleaned, washed & soaked for 2 hrs. & drained)
3 whole red chillies
15 curry leaves
¾ cup water
1 tbsp tamarind pulp
1 tsp jaggery
1 medium-sized carrot, peeled & grated
1 medium-sized (125 gms) cabbage, grated
1 medium-sized onion, finely chopped
1 tsp minced green chillies
2 tbsp finely chopped coriander leaves
2 tsp salt
½ tsp asafoetida (*hing)*
Clarified butter (*ghee*) for shallow frying

METHOD
1. Grind all the *dals* in a grinder to form a coarse batter and then remove.
2. Grind the rice, whole red chillies, curry leaves, jaggery and tamarind pulp in a grinder to form a smooth batter, using a little water to ease the churning. Remove.
3. Combine both batters in a bowl and mix well.
4. Add the cabbage, carrot, green chillies, onions, coriander leaves, asafoetida and salt. Mix well.
5. Heat a griddle and grease it with *ghee*. Pour a ladleful of batter in and spread in a circular motion with the back of the ladle to form a disc of 5-6" diameter and ¼" thickness.
6. Smear *ghee* on both the sides and cook till light brown.
7. Remove the *adai* onto kitchen paper to get rid of any excess *ghee*.
8. Repeat the process with the remaining batter.
9. Place the *adai*s on a serving platter and serve hot with coconut chutney (refer Contents) or any other chutney of your choice.

180

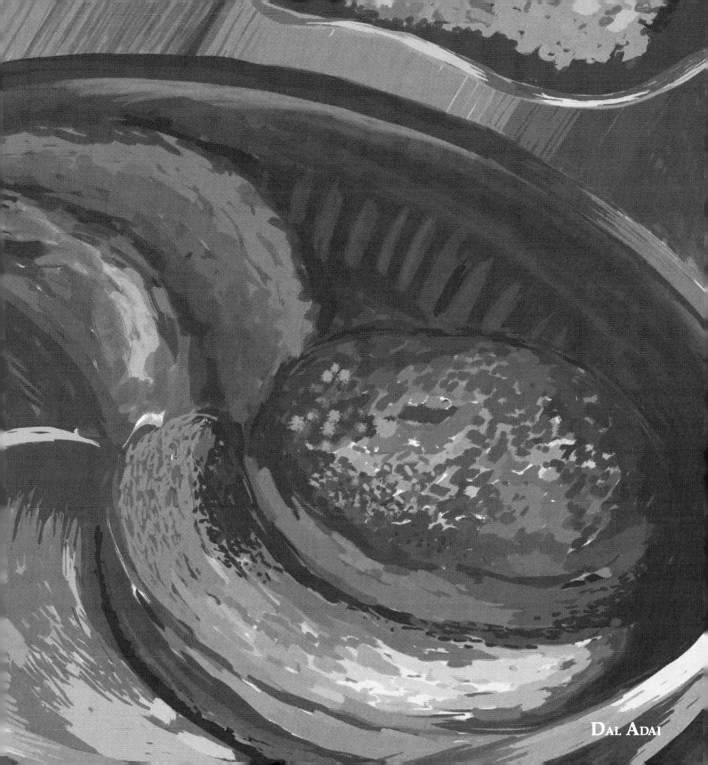

DAL ADAI

DAL BATI
Lentil & Charcoal Grilled Indian Buns

This is a delicacy from the Kutch region of Gujarat State and also very popular in Rajasthan.

INGREDIENTS
Serves: 4
For the *Dal*
100 gms pigeon peas (*tuvar dal*)
75 gms red (*masoor dal*)
75 gms mung beans (*moong dal*)
(Cleaned, washed & soaked separately for ½ hr. & drained)
3 tbsp clarified butter (*ghee*)
1 tsp minced ginger
4 garlic cloves, minced
½ tsp minced green chillies
1 tsp cumin seeds
1 tsp coriander powder
¼ tsp turmeric powder
½ tsp red chilli powder
2 whole red chillies, roasted & pounded coarsely
2 tsp sugar
2 tsp salt
5 cups water

For the Tempering
2 tbsp clarified butter (*ghee*)
A pinch of asafoetida (*hing*)
2 whole red chillies, roasted & pounded
1 medium-sized onion, chopped
1 tbsp finely chopped coriander leaves

182

METHOD

1. Place a heavy-bottomed pan on the stove and heat the clarified butter.
2. Add the cumin seeds. When they splutter, add the ginger, garlic and green chillies. Stir fry for a minute or two.
3. Add the *dals* and stir.
4. Add the cumin, coriander, turmeric and red chilli powders, the whole red chillies, sugar, salt and coriander leaves and mix well. Stir and cook for 2-3 minutes.
5. Add water and stir. Cook covered, stirring occasionally, for 45 minutes or till *dal* is well cooked.
6. Churn with a churner. (If the *dal* is too thick, add ½ - ¾ cup warm water to get the desired consistency.) Simmer for 5-8 minutes on low heat.
7. Heat clarified butter (*ghee*) in a pan and add the asafoetida, whole red chillies, and onions. Stir fry for 2-3 minutes.
8. Pour the tempering over the *dal*. Add the coriander leaves. Stir, mixing well.
9. Remove into a serving bowl and serve hot with the *bati*.

INGREDIENTS
Makes: 12
For the *Bati*
250 gms (2 cups) wheat flour (*atta*)
125 gms (1/2 cup) clarified butter (pure *ghee*)
1 tsp baking powder
2 tsp curd, whisked
1 tsp salt
½ cup water

METHOD
1. Place all the ingredients in a flat dish or *thali*. Rub well, gradually add water and knead to a semi stiff dough.
2. Cover with a wet muslin cloth and set aside for 10 minutes.
3. Knead well again and cover for 10 minutes.
4. Make 12 round balls and place each ball between your palms. Flatten slightly and make a depression with your thumb in the center. Make a slight slit in the center and on the sides.
5. Grease the tray, place the prepared flattened balls over it and bake for about 15-20 minutes at 350°F in a pre-heated oven.

OR

Bake on live charcoal for 2-3 minutes holding with the tongs and turning now and then till fully done.

OR

Place the *bati* in hot charcoal ash and remove when done.
6. Place the *bati* in a bowl, break it open, pour hot clarified butter over it and serve hot immediately with *dal*.

DAL BURGERS
Lentil Burgers

INGREDIENTS
Makes: 6
250 gms (1 cup) mixed *dals* [eg. pigeon peas (*tuvar dal*), mung beans (*moong dal*), Bengal gram (*chana dal*), cleaned, washed & soaked for 2hrs., then drained & ground to a coarse paste
2 tbsp finely chopped French beans
2 medium-sized carrots, peeled & grated
1 small piece cabbage, finely chopped
1 small capsicum, deseeded & finely chopped

(Heat ½ tbsp *ghee* & sauté the vegetables for a few minutes)
2 ½ tbsp clarified butter (*ghee*) & for deep frying
1 medium-sized onion, finely chopped
3 springs onions, finely chopped
2 tsp minced ginger
6 garlic cloves, minced
1½ tsp minced green chillies
1 medium-sized potato (*aloo*), boiled, peeled & mashed
1 tsp salt
2 tbsp finely chopped coriander leaves
1 tbsp cornflour
1 tbsp flour (*maida*)
2 tbsp water
(Combine both the flours & water and beat well into a smooth paste)
4 tbsp breadcrumbs
6 burger buns, slit into 2 (apply ½ tbsp butter on each)
6 tbsp butter
6 tsp garlic chilli spread (available in the market)
6 tsp tomato ketchup
6 tsp whole grain French mustard salad dressing (available in the market)
18 lettuce leaves, stems removed & broken into big pieces
1 large tomato, sliced into 12
2 small onions, sliced into 12
1 large cucumber, peeled & sliced into 12
6 toothpicks
6 slices of carrot
6 sprigs of mint
red cherries
&
6 paper napkins

METHOD

1. Heat the *ghee* in a saucepan and add the onions. Stir fry till light brown.
2. Add the ginger, garlic and green chillies. Stir fry for a few seconds.
3. Add the *dal* paste, vegetables, spring onions, potato, coriander leaves and salt.
4. Stir constantly, scraping the sides and bottom of the pan to prevent sticking and scorching.
5. Remove and divide the mixture into 6 portions.
6. Take one portion and make a round ball and then flatten between your palms to form a thick cutlet.
7. Smear with flour paste and coat with breadcrumbs. Shape and dust off the excess breadcrumbs.
8. Heat *ghee* in a frying pan and fry 2-3 cutlets at a time, basting and turning till they turn a light brown.
9. Remove the cutlets onto kitchen paper to get rid of any excess *ghee*.
10. Repeat the process with the remaining portions and paste.
11. Heat a griddle and heat the buns on both sides. (You can also butter the buns.)
12. Spread 1 tsp each of garlic chilli sauce, tomato ketchup and whole grain French mustard on both halves.
13. Place a lettuce leaf, onion, tomato and cucumber slices on one half of the bun.
14. Place the cutlet on top of this and again place lettuce leaves, onion, tomato and cucumber slices.
15. Cover the top with the other half of the bun. (If desired, wrap in a paper napkin and insert decorated toothpicks to hold it together.)
16. Repeat the process with the remaining buns and cutlets.
17. Serve with sauce.

DAL DHOKLI
Indian Bread cooked with Pigeon Peas

INGREDIENTS
Serves: 4

250 gms (1 cup) pigeon peas (*tuvar dal*), cleaned, washed &
  soaked for 1hr. & drained
2 cups water
1 tsp grated ginger
½ tsp minced green chillies
25 gms tamarind, pulped
2 tbsp grated jaggery
¾ tsp red chilli powder
¼ tsp turmeric powder
1½ tsp salt
1 medium-sized tomato, finely chopped
3 cups water
1 tbsp peanuts, roasted & coarsely pounded
1" cinnamon stick
2 cloves
1 bay leaf
1 tbsp finely chopped coriander leaves

For the Tempering
2 tbsp clarified butter (*ghee*)
½ tsp mustard seeds
1 tsp dry fenugreek leaves (*kasuri methi*)
½ tsp cumin seeds
2 pinches of asafoetida (*hing*)
2 whole red chillies, broken
8-10 curry leaves

½ cup wheat flour (*atta*)
1 tbsp Bengal gram flour (*besan*)
A pinch of turmeric powder
1/8 tsp red chilli powder
2 tbsp finely chopped coriander leaves
1/8 – ¼ cup water
1 medium-sized onion, finely chopped
2 tbsp butter
1 lemon, cut into wedges

METHOD

1. Place the *tuvar dal*, water, salt and turmeric powder in a pressure cooker. Cook under pressure for about 8-10 minutes. Allow the pressure to fall on its own before opening the cooker.
2. Pour the *dal* into another vessel and add the ginger, green chillies, tamarind pulp, jaggery, red chilli powder, tomato, water, peanuts, salt and coriander leaves. Mash well.
3. Heat *ghee* in a pan and add the mustard and cumin seeds. When they splutter, add the dry fenugreek leaves, asafoetida, red chillies and curry leaves. Fry for a minute. Pour the tempering over the *dal*.
4. Combine both flours, the turmeric and red chilli powders, the asafoetida, *ghee*, coriander leaves, salt and water. Mix well and knead into a semi-soft dough.
5. Divide the dough into 4 portions and roll out each into a thin *chapati*. Cut the *chapati*s into square *dhokli*s.
6. Heat a heavy-bottomed pan and pour in the prepared *dal*. When the *dal* reaches boiling point, gradually add in the *dhokli*s. Simmer for 10-15 minutes. If the *dal* thickens, add water till the desired consistency is reached.
7. Remove into a serving bowl and garnish with onions, coriander leaves, butter/*ghee* and lemon wedges. Serve hot.

DAL PAKWAN
Bengal Gram with Fried Savouries

This is a Sindhi delicacy and is a much sought after breakfast.

INGREDIENTS
Makes: 6
For the *Dal*
250 gms (1 cup) Bengal gram (*chana dal*), cleaned, washed
 & soaked for 5-6 hrs. & drained
5 cups water
½ tsp red chilli powder
½ tsp *garam masala* powder
½ tsp black pepper powder
½ tsp mango powder
¼ tsp turmeric powder
1½ tsp salt
3 tbsp oil/clarified butter (*ghee*), for pouring

METHOD
1. Place a heavy-bottomed saucepan on the stove and add the *dal*, water and turmeric powder. Boil the *dal* first on medium heat and then on reduced heat for 30-40 minutes, till soft and slightly mushy.
2. Add salt and stir. Remove into a serving bowl and sprinkle the red chilli, *garam masala*, black pepper powder and mango powders.
3. Heat *ghee* in a pan and pour it over the *dal*.
4. Serve hot with the *pakwan* and sweet chutney (refer Contents).

INGREDIENTS
Makes: 12
For the *Pakwan*
1 cup flour (*maida*)
½ tsp black cumin seeds
1 tsp clarified butter (*ghee*)
1 tsp salt
¼ cup water
Oil/clarified butter (*ghee*) for deep frying

METHOD
1. Combine the flour and *ghee* and rub well.
2. Add the salt, black cumin seeds and water. Knead into a semi-soft smooth dough.
3. Divide the dough into 12 portions. Make into round balls and roll out, dredging flour, into thin discs of about 4-5" diameter. Prick with a fork.
4. Heat oil/*ghee* in a frying pan and fry 1 *pakwan* at a time first on medium heat and then on reduced heat, turning frequently (using tongs or a ladle), till the *pakwan*s are crisp and light pink.
5. Remove and serve hot with the *dal* and a sweet chutney.

190

DAL ROTI ROLLS
Lentil Frankies

INGREDIENTS

Makes: 6

¼ cup mung beans (*moong dal*)
¼ cup Bengal gram (*chana dal*)
(Cleaned, washed & soaked for 2-3 hrs. & drained)
1 cup water
2 tbsp shelled peas
2 tbsp finely chopped cauliflower
2 tbsp finely chopped French beans
3 tbsp finely chopped onions
2 tsp minced ginger
8 garlic cloves, minced
1½ tsp minced green chillies
3 tbsp finely grated carrot
1 tsp salt
2 tbsp finely chopped coriander leaves
4 tbsp clarified butter (*ghee*)
6 slices of bread, soaked in water & squeezed lightly in a cloth
2 medium-sized potatoes (*aloo*), boiled, peeled & mashed
Oil for shallow frying
½ cup wheat flour (*atta*)
¾ cup flour (*maida*)
½ tsp salt
¼ tsp baking powder
1 tbsp clarified butter (*ghee*), melted
1 cup water
9 tsp tomato chilli sauce (1½ tsp for each frankie)
3 tbsp finely chopped coriander leaves

6 tbsp finely chopped onions

2 tsp *chaat masala* (approx. ¼ tsp for each frankie)

Butter/ clarified butter (*ghee*) for shallow frying

&

6 tissue papers

5 polythene bags

METHOD

1. Place the *dal*s and water into a saucepan and boil till ¾ done. Drain and coarsely grind the *dal* and remove.
2. Heat a dry pan and add the cauliflower, cabbage, peas and French beans. Sprinkle 2 tbsp water and cook till ¾ done. Remove from fire and set aside.
3. Heat *ghee* in a frying pan and add the onions and fry till light brown.
4. Add the ginger, garlic and green chillies. Stir, mixing well.
5. Add the cooked vegetables, carrots and potatoes and stir for a few minutes.
6. Add the *dal* and salt and stir constantly for a few minutes, scraping the sides and bottom of the pan to prevent sticking and scorching.
7. Remove into a bowl and add the coriander leaves and bread. Mix well.
8. Divide the mixture into 6 portions and roll each portion into 4″ length and 2″ thickness i.e. oval shapes.
9. Heat oil in a non-stick heavy-bottomed pan and put 2-3 rolls in at a time and shallow fry on all sides, holding the handle and slightly shaking the pan over reduced heat, till the rolls turn brown.
10. Remove the rolls onto kitchen paper to get rid of any excess butter/*ghee*.
11. Combine both the flours, the salt, baking powder, *ghee* and water. Mix well.
12. Beat with your hands or in a blender to form a smooth batter without lumps. (In case of a blender, adjust the quantity of water.)
13. Heat a non-stick griddle and grease with ¼ tsp *ghee*. Then pour in one ladleful of the batter and spread in a circular motion with the back of the ladle to get a diameter of 6″but not too thick.
14. Cook all the pancakes, turning over and smearing *ghee*, till cooked.

15. Place a pancake on a wooden board and spread 1½ tsp tomato chilli sauce, 1 tbsp onions, ½ tbsp coriander leaves and a pinch of *chaat masala* on it.
16. Place a vegetable roll on the top of it and roll into the *frankie*. Tuck in both ends.
17. Shallow fry the rolled frankies in a thick non-stick saucepan/griddle with butter/*ghee,* till light brown.
18. Wrap each frankie in a paper napkin and put into a polythene bag.
19. Place the wrapped frankies on a serving dish or cane *tokri* (basket) and serve hot with soft drinks.

DAL THEPLA
Lentil Pancakes

This is popular dish from Gujarat. It is a breakfast time savoury as well and goes well with afternoon tea time which is called "*Bapori*" in the local dialect.

INGREDIENTS
Makes: 6
125 gms (½ cup) pigeon peas (*tuvar dal*), washed &
  soaked in 2½ cups water for 1 hr.
½ cup wheat flour
2 tsp minced ginger
½ tsp minced green chillies
1 tsp coriander seeds, roasted & pounded
1 tsp cumin seeds, roasted & pounded
¼ tsp turmeric powder
1 tsp salt
3 tbsp finely chopped coriander leaves
1/8 cup water

METHOD
1. Place the *tuvar dal* with the same water in a saucepan and boil till soft. Remove and cool.
2. Combine the *dal*, turmeric powder, salt, pounded coriander and cumin seeds, ginger, green chillies and coriander leaves. Grind till mushy. Remove into a bowl.
3. Combine the *dal* mixture with the wheat flour. Gradually add water and knead to form a smooth dough.
4. Divide the dough into 12 portions and shape into round balls.
5. Grease the rolling board with oil and roll the balls out into *thepla*s of 4-6" diameter and about 1/8th inch thick.

6. Heat a griddle and put in a *thepla*. Shallow fry, smearing a little oil from the edges onto the centre. Flip and do the same. Keep turning till it has cooked and turned a light brown.
7. Remove onto a serving dish and serve piping hot with pickle or curd.

MALVANI VADE
Fried Discs with Lentils

Called *Komdi Vade* in the Konkan region, these thick, fried *puris* are best served with a semi-dry chicken curry.

INGREDIENTS
Makes: 15
6 tbsp rice flour (*chawal ka atta*)
2 tbsp black beans flour (*urad dal atta*)
2 tbsp Bengal gram flour (*besan*)
2 tbsp milo flour (*jawari ka atta*)
½ powdered dry fenugreek leaves (*kasuri methi*)
½ tsp powdered aniseeds
½ tsp powdered coriander seeds
½ tsp salt
2 tbsp luke warm oil
½ cup hot water
Oil for deep frying

METHOD

1. Combine all the dry ingredients and mix well. Add the luke warm oil and rub well. Add water and knead into a smooth dough. Set aside for 1 hr.
2. Divide the dough into 15 portions. Moisten your palms and shape the dough into small balls.
3. Place a plastic sheet on a wooden board and grease with a little oil.
4. Place a ball on this and flatten with a moist palm to 3" in diameter and ¼" thick.
5. Heat oil in a frying pan. Lift the plastic sheet with one hand and remove the *vada* by inverting it onto the other hand. Then slide it into the oil.
6. Fry 2-3 *vada*s at a time, pressing lightly with the back of a ladle, till it puffs up and turns brown.
7. Remove the *vada* onto kitchen paper and repeat the process for all the balls.
8. Place the *vada*s on a serving dish and serve hot. Best with semi-dry chicken curry.

MASOOR DAL KHICHDI
Red Lentil & Rice

Khichdi is an Indian sub-continent-specific word which signifies a dish of rice and lentils cooked together. It is made with all types of lentils – some lentils are preferred for a light meal, whereas others are popular for their therapeutic value.

INGREDIENTS
Serves: 4
200 gms (1 cup) rice, cleaned & washed
125 gms (½ cup) red lentil (*masoor dal*), cleaned,
  washed & soaked for 1 hr. & drained
3 tbsp clarified butter (*ghee*)
1 tsp cumin seeds
A pinch of asafoetida (*hing*)
2 medium-sized onions, finely chopped
1 medium-sized tomato, finely chopped
1 tsp minced ginger
½ tsp garlic cloves, minced
½ tsp minced green chillies
6 black peppercorns
2 big cardamoms, pounded
2 bay leaves
2 cloves
1" cinnamon stick
A small pinch of turmeric powder
1½ tsp salt
3½ cups water

METHOD

1. Heat the *ghee* in a saucepan and add the cumin seeds, asafoetida, black pepper corns, cloves, cardamoms, cinnamon and *dal*. Stir for a while.
2. Add the onions, ginger, garlic and green chillies. Stir till light brown. Then add the tomatoes and stir for a minute or two.
3. Add the rice, *dal* turmeric powder, salt and water. Mix well and first cook covered for 8-10 minutes on medium heat and then 8-10 minutes on reduced heat.
4. Serve hot with warm *ghee*, curd or pickle.

MOONG DAL KHICHDI
Mung Beans & Rice

198

INGREDIENTS

Serves: 4

125 gms (½ cup) mung beans (*moong dal*), cleaned, washed
  & soaked for 1 hr. & drained
¼ cup rice, cleaned, washed & soaked for 10 minutes, then drained
2 tbsp clarified butter (*ghee*)
1 tsp cumin seeds
1" cinnamon stick
2 big cardamoms
½ tsp red chilli powder
1 tsp cumin powder
½ tsp *garam masala* powder
1½ tsp salt
4 cups water

For the Tempering
2 tbsp clarified butter (*ghee*)
1 tsp minced ginger
1 medium-sized onion, finely chopped
A pinch of asafoetida (*hing)*

METHOD

1. Heat clarified butter (*ghee*) in a deep saucepan and add the cumin seeds. When they splutter, add the big cardamoms and cinnamon, and stir for a minute.
2. Add the *dal* and rice. Stir. Add the red chilli, cumin and *garam masala* powders and salt. Stir, mixing well for a minute or two.
3. Add water and cook covered for 5 minutes on medium heat and 8-10 minutes on reduced heat, till well done.
4. Heat clarified butter (*ghee*) in a pan and add the onions, asafoetida and ginger. Stir till light brown. Pour this over the *khichdi* and mix lightly.
5. Serve hot with pickle or curd.

MOONG DAL PARATHA
Mung Beans Stuffed Fried Breads

INGREDIENTS
Makes: 8
For the *Dal* Filling
¾ cup mung beans (*moong dal*), cleaned, washed   &
soaked for 2-3 hrs. & drained
1/8 tsp turmeric powder
¾ tsp salt
1 cup water
¼ tsp red chilli powder

¾ tsp black pepper powder
½ tsp *garam masala* powder
1 tbsp finely chopped coriander leaves

For the Dough
2 cups wheat flour
1 tsp clarified butter (*ghee*)
¾ tsp salt

200

METHOD
1. Place the *dal*, salt, turmeric powder and water in a saucepan and boil for 10-12 minutes till the *dal* is soft.
2. Add in all the spices and stir lightly. Remove, cool and divide into 8 portions.
3. Combine the flour, salt and *ghee*. Gradually add water and knead into a pliable dough. Divide the dough into 8 portions.
4. Make a depression and stuff the *dal* filling in and then seal it. Do the same for all.
5. Shape these into round balls and roll out with a rolling pin, dredging flour, making *paratha*s of 5-6" diameter.
6. Heat a griddle and grease it with *ghee* and put in the *paratha*s one at a time. Cook both sides, pouring a little *ghee* around the edges and on the surface. Turn and press with the spatula till the *paratha* is cooked on both sides.
7. Place the *paratha*s on a serving dish and serve hot with curd, pickle or *raita*.

MOONG DAL PURIS
Mung Beans Fried Thin Breads

INGREDIENTS
Makes: 12-15
For the Filling
125 gms (½ cup) mung beans (*moong dal*), cleaned, washed
  & soaked for 2 hrs., then drained & wiped dry with a napkin &
  ground into a coarse batter
1 tbsp clarified butter (*ghee*)
1 tsp minced ginger
¾ tsp minced green chillies
1½ tsp red chilli powder
½ tsp salt
1 tbsp finely chopped coriander leaves

For the Dough
1¼ cup wheat flour
½ tsp salt
½ cup water
Clarified butter (*ghee*) for deep frying

METHOD
1. Heat *ghee* in a frying pan and add the ginger and green chillies. Fry for a minute or two till slightly crisp.
2. Add the *dal*, salt, red chilli powder and coriander leaves. Stir constantly for 2-3 minutes, scraping the sides and bottom of the pan to prevent sticking and scorching. Remove the *dal* into a bowl and divide into 12-15 portions.
3. Combine the flour and salt and gradually adding water, knead into a smooth dough. Divide the dough into 12-15 portions.

4. Take a portion of the dough and make a depression. Stuff the *dal* filling in and seal it. Do the same for all the portions.
5. Now shape them into round balls and roll out with a rolling pin into small *puris* of 4" diameter and ¼" thickness.
6. Heat *ghee* in a frying pan and put in 1 puri at a time. When specks of *ghee* appear on top of the *puri*, press lightly with the back of the ladle till it puffs up, then turn it. Fry, basting with the *ghee*, till it turns a light brown.
7. Remove the *puris* onto kitchen paper to absorb any excess *ghee*.
8. Repeat the process with the remaining *puris*.
9. Place the *puris* on a serving platter and serve hot with curd, pickle or *raita*.

THALIPEETH
Flour & Lentils Savoury Indian Breads

INGREDIENTS
Makes: 12
3½ cups *thalipeeth* flour (refer Contents)
3 tbsp lukewarm oil/clarified butter (*ghee*)
3 medium-sized onions, finely chopped
3 tbsp finely chopped coriander leaves
¼ tsp turmeric powder
1 tsp red chilli powder
1½ tsp salt
1¼ cups water
Oil/clarified butter (*ghee*) for cooking

METHOD

Combine the flour and oil/*ghee* and rub well.

1. Add the onions, coriander leaves, salt, turmeric and red chilli powders.
2. Gradually add the water and knead to form a smooth dough. Divide the dough into 12 portions.
3. Place a plastic sheet on a wooden board and grease it with *ghee*/oil. Take a portion of the dough and pat lightly with your palms to shape into 1/8" thick circle of 6-7" diameter.
4. Make a few dents/marks with the tip of your finger.
5. Take the sheet in your left hand and place your right hand over the *thalipeeth*. Invert the sheet and then invert your right hand over a hot greased griddle.
6. Smear *ghee*/oil around the edges and on the surface of the *thalipeeth*, turning and pressing with the spatula till it is cooked on both sides.
7. Repeat the process with the remaining dough.
8. Place the *thalipeeth*s on a serving platter or on tissue paper in a bamboo basket (*tokri*) and serve hot with curd or pickle. (They can also be cooled and stored in an airtight tin.)

DAL WITH VEGETABLES

- Chana Dal Aur Baigan
- Chana Dal Aur Lauki
- Chana Dal Aur Paneer
- Chana Dal Aur Turi
- Chana Dal Makhanas
- Chana Dal Simla Mirch
  Aur Tamater
- Dal Aur Sabji
- Dal Kofta Palak Ke Sath
- Dhan Shak Dal
- Gobi Methi Chana Dal
- Masoor Dal Aur Baigan Curry

- Masoor Dal Tale Hue Pyaaz
  Ke Sath
- Matki Dal Aur Phansi
- Moong Dal Aur Gobi
- Moong Dal Mooli Ke Sath
- Moong Dal Palak Ki Parut Mein
- Sambar
- Sengue Baigan Dal
- Tuvar Dal Aur Karela
- Tuvar Dal Aur Palak Ki
  Sukhi Sabji
- Tuvar Dal Aur Mishra Sabji

CHANA DAL AUR BAIGAN

Split Bengal Gram & Aubergine

INGREDIENTS
Serves: 6

250 gms (1 cup) Bengal gram (*chana dal*), cleaned, washed
  & soaked for 30 mins & drained
4 cups water
400 gms aubergine (*baigan*), cut into 12-14 pieces
2 tbsp clarified butter (*ghee*)
1 tsp salt
A pinch of turmeric powder
2 tsp cumin seeds
2 medium-sized onions, finely chopped
2 medium-sized tomatoes, cut into 8 pieces
1 tsp red chilli powder
1 tsp coriander powder
1 tsp *garam masala* powder
4 tbsp curd, whisked
1 tbsp finely chopped coriander leaves

METHOD
1. Put the *chana dal* and water into a saucepan and cook till *dal* is tender. Remove.
2. Heat the *ghee* in a frying pan and add the cumin seeds. When they splutter, add in the onions and fry till they turn light brown.
3. Add the *baigan* and tomatoes. Stir and cook for a few minutes.
4. Add the red chilli, coriander and *garam masala*. Stir till well mixed.
5. Add the *dal*, salt, curd and stir. Cook on reduced heat for 5-6 minutes.
6. Remove into a serving bowl and garnish with coriander leaves. Serve hot with rice or *rotis*.

CHANA DAL AUR LAUKI
Bengal Gram & Bottle Gourd

INGREDIENTS
Serves: 6

250 gms (1 cup) Bengal gram (*chana dal*), washed
  & soaked for 2 hrs. & drained
1 tsp salt
¼ tsp turmeric powder
3 cups water
1 cup bottle gourd (*lauki*), washed, peeled & cubed
3 tbsp clarified butter (*ghee*)
1 tsp mustard seeds
2 medium-sized onions, finely chopped
½ tsp asafoetida (*hing*)
2 tsp minced ginger
8 garlic cloves, minced
6-8 curry leaves
1 tsp red chilli powder
2 tbsp finely chopped coriander leaves

206

METHOD
1. Place the *chana dal*, salt, turmeric powder and water in a pressure cooker. Cook under pressure for 6-8 minutes. Allow the pressure to fall on its own before opening the cooker. Remove.
2. Heat 2 tbsp *ghee* in a frying pan and add *lauki*. Stir fry for a few minutes till tender and then remove *lauki* from frying pan and set aside.
3. Add the remaining *ghee* to the frying pan and put in the mustard seeds. When they splutter, add the onions and fry till light brown. Add the asafoetida, ginger, garlic, curry leaves and red chilli powder. Stir fry for a few minutes.

4. Add the *dal* and *lauki*. Mix well. Add salt and water. Stir till specks appear on the surface.
5. Add the coriander leaves and stir. Cook covered for 5 minutes on reduced heat.
6. Remove into a serving bowl and serve hot with rice or *rotis*.

CHANA DAL AUR PANEER
Bengal Gram & Cottage Cheese

INGREDIENTS
Serves: 6
250 gms (1 cup) Bengal gram (*chana dal*), washed,
  soaked for 2 hrs. & drained
1 tsp salt
1 tsp turmeric powder
2 cups water
300 gms cottage cheese (*paneer*), cubed
Oil for deep frying
3 tbsp clarified butter (*ghee*)
4 bay leaves
4 whole red chillies, broken
4 big cardamom
4 cinnamon sticks
8 cloves
12 curry leaves
2 medium-sized onions, finely chopped
2 tsp minced ginger
8 garlic cloves, minced
4 medium-sized tomatoes, finely chopped

½ tsp *garam masala* powder
½ tsp cumin powder
2 tbsp finely chopped coriander leaves

METHOD

1. Place the *chana dal*, salt, water and turmeric powder in a saucepan and cook till the *dal* is tender but the grains remain separate. Remove and set aside.
2. Heat oil in a frying pan and fry the *paneer* pieces till light brown. Remove.
3. Heat *ghee* in a saucepan and add the bay leaves, red chillies, cardamoms, cinnamon, cloves and curry leaves. Stir fry for a few minutes.
4. Add the onions and stir fry till light brown.
5. Add the ginger and garlic and stir fry till the raw aroma disappears.
6. Add the tomatoes and stir. Cook till tender.
7. Add the *dal*, salt, *garam masala* and cumin powders. Stir and cook till well mixed.
8. Add water and cook covered for 1 minute.
9. Add in the *paneer* and mix lightly. Simmer for 2-3 minutes till the *paneer* is soft.
10. Sprinkle the coriander leaves and mix well.
11. Remove into a serving bowl and serve hot with rice or *paratha*s.

CHANA DAL AUR TURI
Split Bengal Gram & Ridge Gourd

INGREDIENTS
Serves: 6

250 gms (1 cup) split Bengal gram (*chana dal*), washed,
  soaked for 4 hrs. & drained
12 tbsp oil
2 tsp minced ginger
1½ tsp minced green chillies
4 medium-sized onions, finely chopped
1 tsp red chilli powder
¼ tsp turmeric powder
1 tsp *garam masala* powder
2 tsp cumin powder
2 tsp salt
800 gms ridge gourd (*turi*), peeled, washed & finely chopped
2 medium-sized tomatoes, puréed
2 medium-sized tomatoes, finely chopped
3½ tbsp finely chopped coriander leaves
1½ cup water

METHOD
1. Heat oil in a saucepan and add the ginger and green chillies. Stir fry for a minute or two then add the onions. Stir fry till light brown. Add salt and the red chilli, turmeric, *garam masala* and cumin powders. Stir fry for a minute or two.
2. Add the *dal*, mixing well. Add the tomato purée and stir. Cook for few minutes.
3. Add the *turi* and cook for a few minutes. Add the tomatoes and coriander leaves.

4. Transfer into a pressure cooker, add water and mix well. Cook under pressure for 6-8 minutes. When the pressure falls, move into a serving bowl, garnish with coriander leaves and serve hot with rice or *rotis*.

CHANA DAL MAKHANAS
Bengal Gram & Fox Nuts

INGREDIENTS

Serves: 6

For Boiling the *Dal*

250 gms Bengal gram (*chana dal*), washed,
  soaked for 1½ hrs & drained

¼ tsp turmeric powder

1½ tsp salt

6 cups water

For Frying the *Makhana*

2½ tbsp clarified butter (*ghee*)

100 gms foxnuts (*makhanas*), available in the market

For the Gravy

1 tbsp clarified butter (*ghee*)

1 medium-sized onion, finely chopped

2 tsp dry fenugreek leaves (*kasuri methi*)

2 tsp ginger paste

8 garlic cloves, made into a paste

4 medium-sized tomatoes, blanched & puréed

1 tsp garam masala powder

210

1 tsp cumin powder
1 tsp red chilli powder
1 tsp salt
6 cups water
1 tbsp butter
1 tbsp finely chopped coriander leaves
4 – 5 cups water

METHOD

1. Place the *chana dal*, turmeric powder, salt and water in a saucepan and cook covered for 15-20 minutes till the water evaporates and the *dal* is 3/4th done, ensuring that the grains are separate. Remove any scum. Remove from the stove and set aside.
2. Heat *ghee* in a shallow frying pan and fry the *makhanas* on medium heat till light brown. Remove and set aside.
3. Heat *ghee* in a heavy-bottomed saucepan and add the onions. Stir-fry till light brown. Then add the fenugreek leaves, ginger paste, garlic paste, *garam masala*, cumin and red chilli powder and the rest of the salt. Stir-fry for 6 – 8 minutes.
4. Add the tomatoes and stir, mixing well.
5. Add the prepared *dal* and water and stir. Bring to a boil and cook covered for 5-6 minutes.
6. Add prepared *makhanas*, cook and stir for 3 – 4 minutes till well mixed and the gravy is semi liquid.
7. Add butter and cook for another minute or two. Remove into a serving bowl and garnish with coriander leaves. Serve hot with assorted *rotis* or rice.
8.

CHANA DAL SIMLA MIRCH AUR TAMATER
Bengal Gram, Capsicum & Tomatoes

INGREDIENTS
Serves: 6

250 gms (1 cup) Bengal gram (*chana dal*), washed,
  soaked for 2 hrs. & drained
1 tsp turmeric powder
1 tsp salt
2 cups water
2 medium-sized capsicum, deseeded & cut into 8 pieces
2 medium-sized tomatoes, cut into 8 pieces
7 tbsp oil
2 tsp minced ginger
3 garlic cloves, minced
½ tsp minced green chillies
½ tsp cumin powder
15 gms tamarind, pulped
½ tsp sugar
1 tsp dry fenugreek leaves (*kasuri methi*)
4 whole red chillies, roasted & pounded
2 tbsp finely chopped coriander leaves

METHOD
1. Place the *chana dal,* turmeric powder, salt and water in a saucepan and boil till the *dal* is tender. Remove.
2. Heat oil in a saucepan and add the capsicum and tomatoes.
3. Add the salt and turmeric powder and stir fry for a few minutes. Remove.
4. Heat oil in a saucepan and add the ginger, garlic and green chillies. Stir for a minute or two.

CHANA DAL SIMLA MIRCH AUR TAMATER

5. Add the *dal, garam masala* and cumin powders. Stir and cook for a few minutes.
6. Add the tamarind pulp, sugar, capsicum and tomatoes.
7. Add the red chillies and fenugreek leaves. Stir and mix well. Cook covered for a few minutes and then add the coriander leaves, mixing well.
8. Remove into a serving bowl and serve hot with rice or *parathas*.

DAL AUR SABJI
Lentil & Vegetables

INGREDIENTS
Serves: 6

125 gms (½ cup) pigeon peas (*tuvar dal*), washed, soaked for 10 mins & drained

125 gms (½ cup) red lentil (*masoor dal*) washed, soaked for 10 mins & drained

3 cups water

For the *Masala*

2 tsp coriander seeds

2 tsp cumin seeds

8 whole red chillies

2 tsp mustard seeds

1 cup finely grated fresh coconut

3 tsp chopped ginger

12 garlic cloves, chopped

(Sautéed in oil separately & ground together to form a fine paste)

For the Vegetables

60 gms yam (*suran*), cubed
60 gms bottle gourd (*lauki*), cubed
2 drumsticks (*munga*), cut into 4" pieces
2 small aubergine (*baigan*), cubed
2 small potatoes (*aloo*), cubed
4 tbsp tamarind, pulped
3 tbsp clarified butter (*ghee*)
1½ tsp salt
2 tbsp dry fenugreek leaves (*kasuri methi*)
1 tbsp grated jaggery (*gur*)

METHOD

1. Place the *tuvar dal*, *masoor dal* and water in a pressure cooker. Cook under pressure for about 6-8 minutes. Allow the pressure to fall on its own before opening the cooker. Remove.
2. Heat oil in a frying pan and add the *suran, lauki, munga, baigan* and *aloo*. Stir fry till the vegetables are parboiled. Remove.
3. Heat *ghee* in a saucepan and add the *masala paste*. Stir fry for a few minutes.
4. Add the vegetables and cook for a few minutes.
5. Add the *dal*, salt and tamarind pulp. Cook till the vegetables are tender. If desired, add extra water.
6. Add the dry fenugreek leaves and jaggery. Mix well and then cook covered for a few minutes on reduced heat.
7. Remove into a serving bowl and serve hot with plain boiled rice.

DAL KOFTA PALAK KE SATH
Dal Balls with Spinach

INGREDIENTS
Serves: 6

125 gms (½ cup) mung beans (*moong dal*) washed,
  soaked for 2 hrs. & drained
125 gms (½ cup) Bengal gram (*chana dal*)
2 tsp ginger, roughly chopped
6 garlic cloves, roughly chopped
6 garlic cloves, minced
1¼ tsp green chillies, roughly chopped
¾ tsp minced green chillies
1 tsp coriander seeds, roasted
1 tsp aniseeds, roasted
2 tsp salt
2 tbsp clarified butter (*ghee*) & for frying
2 large potatoes (*aloo*), boiled, peeled & mashed
25 gms raisins, pounded
500 gms spinach (*palak*), stems removed, washed & drained
3 medium-sized tomatoes, blanched & puréed
1 tsp minced ginger
1½ tsp red chilli powder
1 tsp cumin powder
1½ tbsp white butter
1 cup coconut milk (refer Contents)
4 tbsp grated fresh coconut

216

METHOD

1. Combine *moong dal*, *chana dal*, ginger, garlic, green chillies, coriander seeds, aniseeds and salt. Grind in a grinder to a fine paste.
2. Heat *ghee* in a frying pan, add *dal* mixture and cook for few minutes stir constantly scraping the sides and bottom of the pan to prevent sticking and scorching. When done remove.
3. Add potatoes and salt to *dal* mixture. Mix well. Divide the mixture into 30 portions.
4. Make round ball of each portion, with a depression in the center and fill it up with raisins. Give a proper round shape.
5. Heat *ghee* in a frying pan and slide few *koftas* at a time in the oil. Fry basting oil on it with a perforated spoon on medium heat till light brown in colour.
6. Remove *koftas* on a kitchen paper.
7. Place spinach in a pan. Place the pan on fire. Cook without water for 5-6 minutes. Remove, cool and grind in a grinder to a rough paste.
8. Heat *ghee* in a sauce pan, add green chillies stir and fry for a minute or two.
9. Add ginger, garlic, stir and fry for a minute or two.
10. Add red chilli and cumin powders.
11. Add spinach, tomatoes, butter and salt. Stir and cook till specks appear on the surface.
12. Add coconut milk. Stir and cook for 6-8 minutes.
13. Add *dal koftas* and cook covered for few minutes.
14. Remove in a serving bowl, garnish with coriander leaves and serve hot with *rotis* or *parathas*.

DHAN SHAK DAL

This is a Parsee delicacy. Apart from vegetables in it, it is also cooked with mutton or chicken and hugely popular with non-Parsees as well.

INGREDIENTS

Serves: 6

2 tbsp oil/butter

1 tbsp ginger paste

10 garlic cloves, made into a paste

½ tsp green chilli paste

¼ turmeric powder

4 medium-sized tomatoes, puréed

2 tsp salt

For the *Dals & Vegetables*

¼ cup each, washed, soaked separately for 2 hrs. & drained

    Field beans (*val*)

    Red lentil (*masoor dal*)

    Mung beans (*moong dal*)

    Pigeon peas (*tuvar dal*)

    Bengal gram (*chana dal*) or black beans (*urad dal*)

50 gms (½ bunch) fenugreek leaves, chopped

1 medium-sized tomato, quartered

1 small aburgine (*baigan*), quartered

1 small piece of red pumpkin (*bhopla*), peeled & quartered

1 small potato (*aloo*), quartered

1 small sweet potatao *(shakarkand)*, quartered

1 small bottle gourd (*turi*), peeled & quartered

1 medium-sized onion, quartered

4 spring onions with leaves, chopped

4 tbsp chopped coriander leaves
4 sprigs mint leaves, chopped
5 cups water

For the Powdered Spices
2 whole red chillies
3 black peppercorns
2 cloves
2 big cardamoms
½ tbsp cumin seeds
1 tbsp coriander seeds
1" stick cinnamon
(Ground into a powder)

For the *Dhan Shak Masala*
1 tbsp dry fenugreek leaves (*kasuri methi*)
1 tbsp cumin seeds
½ tsp cloves
(roasted & ground into a fine powder)

For the Garnish
2 tbsp clarified butter (*ghee*)
2 medium-sized onions, wedged

METHOD
1. Place all the *dals*, vegetables and water in a pressure cooker. Cook under pressure
2. for about 10-12 minutes. Allow the pressure to fall on its own before opening the cooker. Remove into a bowl and cool.
3. Blend in a blender till a liquid consistency has been achieved. Remove.
4. Heat oil/butter in a heavy-bottomed saucepan and add the ginger, garlic and green chilli paste. Stir fry for a few minutes.

5. Add all the powdered spices, the turmeric powder, and *dhan shak masala*. Stir fry for few minutes.
6. Add the tomato purée and stir well.
7. Add the *dal*, vegetables and salt. Stir and cook for 5-8 minutes.
8. Heat the *ghee* in a frying pan and add the onions. Stir fry till brown. Remove.
9. Pour the *dhan shak dal* into a serving bowl and garnish with fried onions. Serve hot with brown rice and cucumber.

GOBI METHI CHANA DAL
Bengal Gram with Cauliflower & Fenugreek

220

INGREDIENTS
Serves: 6
For Frying Cauliflour
750 gms (2 medium-sized) cauliflower (*phool gobi*), cut into sprigs & washed
½ tsp red chilli powder
½ tsp dry mango powder
1 tsp salt
3½ tbsp oil for shallow frying

For Cooking Fenugreek Leaves
1¼ tbsp oil
400 gms (2 bunches) fenugreek leaves, chopped
1 tsp minced ginger
4 garlic cloves, minced
¼ tsp turmeric powder
¼ cups water
1¼ tbsp oil

For Cooking *Dal*

¾ cup Bengal gram (*chana dal*), washed, soaked for 25-30 minutes & drained
½ tsp salt
¼ tsp turmeric powder
1 cup water

For the Final Dish

3 tbsp oil
3 tsp minced ginger
10 garlic cloves, minced
4 medium-sized tomatoes, chopped
¾ tsp salt
1 tsp red chilli powder
2 tsp cumin powder
½ tsp *garam masala* powder
2 tbsp finely chopped coriander leaves

METHOD

1. Combine the salt, red chilli and dry mango powders and sprinkle over the cauliflower. Mix well.
2. Heat oil in a pan and shallow fry the cauliflower till it turns a light brown. Remove onto kitchen paper.
3. For cooking cauliflour, heat oil in a pan and add half the ginger and garlic and stir for a few seconds.
4. Add the fenugreek leaves, turmeric powder and salt and stir well.
5. Add water and cook covered till fenugreek leaves are tender. Remove.
6. Combine the *chana dal* with salt, turmeric powder and water in a saucepan and cook for 8-10 minutes till the *dal* is soft. Remove.
7. Heat oil in a frying pan and add ginger and garlic and stir for 1-2 minutes.
8. Add the tomatoes, salt, red chilli, cumin and *garam masala* powders. Mix well.

9. Immediately add in the fried cauliflower and cooked fenugreek leaves and *chana dal*. Stir on reduced heat. Cook covered for a few minutes.
10. Remove into a serving bowl and garnish with coriander leaves. Serve hot with *rotis* or rice.

MASOOR DAL AUR BAIGAN CURRY
Red Lentil & Aubergine Curry

INGREDIENTS
Serves: 6
250 gms (1 cup) red lentil (*masoor dal*), cleaned, washed & drained
½ tsp turmeric powder
1½ tsp salt
7 cups water
2 tbsp finely chopped coriander leaves
400 gms 2 large aubergine (*baigan*), washed, stems removed & cut into 8 pieces
Oil for deep frying

For the *Masala*
4 tbsp grated dry coconut
4 tsp coriander seeds
6 whole red chillies
1 tsp cumin seeds
25 gms tamarind, cleaned & washed
            OR
100 gms grated mango
¼ tsp turmeric powder
½ tsp salt

222

6 tbsp oil
¾ cup water
(Ground into a fine paste)

For the Tempering
3 medium onions, finely chopped
2 tsp minced ginger
6 garlic cloves, minced
4 tbsp oil

For the Garnish
½ tbsp finely chopped coriander leaves

METHOD
1. Place the *masoor dal*, salt, turmeric powder and water in a saucepan and cook covered till the *dal* is soft. Remove any scum that collects on the surface.
2. Mash the *dal* with a wooden churner and add the coriander leaves. Stir and cook for a few minutes. Remove.
3. Rub salt and turmeric powder on the *baigan* pieces and then heat oil in a frying pan and fry the *baigan pieces* till half done. Remove.
4. Heat oil in a saucepan and add in the *masala*. Stir and cook till the raw aroma disappears.
5. Add in the *baigan pieces* and stir till well mixed.
6. Add the *dal* and mix well. Cook covered for a few minutes on reduced heat. If the *dal* is thick, add more hot water and cook for a few minutes more. Remove.
7. Heat oil in a frying pan and add the onions. Stir fry till light brown.
8. Add in the ginger and garlic and stir fry for a minute or two.
9. Pour the *dal & baigan* curry into the tempering ingredients and stir. Cook for a few minutes.
10. Remove into a serving bowl and garnish with coriander leaves. Serve hot with *jeera* rice.

MASOOR DAL TALEHUE PYAAZ KE SATH

Red Lentil with Fried Onions

INGREDIENTS

Serves: 6

250 gms (1 cup) red lentil (*masoor dal*), washed,
  soaked for 15 minutes & drained
A pinch of turmeric powder
2 tsp salt
2 cups water
4 tbsp white butter
4 medium-sized onions, wedged
4 medium-sized tomatoes, blanched & puréed
1 tbsp finely chopped coriander leaves

224

METHOD

1. Place the *masoor dal*, salt, turmeric powder and water in a saucepan and boil till the *dal* is half done. Remove.
2. Place a pan on the stove and add the tomato purée and salt. Stir and cook for a few minutes. Remove.
3. Heat the butter in a saucepan and add the onions. Stir fry till light brown.
4. Add in the cooked *dal* and tomato purée. Stir and cook for a few minutes.
5. Remove into a serving bowl and garnish with dots of white butter and coriander leaves. Serve hot with *rotis* and rice.

Matki Dal aur Fransbean
Moth & French Beans

Ingredients
Serves: 6
200 gms French beans (*fransbean*), washed & chopped
1 tsp minced green chillies
¼ tsp turmeric powder
1½ tsp salt
8 tbsp oil
250 gms (1 cup) moth (*matki dal*), washed, soaked for 2 hrs. & drained
100 gms raw mango, grated
½ tsp turmeric powder
1 cup water
1 tbsp finely chopped coriander leaves

For the Coconut *Masala*
2 tbsp grated dry coconut
4 whole red chillies
1 tbsp chopped coriander leaves
2 tsp chopped ginger
6 garlic cloves, chopped,
(Ground into a smooth paste)

METHOD

1. Heat oil in a pan and add the green chillies. Stir fry for a minute or two.
2. Add in half the salt and turmeric powder and the *fransbean*. Stir, then cook covered till half done. Remove.
3. Heat oil in the same saucepan and add the ground *masala*. Stir fry till fat oozes.
4. Add the moth, the rest of the turmeric powder and salt. Stir fry till well mixed.
5. Add water and mix well. Cook covered for a few minutes on reduced heat.
6. When half done, add the cooked *fransbean*, mango and coriander leaves. Stir for a few more minutes.
7. Remove into a serving bowl and serve hot with *roti*s or *paratha*s.

226

MOONG DAL AUR GOBI
Mung Beans & Cauliflower

INGREDIENTS
Serves: 6
For the Cauliflower
1 kg cauliflower (*phool gobi*), cut into sprigs & washed
¼ tsp turmeric powder
1 tsp salt
2 cups water
Oil for frying

For the *Dal*
250 gms (1 cup) mung beans (*moong dal*), washed,
  soaked for 20 mins & drained

½ tsp turmeric powder
1 tsp salt
4 bay leaves
3½ cups water

For the Coconut *Masala*
125 gms (½ cup) grated dry coconut
2 tsp cumin seeds
1½ tsp minced green chillies
4 whole red chillies
¼ tsp turmeric powder
½ tsp salt
(Ground into a smooth paste)

For the Tempering
2 tbsp clarified butter (*ghee*)
1 tsp mustard seeds
½ tsp asafoetida (*hing*)
10-15 curry leaves
1 tsp dry fenugreek leaves (*kasuri methi*)
2 tbsp finely chopped coriander leaves

METHOD
1. Place the cauliflower, salt, turmeric powder and water in a saucepan and cook till half done. Remove and cool.
2. Heat oil in a frying pan and fry the cauliflower till light brown. Remove.
3. Put the *moong dal*, salt, turmeric powder, bay leaves and water into a saucepan and cook till the *dal* is tender tender. Remove any scum that rises to the surface.
4. Mash the *dal* with the back of a ladle.
5. Add the coconut *masala* and stir. Cook for a few minutes.

6. Add the cauliflower (if desired, add 1 cup water), stir and cook for a few minutes before removing from the stove.
7. Heat the *ghee* in a frying pan and add in the mustard seeds. When they splutter, add the asafoetida, curry leaves and dry fenugreek leaves. Stir fry for a minute.
8. Add in the cooked *dal* and cook covered for a few minutes.
9. Remove into a serving bowl and garnish with coriander leaves. Serve hot with *roti*s or rice.

MOONG DAL MOOLI KE SATH
Mung Beans with Radish

INGREDIENTS
Serves: 6

228

250 gms (1 cup) mung beans (*moong dal*), washed & soaked for 3 hrs. & drained (Preserve the water)
¾ tsp turmeric powder
1½ tsp salt
2 cups water
5 medium-sized radish (*mooli*) with tender leaves, peeled & cubed & leaves finely chopped
2 whole red chillies, powdered
4 minced green chillies
4 tbsp oil
4 tbsp tamarind pulp (refer Contents)

For the Tempering
3 tbsp oil
¼ tsp asafoetida (*hing*)
1 tsp cumin seeds
1 tsp minced ginger

METHOD

1. Place the *moong dal* and preserved water into a saucepan and add the water and half the salt and turmeric powder. Cook till the *dal* is half done, remove any scum that floats to the surface. Remove from the stove.
2. Heat oil in a pan and add the green chillies and stir for 1-2 minutes.
3. Add the radish and leaves, the remaining salt and turmeric powder. Stir for 2 minutes.
4. Add the red chilli powder and stir. Cook till half done, then remove.
5. Heat oil in a pan and add the half cooked *dal* and radish. Stir for a few minutes.
6. Add the tamarind pulp and cook for a few minutes.
7. Heat oil in a pan and add the asafoetida, cumin seeds and ginger. Stir for 1-2 minutes.
8. Pour in the *dal* and radish over the tempering and stir lightly for a few seconds.
9. Remove into a serving bowl and serve hot with *chapati*s or *paratha*s.

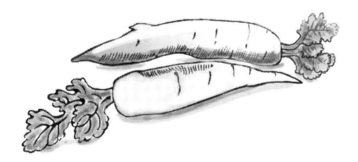

MOONG DAL PALAK KI PARUT MEIN
Mung Beans in Spinach Layers

INGREDIENTS

Serves: 6

For the *Dal*

250 gms (1 cup) mung beans (*moong dal*), washed,
  soaked for 1 hr. & drained. (Preserve the water)

1 tbsp butter

A pinch of turmeric powder

1½ tsp salt

For the Spinach

100 gms (4 bunches) spinach (*palak*), stems removed & washed

2 tsp minced ginger

4 garlic cloves, minced

2 tsp minced green chillies

½ tsp salt

2 tbsp butter

4 medium-sized tomatoes, puréed

200 gms cream, lightly whipped

½ tsp salt

For the Garnish

1 tbsp white butter

2 large tomatoes, sliced

½ tsp black pepper powder

½ tsp salt

1 tbsp finely chopped coriander leaves

METHOD

1. Place the *moong dal* and preserved water into a saucepan. Add butter, salt and turmeric powder. Cook till the *dal* is tender but the grains separate. Remove from the stove.
2. Place the spinach, ginger, garlic, green chillies and salt in a saucepan and cook covered for a few minutes till slightly tender. Remove and cool.
3. Grind the spinach into a coarse paste.
4. Heat butter in a saucepan and add the tomato purée. Stir and cook for a few minutes.
5. Add the spinach, cream and salt. Stir and cook for a few minutes. Remove.
6. Heat the white butter in a pan and add in the tomato slices, black pepper powder and salt. Fry till slightly soft. Remove.
7. Place a ladleful of *dal* into a dish. Cover with a ladleful of the spinach.
8. Repeat the process with the remaining *dal* and spinach so that there is a layer of *dal* at the top.
9. Place prepared tomato slices over this and garnish with coriander leaves. Serve hot with *roti*s or rice.

SAMBAR

Spicy Lentil & Vegetable Accompaniment from South India.

INGREDIENTS
Serves: 6
For the *Dal*
175 gms (¾ cup) pigeon peas (*tuvar dal*), washed &
  soaked for 15 mins & drained
3½ cups water
½ tsp turmeric powder

½ tsp cumin powder
½ tsp coriander powder
1 whole red chilli, broken
6 curry leaves
1½ tsp desiccated coconut
1 tsp salt

For the *Sambar*
1¼ tbsp oil
6 curry leaves
1 small tomato, chopped
1 drumstick (*munga*), chopped
1 medium-sized aubergine (*baigan*), chopped
6 Madras onions, chopped
3 small pieces pumpkin (*bhopla*) , chopped
¼ cup shelled peas
4 small pieces bottle gourd (*lauki*), chopped
1 tsp *sambar masala* (refer Contents)
1 tsp desiccated coconut
½ tsp jaggery (gur)
25 gms tamarind, pulped
½ tsp salt
3 cups water

For the Tempering
2 tbsp oil
½ tsp mustard seeds
6-8 curry leaves
1 whole red chilli, broken
½ tsp asafoetida (*hing*)
½ tsp *sambar powder masala*
1 tsp desiccated coconut

232

METHOD

1. Place all the *dal* ingredients into a pressure cooker and cook under pressure for about 10-15 minutes. Allow the pressure to fall on its own before opening the cooker. Remove.
2. Heat oil in the pressure cooker and the add curry leaves, tomato, *munga*, *baigan*, Madras onions, *bhopla*, peas and *lauki*. Stir and cook for a few minutes.
3. Add salt, the *sambar powder*, coconut, jaggery, tamarind pulp and water. Stir and mix well. Cook under pressure for about 5-6 minutes, then remove sambar from fire.
4. Heat oil in a pan and add the mustard seeds. When they splutter, add the whole red chilli, curry leaves, asafoetida, *sambar powder masala* and desiccated coconut. Stir for a few seconds.
5. Pour the *sambar* into the tempering. Stir and mix well.
6. Remove into a serving bowl and serve hot with *idli*s, *vada*s or *dosa*s.

SENGUE BAIGAN DAL
Drumsticks, Aubergine & Lentils

INGREDIENTS

Serves: 6

250 gms (1 cup) mixed *dals*, eg. mung beans (*moong dal*), pigeon peas (*tuvar dal*), black beans (*urad dal*), washed & soaked for 1 hr. & drained

3 tbsp clarified butter (*ghee*)

2 tsp minced ginger

13 cups water

2 medium-sized aubergine (*baigan*), cubed

4 drumsticks (*munga or sengue as called in Sindhi language*), scraped & cut into pieces

4 medium-sized tomatoes, blanched & chopped

20 curry leaves

1 tsp *garam masala* powder

2 tsp red chilli powder

1 tsp sugar

1 tsp salt

For the Tempering

2 tbsp clarified butter (*ghee*)

1 tsp cumin seeds

1 tsp mustard seeds

¼ tsp asafoetida (*hing*)

2½ tsp salt

1 cup water

1 tbsp finely chopped coriander leaves

METHOD

1. Heat *ghee* in a saucepan and add the ginger and fry for a minute or two.
2. Add the *dal*s. Stir fry for a few minutes then add water and mix well. Cook covered for 30 minutes.
3. Remove from the stove, mash and strain.
4. Heat *ghee* in a pan and add the tomatoes, salt and drumsticks, Stir and cook for few a minutes.
5. Add the *baigan*, curry leaves, *garam masala* and red chilli powders, and sugar. Stir and cook for a few minutes.
6. Add water and mix well. Cook covered till the vegetables are tender. Remove.
7. Heat *ghee* in a saucepan and add the cumin and mustard seeds. When they splutter, add the asafoetida and stir for a minute or two.
8. Add the *dal*s, vegetables and salt. Mix well. Cook covered till the *dal*s and vegetables are well mixed (if the *dal* becomes thick, add hot water as necessary).
9. Remove into a serving bowl and garnish with coriander leaves. Serve hot with plain boiled rice.

TUVAR DAL AUR KARELA
Pigeon Peas & Bitter Gourd

INGREDIENTS
Serves: 6
125 gms (½ cup) pigeon peas (*tuvar dal*)
2 pinches turmeric powder1 tsp salt
1½ cups water
1 cup tender bitter gourd (*karela*), sliced
50 gms tamarind, pulped

For the *Masala*
½ tbsp oil
4 tsp black beans (*urad dal*)
4 tbsp grated dry coconut
4 whole red chillies
3 tbsp coriander seeds
8 black peppercorns
5 tbsp water
(Fried in oil and ground into a smooth paste)
2 tbsp oil
A pinch of turmeric powder
½ tsp salt
2 tbsp hot oil
1 tbsp finely chopped coriander leaves

236

METHOD
1. Place the *tuvar dal*, salt, turmeric powder and water into a pressure cooker. Cook under pressure for about 6-8 minutes. Allow the pressure to fall on its own before opening the cooker. Remove.
2. Rub salt with the turmeric powder on *karela* and leave overnight.
3. Next morning, wash the *karela* slices and add the tamarind pulp. Set aside for 5-8 minutes.
4. Heat oil in a frying pan and add the *karela*. Stir fry for 5 minutes.
5. Add salt and turmeric powder. Stir fry for a minute or two.
6. Add the *masala* and hot oil. Mix well.
7. Cook covered on reduced heat for 5 minutes.
8. Remove into a serving bowl and garnish with coriander leaves. Serve hot with *roti*s or rice.

Tuvar Dal aur Palak ki Sukhi Sabji
Pigeon Peas & Spinach

Ingredients
Serves: 6

250 gms (1 cup) pigeon peas (*tuvar dal*), washed &
  soaked for 1 hr. & drained
6 whole red chillies
2 tbsp grated fresh coconut
8 pieces tamarind, cleaned & washed
2 tsp salt
(Ground into a coarse paste)
400 gms (2 bunches) spinach (*palak*), stems removed,
  washed & finely chopped
10 tbsp oil
1/8 tsp turmeric powder
100 gms cottage cheese (*paneer*), grated

Method
1. Combine the *dal* paste and spinach. Mix well.
2. Heat oil in a saucepan and add the *dal* and spinach mixture. Stir fry for a
    few minutes.
3. Add the turmeric powder and salt. Stir constantly for 6-8 minutes on
    medium heat, scraping the sides and bottom of the pan to prevent
    sticking and scorching.
4. Remove into a serving dish and garnish with the *paneer*. Serve hot with
    *paratha*s.

Tuvar Dal aur Mishra Sabji
Pigeon Peas & Mixed Vegetable

Ingredients
Serves: 6
250 gms (1 cup) pigeon peas (*tuvar dal*)
½ tsp turmeric powder
9 cups water
1 tbsp oil
125 gms aubergine (*baigan*), cut into pieces
3 drumsticks (*munga*), cut into 4 pieces
1 medium-sized onion, chopped
1½ tsp salt
2 tsp curry powder (refer Contents)
2 tbsp desiccated or grated dry coconut
15 garlic cloves, minced
1 tamarind, pulped
1 medium-sized tomato, cut into pieces

For the Tempering
1 tbsp oil
1 tbsp clarified butter (*ghee*)
¼ tsp asafoetida (*hing*)
1 tsp mustard seeds
10-15 curry leaves

METHOD

1. Place water in a heavy-bottom saucepan and bring to boiling point.
2. Add the *tuvar dal*, turmeric powder and oil and cook covered over medium heat for 45 minutes till the *dal* is soft. Remove from the stove.
3. Pour out the top thin watery surface *dal* into a separate pan.
4. Mash the remaining thick *dal* with wooden churner, into a smooth consistency.
5. Pour in the thin watery layer and mix well. Place on the stove.
6. Add the *baigan*, *munga*, salt, onion, curry powder, coconut, turmeric powder and garlic. Stir and mix well. (If the *dal* turns thick after adding the vegetables, pour in 2 cups of hot water and mix well.)
7. Cook covered over medium heat till the vegetables become tender.
8. Add the tamarind pulp and cook covered for a few minutes.
9. Add the tomatoes and cook covered over medium heat till the *dal* reaches the thickness desired.
10. Heat oil and *ghee* in a frying pan and add the mustard seeds. When they splutter, add the asafoetida and curry leaves. Fry for a few minutes.
11. Pour a ladleful of *dal* over the tempering and stir. Pour all the tempering over the *dal*. Stir and cook covered for a few minutes.
12. Remove into a serving bowl and serve hot with plain boiled rice.

SEMI-LIQUID DALS

- Chana Dal
- Moong Dal
- Moong Dal Aur Sabut Moong Mithi Chutney Ke Sath
- Palakwali Moong Dal
- Sabut Urad Aur Rajma
- Sabut Urad Lajawab
- Sabut Urad Pakhtooni
- Shahi Sabut Urad
- Sukhi Moong Dal
- Urad Dal Talehue Pyaaz Ke Sath
- Tridali Dal Kokumwali

CHANA DAL
Bengal Gram

INGREDIENTS
Serves: 6

¾ cup Bengal gram (*chana dal*), washed
  & soaked for 25-30 mins & drained
2 cups water
A pinch of turmeric powder
1 tsp salt
2 tsp oil
A pinch of asafoetida (*hing*)
1 tsp cumin seeds
4 whole red chillies
6 curry leaves
1 bay leaf
2 black cardamoms
8 black peppercorns
4 cloves
1" stick cinnamon
1 tsp minced ginger
4 garlic cloves, minced
¼ cup groundnuts, roasted, peeled & ground to a powder.
½ tsp jaggery (*gur*)
1½ tbsp desiccated coconut
25 gms tamarind, pulped
1 tbsp finely chopped coriander leaves

METHOD

1. Place a heavy-bottomed pan on the stove and add the *dal*, water, salt and turmeric powder. Boil, stirring occasionally, for 10-15 minutes on medium heat and then for 10 minutes on low heat, till the *dal* is soft but the grains separate. When the *dal* is ¾ done, remove from the stove.
2. Remove 3 tbsp *dal* from the whole and mash it.
3. Heat oil in a pan and add all the spices, herbs and the mashed *dal*. Stir and cook for a few minutes.
4. Pour in the remaining *dal* and stir. Cook for a few minutes on low heat.
5. Remove into a serving bowl and serve hot, garnished with coriander leaves.

242

MOONG DAL
Mung Beans

INGREDIENTS
Serves: 6
For the *Dal*
250 gms (1 cup) mung beans (*moong dal*), washed
  & soaked in 2½ cups water for 1 hour (preserve the water)
2 tbsp oil
4 green chillies, minced
2 tsp minced ginger
¼ tsp turmeric powder
1 tsp salt
2 tbsp finely chopped coriander leaves
1 small raw mango, grated
OR
2 tsp lime juice

For the Tempering
2 tsp clarified butter (*ghee*)
6 cloves garlic, minced
A pinch of asafoetida (*hing*)
1 tsp cumin seeds

METHOD

1. Heat oil in a saucepan and add the green chillies and ginger. Stir fry till the raw aroma disappears.
2. Add the *moong dal* along with the water in which it has been soaked, the turmeric and salt. Cover the saucepan and cook till the *dal* is tender but the grains remain separate. Remove from the stove and set aside the cooked *dal*.
3. Heat *ghee* in frying pan and add the *garlic* and *hing*. Stir for a few seconds.
4. Add the cumin seeds and fry till they splutter.
5. Pour the tempering over the cooked *moong dal*.
6. Add the coriander leaves to the *dal*. Stir and mix lightly.
7. Add the grated mango. Stir and mix lightly.
8. Serve hot with *chapati*s.

Moong Dal aur Sabut Moong Mithi Chutney ke Sath
Mung Beans & Whole Mung Beans with Sweet Sauce

This is combination of *dals* with a sweet sauce, served on green leaves.

INGREDIENTS
Serves: 6
For the ***Moong Dal***
125 gms (½ cup) mung beans (*moong dal*) washed & soaked for 4 hrs
A pinch of turmeric
1 tsp salt
2½ cups water

For the ***Sabut Moong***
125 gms (½ cup) whole green gram (*sabut moong*) washed & soaked for 4 hrs
A pinch of turmeric
1 tsp salt
2½ cups water

For the Sweet Chutney
100 gms jaggery (*gur*), grated
½ cup water
8 tbsp tamarind pulp
¼ tsp salt
1 tsp red chilli powder
1 tsp cumin seed powder

For the Garnish
½ tsp red chilli powder
½ tsp black pepper powder
½ tsp dry mango powder (*amchur*)

For the accompaniment & to serve
3 tbsp butter
12 small buns (*pav*), slit or bread slices
6 bowls made of dry almond leaves (*badam patta dona*), available in the market

METHOD

1. Place the *moong dal* and all the ingredients in a pressure cooker and cook under pressure for 5-6 minutes. Allow the pressure to fall on its own before opening the cooker. Remove into a bowl, mash and set aside.
2. Place the *sabut moong* and all its ingredients in a pressure cooker and cook under pressure for 6-8 minutes. Allow the pressure to fall on its own before opening the cooker. Remove into a bowl and set aside.
3. Place the jaggery, water, tamarind pulp and salt in pan. Stir and cook for a minute or two.
4. Add the red chilli and cumin powder. Stir and cook till the chutney becomes slightly thick. Remove into a bowl and set aside.
5. Spread ¼ tbsp butter on each *pav* all over and in the slits. Heat a griddle and roast the *pav* till slightly brown all over. Repeat the process for all the *pavs*. Set aside.
6. On a serving platter, place *badam patta dona*.
7. Pour in layers: ½ tbsp of moong *dal*, then ½ tbsp of *sabut moong* and then the chutney.
8. Sprinkle red chilli powder, black pepper powder and *amchur*. Serve with the buttered and roasted *pavs*.

PALAKWALI MOONG DAL
Spinach with Mung Beans

INGREDIENTS
Serves: 6
250 gms (1 cup) mung beans (*moong dal*), washed
 & soaked for 30 mins & drained
2 cups water
1 tsp salt
1 tsp turmeric powder
1 (150 gms) small bunch spinach, cleaned & washed
¼ tsp soda
1 tsp salt
3 tbsp butter
2 tsp minced ginger
1 tsp minced green chillies
2 medium-sized tomatoes, blanched & puréed
½ tsp red chilli powder
1 tsp cumin powder

METHOD
1. Place a heavy-bottomed pan on the stove and add the *dal*, water, salt and half the turmeric powder. Stir and cook for 10-15 minutes on medium heat, then simmer for 10 minutes on low heat till the *dal* becomes soft but the grains remain separate. Remove.
2. Rub the spinach with the soda. Add salt and cook in a pan with water till tender. Remove, cool and coarsely grind.
3. Heat butter in a pan and add the ginger and green chillies. Stir for a minute.
4. Add the tomato purée, spinach, salt, red chilli, rest of the turmeric and cumin powder. Cook for a few minutes. Pour in the boiled *dal*. Stir over low heat.
5. Remove into a serving bowl and serve hot with *rotis*.

SABUT URAD AUR RAJMA
Whole Black Beans & Red Kidney Beans

INGREDIENTS
Serves: 6

250 gms (1 cup) whole black beans (*sabut urad dal*), washed
  & soaked for 25-30 mins & drained

7½ cups water

2 tsp ginger paste

2 tsp minced ginger

10 garlic cloves, made into a paste

15 garlic cloves, minced

2 medium-sized tomatoes, finely chopped

½ tsp turmeric powder

2 tsp salt

125 gms (½ cup) red kidney beans (*rajma*), washed & soaked for 8 hrs. &
drained

2½ tbsp butter/ clarified butter (*ghee*)

2 tbsp knobs of white butter

A pinch of asafoetida (*hing*)

1½ tsp minced green chillies

1 tsp red chilli powder

1 tbsp finely chopped coriander leaves

METHOD

1. Place the *urad dal*, water, minced ginger and garlic, tomatoes, turmeric
    powder and salt into a pressure cooker. Cook under pressure for 10
    minutes on medium heat. Simmer on low heat for 10 minutes. Allow the
    pressure to fall before opening the cooker. Remove.

2. Place the beans and water in the pressure cooker and cook under pressure
    for 10-15 minutes. Allow the pressure to fall before opening the cooker.
    Remove.

3. Heat the butter/*ghee* in a pan and add the asafoetida, ginger and garlic pastes, green chillies and red chilli powder. Stir for a minute.
4. Pour in the prepared *dal* and *rajma* and mix well. Cook covered for 5 minutes.
5. Remove into a serving bowl and serve hot, garnished with knobs of white butter and coriander leaves.

SABUT URAD LAJAWAB
Whole Black Beans

INGREDIENTS
Serves: 6

For the *Dal*

250 gms (1 cup) whole black beans *(sabut urad),* washed & soaked for 2 hrs
1 tsp salt
½ tsp turmeric
4¾ cups water
2 tbsp clarified butter (*ghee*)
8 cloves garlic, finely chopped
2 tsp finely chopped ginger
1 tsp cumin seeds, roasted & pound into a powder
2 tsp coriander seeds, roasted & pound into a powder
4 whole red chillies, roasted & pound into a powder
½ tsp *garam masala*
6 medium-sized tomatoes, puréed
2 tbsp butter
2 tsp dried fenugreek leaves (*kasuri methi*)
1 tsp lime juice

For the Garnish
1 tbsp finely chopped coriander leaves

METHOD
1. Place the *sabut urad*, salt, turmeric and 4 cups of water in a pressure cooker and cook under pressure for 8-10 minutes. Allow the pressure to fall before opening the cooker. Remove and set aside.
2. Heat *ghee* in a pan and add in the garlic, ginger, cumin and coriander seeds, red chillies and *garam masala*. Stir fry for a few minutes.
3. Add the tomato purée and *sabut urad*. Stir and cook for a few minutes.
4. Add the remaining water, butter, fenugreek leaves and lime juice. Mix lightly and simmer for 8-10 minutes. Remove.
5. Garnish with coriander leaves and serve hot, preferably with *tandoori roti*s (Indian bread baked in a *tandoor* oven).

SABUT URAD PAKHTOONI
Whole Black Beans with Cream – Afghan Style

INGREDIENTS
Serves: 6
For the *Dal*
50 gms. (1 cup) whole black beans (*sabut urad*), washed
  & soaked overnight
2½ tsp salt
2 tsp red chilli powder
2 tsp ginger paste, mixed with ¼ cup water
2 tsp garlic paste, mixed with ¼ cup water
8 cups water
4 tbsp white butter
4 large tomatoes, puréed
1 tsp *garam masala*

For the Garnish
2 tbsp finely chopped coriander leaves
100 gms cream, whipped

METHOD
1. Place the *sabut urad*, 2 tsp salt, red chilli powder, ginger and garlic paste, and water, into a pressure cooker and cook under pressure for 20-30 minutes. Allow the pressure to fall before opening the cooker. Remove and set aside.
2. Heat the white butter in a sauce pan and add the tomato purée, *garam masala* and remaing salt. Stir and cook for a few minutes.
3. Add the *sabut urad* mixture. Cover and simmer on low heat for about 25-30 minutes, occasionally stirring with a ladle, till mushy.
4. Remove into a serving bowl. Garnish with coriander leaves and swirls of cream. Serve hot with assorted *rotis* or *jeera* rice.

SHAHI KALI URAD
Royale Whole Black Beans

INGREDIENTS
Serves: 6
For the *Dal*
250 gms (1 cup) whole black beans (*sabut urad*), washed
  & soaked for 30 mins
4 cups water
½ tsp turmeric powder
1 tsp salt
½ cup curd (*dahi*)
2 medium-sized tomatoes
1 tsp ginger paste
1 tsp finely chopped coriander leaves
2 cups hot water

For the Tempering
1 tbsp butter
¼ tsp asafoetida (*hing*)
4 green chillies, chopped
10 cloves garlic, crushed
1 tsp finely chopped ginger
2 tsp red chilli powder

For the Garnish
3 tbsp butter
2 medium-sized onions, thinly sliced into rings
1 tbsp finely chopped coriander leaves

METHOD

1. Place the *sabut urad*, water, turmeric and salt, into a pressure cooker and cook for 10-15 minutes. Allow the pressure to fall before opening the cooker. Remove and set aside.
2. Place a pan on the stove and add the boiled *sabut urad*, curd, tomatoes, ginger paste & coriander leaves. Stir and mash.
3. Add hot water and cook till slightly thick. Remove and set aside.
4. Heat butter in a saucepan and add all the tempering ingredients and fry for a minute.
5. Pour the cooked *dal* mixture over the tempering. Stir and cook for a few minutes on reduced heat and then remove into a serving bowl.
6. Heat 3 tbsp butter in a pan and add the onion rings. Fry till golden brown, stirring constantly. Remove and drain.
7. Serve the *shahi sabut urad* hot, garnished with fried onions and chopped coriander leaves.

SUKHI MOONG DAL
Dry Mung Beans

INGREDIENTS
Serves: 6
For the *Dal*
250 gms (1 cup) mung beans (*moong dal*), washed
  & soaked for 10 mins
¼ tsp turmeric
1 tsp salt
3 cups water

For the Tempering
2 tbsp oil or 1 tbsp butter
3 green chillies, minced
1 tsp black cumin seeds (*shahjeera*)
½ tsp black pepper powder

For the Garnish
1 tbsp finely chopped coriander leaves

METHOD
1. Place the *dal*, turmeric, salt and water into a saucepan. Boil till the *dal* becomes tender yet the grains remain separated. Remove and set aside.
2. Heat oil in a pan and add the green chillies. Stir fry for a few seconds.
3. Add the *shahjeera.* When it splutters, pour in the *dal*. Lightly mix with a fork.
4. Remove into a serving bowl and sprinkle black pepper powder on top.
5. Serve hot, garnished with coriander leaves.

Urad Dal Tale Hue Pyaaz ke Sath
Black Beans with Fried Onions

Ingredients
Serves: 6
For the *Dal*
250 gms (1 cup) black beans (*urad dal*), washed
  & soaked for 20 mins & drained
2 cups water
1 large tomato, chopped
A pinch of turmeric powder
1 tsp salt

254

For the Tempering
1 tbsp butter
A pinch of asafoetida (*hing*)
1 whole red chilli, broken
1 tsp minced ginger
3 garlic cloves, minced
1 medium-sized tomato, finely chopped
½ tbsp finely chopped coriander leaves

For the Onions
3 tbsp butter
1 large onion, cut into wedges

For the Garnish
3 tbsp finely chopped coriander leaves

METHOD

1. Place a heavy-bottom pan on the stove and add the *dal*, water, tomatoes, salt and turmeric powder.
2. Stir and cook for 10 minutes on medium heat and simmer for 10 minutes on low heat, till the *dal* becomes tender but the grains remain separated. Remove.
3. Heat butter in a pan and add the asafoetida, ginger, garlic and red chilli. Stir for a minute and add the tomato. Stir for 1-2 minutes.
4. Add the coriander leaves and stir for a few seconds.
5. Pour in the boiled *dal* and stir. Cook for a few minutes on low heat. Remove the *dal* into a serving bowl.
6. Heat butter in a pan and add the onions. Fry till golden brown, stirring constantly. Drain and remove. Sprinkle over the *dal*.
7. Sprinkle coriander leaves over the *dal and fried onions* and serve hot with *roti*s.

TRIDALI DAL KOKUMWALI
Tangy Three-Lentil Soup

In this dish, three varieties of lentils are cooked together with Garciana Indica – a fruit with a wonderfully tangy taste. It is indigenous to the west coast of India.

INGREDIENTS
Serves: 6
250 gms (1 cup) three mixed lentils, washed & soaked for 1 hr. Preserve the water.
  Split mung beans (*moong dal chilka*)
  Black beans (*urad dal*)
  Bengal gram (*chana dal*)
3 tbsp oil
garlic cloves, roughly crushed

¼ tsp asafoetida (*hing*)
2 tsp roughly crushed ginger
2 green chillies, roughly crushed
4 Garciana Indica (*kokum*)
1 medium-sized tomato, cut into 4 pieces
¼ tsp turmeric powder
1 tsp red chilli powder
1 tsp dry coriander powder (*dhania* powder)
1½ tsp salt
1 tbsp finely chopped coriander leaves
3 cups water

METHOD

1. Heat oil in a pan and add the *hing*.
2. Add the garlic, ginger and green chillies. Stir for a minute or two till the raw aroma disappears.
3. Add the tomato and stir for a minute or two.
4. Add the *kokum* and stir.
5. Add the soaked *dal* mixture and stir well.
6. Add all the remaining ingredients including the water in which the *dals* have been soaked. Stir and mix well.
7. Transfer the mixture into a pressure cooker and cook under pressure for 8-10 minutes. Allow the pressure to fall before opening the cooker.
8. Open the lid and stir, mixing well.
9. Remove and serve hot with rice or *chapatis*.

LIQUID DALS

- Aam Aur Tuvar Ki Dal
- Masoor Dal
- Masoor Tamater Dal Sar
- Panchratni Dal
- Tamater Aur Tuvar Dal
- Tuvar Dal Amboat
- Varan

AAM AUR TUVAR KI DAL
Pigeon Peas with Mango

INGREDIENTS

Serves: 6

250 gms (1 cup) pigeon peas (*tuvar dal*), washed

2 tsp salt

¼ tsp turmeric powder

5 cups of water

2 tbsp clarified butter (*ghee*)

4 tbsp of *panch phoran* (refer Contents)

A pinch of asafoetida (*hing*)

8 curry leaves

1 tsp red chilli powder

6 small raw mangos, grated

50 gms (2 tbsp) jaggery (*gur*), grated

1 tbsp finely chopped coriander

258

METHOD

1. Place the *tuvar dal*, turmeric, salt and water into a pressure cooker and cook under pressure for 6-8 minutes. Allow the pressure to fall before opening the lid. Remove the cooked *dal* and set side.
2. Heat *ghee* in a pan and add the *panch phoran*, asafoetida and curry leaves. Stir for 1-2 minutes till they splutter.
3. Add the cooked *dal*, red chilli powder, mango and jaggery. Blend the mixture with a wooden churner or a beater till well mixed and cook for a few minutes.
4. Add the coriander leaves and mix well.
5. Remove into a serving bowl and serve hot with plain boiled rice.

MASOOR DAL
Red Lentil

INGREDIENTS
Serves: 6
For the *Dal*
125 gms (½ cup) red lentil (*masoor dal*), washed
1 medium-sized onion, finely chopped
4 garlic cloves, minced
½" cinnamon stick (*dalchini*)
¼ tsp whole black peppercorns
2 bay leaves (*tej patta*)
6 cups water

For the Tempering
2 tbsp clarified butter (*ghee*)
1 medium-sized onion, cut into wedges
1 tsp minced ginger
6-8 curry leaves
¼ tsp turmeric powder
½ tsp *garam masala*
¼ tsp black pepper powder
1½ tsp salt
½ cup coconut milk (refer Contents)
½ tbsp finely chopped coriander leaves

METHOD

1. Place a heavy-bottomed saucepan on the stove and put in all the *dal* ingredients. Boil for 15 minutes. Then cook the *dal* with the pan covered, for 15 minutes, stirring occasionally, till the *dal* becomes soft and mushy.
2. Mash the *dal* well and strain through a muslin cloth. Add 1 cup of water to the residue, mash well and liquidise. Strain again. Discard the residue. Set aside the strained *dal*.
3. Melt the *ghee* in heavy-bottomed pan and add the onion wedges, ginger and curry leaves. Stir till the onions are brown.
4. Add the turmeric powder, *garam masala*, black pepper powder and salt. Stir well.
5. Pour the *dal* over the tempering and cook for 5-6 minutes (bringing it to the boil twice).
6. Add the coconut milk (refer Contents) and the coriander leaves. Mix well and cook for a few minutes.
7. Remove and serve hot with rice.

Note This preparation can be served on its own as a rich soup

260

MASOOR TAMATER DAL SAR
Red Lentil with Tomato

INGREDIENTS
Serves: 6
For the *Dal*
250 gms (1 cup) red lentil (*masoor dal*), washed
6 medium-sized tomatoes, finely chopped
1 tsp salt
½ tsp turmeric
4 cups water

For the Tempering & Garnish
2 tbsp oil
1 tsp mustard seeds
1 tsp cumin seeds
4 whole red chillies, broken
4 garlic cloves, minced
6 curry leaves
2 tbsp finely chopped coriander leaves

METHOD
1. Place all the *dal* ingredients into a pressure cooker and cook under pressure for 8-10 minutes. Allow the pressure to fall before opening the lid. Mash the mixture and strain through a muslin cloth. Set aside strained *dal* liquid and discard the residue.
2. Heat oil in a pan and add the remaining tempering ingredients. Stir fry for a few seconds then pour in the strained *dal* liquid. Stir, mixing well. Simmer for 6 minutes with the pan covered.
3. Remove, garnish with coriander leaves and serve hot with rice.

PANCHRATNI DAL
Five Lentils Curry

INGREDIENTS
Serves: 6
For the *Dal*
250 gms (1 cup) 5 mixed *dals*, eg. 2 tbsp each of:
  Whole black beans (*sabut urad*)
  Whole mung beans (*sabut moong*)
  Whole red lentil (*sabut masoor*)
  Pigeon peas (*tuvar dal*)
  Bengal gram (*chana dal*)
washed & soaked together for 2 hours
4 tbsp clarified butter (*ghee*)
1 tsp cumin seeds
1 medium-sized onion, finely chopped
¼ tsp turmeric powder
2 tsp coriander seeds powder (*dhania powder*)
1 tsp cumin powder
1 tsp red chilli powder
4 cups water
2 tbsp finely chopped coriander leaves

For the Tempering
4 tbsp white butter (*makkhan*)
1 tsp black cumin seeds
1 tsp aniseeds (*saunf*) powdered
1 medium-sized tomato, finely chopped
6 tbsp curd (*dahi*), whipped
1 tsp *garam masala* powder
1 tbsp finely chopped coriander leaves

METHOD

1. Heat *ghee* in a pressure cooker and add the cumin seeds. When they splutter, add the onions and stir for 3-4 minutes, on medium heat, till light brown.
2. Add the soaked *dals* and stir for 2-3 minutes.
3. Add the rest of the *dal* ingredients and mix well. Shut the cooker and cook under pressure for 6-8 minutes. Allow the pressure to fall before opening the cooker. Remove and set aside.
4. Place a heavy-bottomed pan on the stove and melt the white butter. Add all the other tempering ingredients except the coriander leaves. Stir for 4-5 minutes.
5. Pour the *dal* over the tempering and stir. Sprinkle the coriander leaves and stir.
6. Cook with the pan covered for 8-10 minutes, on low heat, stirring occasionally till the *dal* is soft and mushy.
7. Remove and serve hot with *chapati*s or rice.

TAMATER AUR TUVAR DAL
Pigeon Peas with Tomato

INGREDIENTS
Serves: 6
For the *Dal*
250 gms (1 cup) pigeon peas (*tuvar dal*), washed & soaked for 15 mins
2 tsp salt
¼ tsp turmeric powder
4 green chillies, minced
2 tsp minced ginger
6 garlic cloves, minced
6 medium-sized tomatoes, finely chopped
5 cups water

For the Tempering
4 tbsp oil
¼ tsp asafoetida (*hing*)
½ tsp mustard seeds
½ tsp cumin seeds
¼ tsp fenugreek seeds
4 whole red chillies, broken
6 curry leaves
½ tbsp finely chopped coriander leaves

METHOD

1. Place all the *dal* ingredients into a pressure cooker and cook under pressure for 6-8 minutes. Allow the pressure to fall before opening the cooker.
2. Remove the cooked *dal* into a bowl and lightly mash with a spoon. Set aside.
3. Heat oil in a pan and add the asafoetida, mustard seeds and cumin seeds. Stir.
4. When the seeds splutter, add the fenugreek seeds, red chillies and curry leaves. Stir fry for a few seconds.
5. Pour the cooked *dal* over the tempering. Stir and cook till the spices are well mixed.
6. Add the coriander leaves and mix well.
7. Remove and serve hot with rice.

264

TUVAR DAL AMBOAT
Sour Pigeon Peas

INGREDIENTS
Serves: 6
For the *Dal*
250 gms (1 cup) pigeon peas (*tuvar dal*), washed
6 cups water
2 medium-sized onions, finely chopped
6 green chillies, finely chopped
1 tsp red chilli powder
½ tsp turmeric powder
1 tsp *garam masala* powder
1 cup peanuts, pounded
3 tsp salt
100 gms fresh coconut
50 gms tamarind, pulped
50 gms jaggery (*gur*), grated

For the Tempering
2 tbsp oil
½ tsp asafoetida (*hing*)
1 tsp mustard seeds
20 curry leaves

For the Garnish
2 tbsp finely chopped coriander leaves

METHOD
1. Grate the coconut and grind with 3 tbsp water to form a fine paste.
2. Place a heavy-bottomed saucepan on the stove and put in the *tuvar dal*, water, onion, green chillies, red chilli powder, turmeric and *garam masala*. Mix well.
3. Add the peanuts, salt and coconut paste. Stir, mixing well. Cook for 6-8 minutes.
4. Add the tamarind pulp and jaggery. Stir, cover the pan and cook the *dal* for 45 minutes. Remove and set aside.
5. Heat oil in a pan and add the asafoetida and mustard seeds. When they splutter, add the curry leaves. Fry for a few seconds.
6. Add the cooked *dal* and mix well, stirring with the back of the ladle. Cook on low heat for a few minutes.
7. Remove into a serving bowl and garnish with coriander leaves. Serve hot with plain boiled rice.

266

VARAN
Plain Pigeon Peas

This is a simple everyday dish from Maharashtra. It is eaten with rice and usually a spoonful of clarified butter (*ghee* or *tup* in Marathi) is added to the *Varan* which is put on the rice.

INGREDIENTS
Serves: 4
125 gms (½ cup) pigeon peas (*tuvar dal*), washed &
  soaked for ½ hr. & drained
1/8 tsp turmeric powder
½ tsp salt
2½ cups water

METHOD

1. Place all the ingredients into a pressure cooker and cook under pressure for about 8-10 minutes. Allow the pressure to fall before opening the cooker.
2. Churn with wooden churner, mix well and re-heat.
3. Remove into a serving bowl and serve hot with plain boiled rice.

DAL MITHAIS

- Adadya
- Bhune Hue Daalia Ke Laddoo
- Chana Dal Aur Paneer Ki Mithai
- Chana Dal, Khopra Aur Char Magaz Ki Mithai
- Dalia Ki Chikki
- Dal Aur Dudhi Ki Mithai
- Ghari
- Moong Dal Halwa
- Moong Dal Laddoo
- Khajur Aur Daalia Ki Toffee
- Moong Dal Aur Anjeer Ki Burfi
- Moong Dal Pyasam
- Puran Poli
- Tridali Mithai

ADADYA
Lentil Sweet with Edible Gum

INGREDIENTS
Makes: 12

125 gms (½ cup) black beans (*urad dal*), powdered
30 gms (1½ tbsp) edible gum (*gaund*)
5 tbsp clarified butter (*ghee*)
¾ cup sugar
1 cup water
1/8 tsp nutmeg (*jaiphal*)
1/8 tsp mace (*javitri*)
12 gms chironjia nuts (*charoli*)
40 gms mixed dry fruit (eg. almonds, pistachios, cashewnuts), shredded
¼ tsp black pepper powder
½ tsp cardamom powder
1½ tsp dry ginger powder (*saunth*)
¼ cup milk

METHOD
1. Heat the *ghee* in a heavy-bottomed pan. Add the *gaund* and stir. As soon as they puff up, remove, preserve *ghee*, and pound *gaund* in a mortar and pestle, to form a powder.
2. Heat water and sugar in a deep saucepan, stirring occasionally till a one-thread consistency has been achieved.
3. In the same *ghee* used to fry the *gaund,* add the *dal* powder and stir for 8-10 minutes till light brown.
4. Add the *gaund*, all the spices and sugar syrup. Mix well and stir constantly till brown and well cooked. Remove and cool.
5. Divide into 12 portions and form pear shapes. Cool and store in a tin lined with wax paper. Use as required.

BHUNE HUE DAALIA KE LADDOO
Husked-Split-Roasted Bengal Gram Sweetmeat

INGREDIENTS
Makes: 20

100 gms husked split & roasted Bengal gram (*daalia*)
1 tbsp sesame seeds, roasted
4 tbsp grated & roasted dry coconut
150 gms jaggery (*gur*), grated
¼ tsp nutmeg (*jaiphal*)
¼ tsp mace (*javitri*)
3 tbsp clarified butter (*ghee*)
2 tbsp raisins, fried in a few drops of oil & removed when swollen
8 cashewnuts, broken into pieces

270

METHOD

1. Roast the *chana dal* for about 8-10 minutes on reduced heat till light brown and crisp. Remove and cool for a while. Grind into a coarse powder.
2. Place a heavy-bottomed pan on the stove and add *ghee*. When hot, add the *daalia* powder. Stir on reduced heat till a roasted aroma emanates.
3. Add all the remaining ingredients except the jaggery and roast well.
4. Heat another pan on reduced heat and melt the jaggery. Pour the melted jaggery over the roasted mixture and stir, mixing well.
5. Remove onto a plastic sheet and divide into 20 portions immediately while the mixture is hot.
6. Grease your palms and shape into round *laddoo*s, pressing lightly.
7. Store in tin lined with wax paper. Use as required.

CHANA DAL AUR PANEER KI MITHAI
Bengal Gram & Cottage Cheese Sweet

INGREDIENTS
Makes: ½ kg.

¼ cup Bengal gram (*chana dal*) washed,
 soaked for 3-4 hrs. Drained & washed.
½ cup water
250 gms cottage cheese (*paneer*), crumbled
2 tbsp clarified butter (*ghee*)
¾ - 1 cup sugar
2 tbsp milk
2 tsp poppy seeds
¼ tsp coarsely crushed green cardamom powder
2 edible silver foil (*warq*)

METHOD
1. Cook the *dal* in ½ cup water till tender. Remove.
2. Place a heavy-bottomed pan on the stove and add *ghee*. Add the *paneer* and stir over medium heat and then on reduced heat, till the paneer turns a light brown.
3. Add the *dal*, stir and mix well. Add sugar and stir, mixing well.
4. Add the poppy seeds and stir. Add milk if required to soften and stir till it leaves the sides of the pan. Add the cardamom powder and stir, mixing well.
5. Grease a *thali* or flat dish and remove the mixture onto it. Pat lightly into a diameter of 6-7 inches and ½ inch thickness (you can use a square aluminium tray of 6-7 " and ½ " high. This will help to make even pieces of *mithai*).
6. Decorate the pieces with *warq* and cool for ½ an hour. Cut into squares of 2" each (approximately 20) and store in a tin lined with wax paper. Use as required.

CHANA DAL, KHOPRA AUR CHAR MAGAZ KI MITHAI
Split Bengal Gram, Coconut & Kernel Seeds Sweet

INGREDIENTS
Makes: ½ kg.
125 gms (½ cup) split Bengal gram (*chana dal*), washed &
  soaked for 3-4 hrs. & drained
2½ cups water
½ tbsp clarified butter (*ghee*)
125 gms grated coconut
8 tbsp fine sugar
1½ tbsp kernel seeds (*char magaz*), roasted
1½ tbsp pistachios, shredded
1½ tbsp almonds, blanched & shredded
½ tsp green cardamom powder
1/8 tsp nutmeg (*jaiphal*), powdered
1/8 tsp mace (*javitri*), powdered
1 tbsp mixed dry fruit (eg. roasted *char magaz*, shredded almonds &
pistachios)

METHOD

1. Place the *dal* and water in a pan and boil till the *dal* becomes tender and dry. Drain and grind into a rough lump. Remove and crumble with your fingers.
2. Place a heavy-bottomed pan on the stove and add the *ghee*. Add the coconut and sauté for 1-2 minutes. Add the *dal* and sugar and stir for a few minutes on reduced heat till the mixture leaves the sides of the pan and becomes a lump.
3. Add the *char magaz*, almonds, pistachios, nutmeg, mace and cardamom powder. Stir, mixing well for few minutes.
4. Remove onto a board/flat dish and roll with a rolling pin into a 6 x 6" square of ½" thickness. Garnish with nuts and cut into 16 square pieces. Store in a tin lined with wax paper. Use as required.

272

Chana Dal, Khopra aur Char Magaz ki Mithai

CHANA DAL KI CHIKKI
Husked-Split-Roasted Bengal Gram Fudge

INGREDIENTS
Makes: 12

100 gms husked split & roasted Bengal gram (*daalia*),
  roasted again till crisp then cooled
70 gms sugar
70 gms jaggery (*gur*)
½ tsp clarified butter (*ghee*)

METHOD

1. Place a heavy-bottomed pan on the stove and add the sugar. Stir constantly till the sugar has melted and become light brown, occasionally reducing the heat so it does not burn.
2. Add the jaggery and reduce the heat. Stir vigorously till it melts.
3. Add the *ghee* and stir. Add the roasted gram. Turn off the heat and stir vigorously till well mixed.
4. Remove onto a wooden board and cool just for a minute. Roll out with a rolling pin into a square shape of 6" length, 4½" breadth and ½" thickness.
5. Cut into 12 pieces of 1½" length and breadth and ½" thickness.
6. Cool and store, wrapped in cellophane in an airtight tin. Use as required.

274

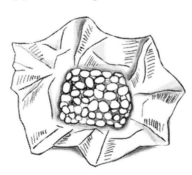

DAL AUR DUDHI KI MITHAI
Lentil & Bottle Gourd Sweet

INGREDIENTS

Makes: ¾ kg.

125 gms (½ cup) mixed *dals*, eg. 1 tbsp each of:
  Bengal gram (*chana dal*)
  Mung beans (*moong dal*)
  Pigeon peas (*tuvar dal*)
  Red Lentil (*masoor dal*)
  Black beans (*urad dal*)
Roasted for 6-8 minutes on reduced heat, cooled & ground
  into a coarse powder.
1 tbsp semolina (*rawa*)
350 gms (1 medium-sized) bottle gourd (*dudhi/lauki*),
  peeled, grated & squeezed
1 tbsp clarified butter (*ghee*)
200 gms condensed milk
3 tbsp almonds, soaked overnight, peeled & shredded
  (set aside 1 tbsp for garnishing)
2 edible silver foil (*warq*)

METHOD
1. Place a heavy-bottomed pan on the stove and heat *ghee*. Add the *dudhi* and
    stir for 4-5 minutes till the moisture evaporates. Remove.
2. In the same pan, heat more *ghee* and add the *dal* powder. Stir for 4-5
    minutes till it turns brown. Add the *dudhi* and mix well on reduced heat.
    Add the condensed milk. Stir well for 3-4 minutes. Stir in the almonds.
3. Remove into a flat dish and roll out with a rolling pin into a 6" diameter
    and ½" thickness. Garnish with almonds and decorate with *warq*.
4. Cut into approximately 20 square pieces. When set, store in a tin lined with
    wax paper. Use as required.

GHARI
Sweet Lentil Doughnuts

INGREDIENTS
Makes: 15
½ cup flour (*maida*), sifted
2½ tbsp clarified butter (*ghee*) & for deep frying
1 tsp milk
1/8 cup water
A pinch of salt
½ cup mixed *dals*, eg. 2 tbsp each of:
  Mung beans (*moong dal*)
  Bengal gram (*chana dal*)
(Roasted till crisp and light brown, cooled & ground into a coarse powder)
100 gms sweet *khoa* or any *khoa burfi*, available in the market
100 gms sugar (powdered)
15 gms pistachios (pounded)
20 gms cashewnuts (pounded)
1 tsp green cardamom powder
18 tsp nutmeg powder (*jaiphal*)
1/8 tsp mace powder (*javitri*)
1½ cups milk

276

METHOD

1. Combine the flour and *ghee* and rub well. Add the salt, milk and water and knead into a very smooth dough. Divide the dough into 5 portions.
2. Heat *ghee* in a heavy-bottomed pan and add the *dal* powder. Stir for 4-5 minutes on medium heat till it releases its roasted aroma and becomes brown.
3. Add the *khoa*, sugar, pistachios, cashewnuts, nutmeg, mace and cardamom powder and stir till well mixed.
4. Take a portion of dough and roll out on a rolling board with a rolling pin dredged in flour, into a diameter of 3".
5. Take the rolled disk in your palm and place a portion of the filling on it.
6. Gather all the edges towards the centre. Join and seal.
7. Twist the pointed, sealed portion to form a knot.
8. Place your left thumb on the knot and left middle finger at the base. Hold the *ghari* with your left hand and place it between the arc made by your right thumb and index finger.
9. Press lightly towards the centre, to create a barrel shape.
10. Repeat the same process for the remaining dough and filling.
11. Heat *ghee* in a frying pan and slide 2-3 *ghari*s in at a time. Fry, basting with oil, over reduced heat, till golden brown.
12. Remove and serve hot.

MOONG DAL HALWA
Mung Beans Dessert

Halwa is a semi-solid Indian dessert. Originally, *halwa* was made from *sooji* (cream of wheat) while the celestial offering in *Gurudwaras* (places of worship for the Sikhs), is known as *Kada Prasad* and is made from *atta* (wheat flour). *Moong Dal Halwa* is a very popular dish in northern and central India.

INGREDIENTS
Makes: ½ kg.
125 gms (½ cup) mung beans (*moong dal*), washed
& soaked for 4 hrs. & drained & ground into a smooth paste
3 tbsp clarified butter (*ghee*)
1¼ cups milk
½ - ¾ cup sugar
½ tsp green cardamom powder
25 gms mixed dry fruits (eg. almonds, cashewnuts & raisins), shredded

278

METHOD
1. Place a heavy-bottomed pan on the stove and heat 2 tbsp *ghee*. Add the *dal* paste and stir over medium heat, constantly scraping the sides and bottom of the pan to prevent sticking and scorching, for 6-8 minutes, till the *dal* is cooked and a greenish-brown
2. In another pan, heat the milk and add sugar. Stir for 5-6 minutes on reduced heat. Pour this over the *dal*.
3. Add 1 tbsp *ghee* and stir for 2-3 minutes.
4. Add the cardamom powder and half of the dry fruits. Mix well.
5. Stir for 3-4 minutes till the *halwa* starts oozing *ghee* and leaves the sides of the pan.
6. Remove into a serving bowl. Garnish with the remaining dry fruits and serve hot.

MOONG DAL LADDOO
Mung Beans Sweetmeat

INGREDIENTS
Makes: 12

50 gms (1 cup) mung beans (*moong dal*), washed
4 tbsp clarified butter (*ghee*)
1 tsp clarified butter (*ghee*), for frying the cashewnuts & raisins
¾ cup powdered sugar (sifted)
12 cashewnuts, broken
1½ tbsp raisins
3 tbsp fresh coconut, grated
8 green cardamoms, powdered
¼ tsp salt
3 tbsp milk (for binding)

METHOD

1. Place a heavy-bottomed pan on the stove and add the *dal*. Roast for 3-4 minutes on medium, then reduced heat, till crisp and light brown. Cool for 5-6 minutes and grind into a thick flour. Remove.
2. Heat *ghee* in a pan and fry the cashewnuts till light brown. Remove. In the same *ghee* fry the raisins till they swell. Remove.
3. Place a heavy-bottomed pan on the stove and add *ghee*. Add the *dal* flour and stir for 2-3 minutes on reduced heat till the *dal* and *ghee* are well mixed.
4. Add the sugar, cashewnuts, raisins, coconut, cardamom and salt. Mix well and remove the pan from the stove. Add milk and stir.
5. Divide into 12 portions and immediately bind while still hot into round balls.
6. Repeat the process for the remaining portions. Store in a tin lined with wax paper. Use as required.

KHAJUR AUR DAALIA KI TOFFEE
Dates & Husked-Split-Roasted Bengal Gram Toffee

INGREDIENTS
Makes: 12

250 gms seedless dates (*khajur*), cut into 4 and
  mashed lightly with a rolling pin
50 gms husked, split & roasted Bengal gram (*daalia*), roasted again & cooled
50 gms mixed dry fruits (eg. almonds, pistachios, walnuts, cashewnuts),
  roasted & thickly shredded
2 tbsp poppy seeds (*khus-khus*), roasted
1 sheet cellophane paper (cut into 12 pieces of 4"x4")

METHOD

1. Combine the *daalia*, dry fruits and dates. Mix well with your hands, mashing the dates lightly so that the *dal* and dry fruits blend well with the dates. Mix till it forms a lump.
2. Make a rectangular cube of 6" length, 2" breadth and 1" height.
3. Cut lengthwise from the centre to get 2 rectangular cubes of 1" breadth.
4. Cut each rectangle into 6 pieces horizontally to get 12 pieces totally, each of 1" length, breadth and height.
5. Now roll each piece in poppy seeds lightly and wrap in a piece of cellophane.
6. Store in a tin and use as required.

MOONG DAL AUR ANJEER KI BURFI
Mung Beans & Fig Sweet

INGREDIENTS
Makes: ½ kg.

125 gms (½ cup) mung beans (*moong dal*), washed
  & soaked for 2-3 hrs. & drained & ground coarsely
4 tbsp clarified butter (*ghee*)
½ cup powdered sugar
3 tbsp milk powder
2 tbsp milk
50 gms mixed dry fruits (eg. almonds, pistachios, cashewnuts),
  finely chopped
3 dry figs (*anjeer*), boiled in 4 tbsp water & pound when soft
1 tsp poppy seeds
2 edible silver foil (*warq*)
A dash of salt

METHOD

1. Place a heavy-bottomed pan on the stove and add 3 tbsp *ghee* and the *dal*. Stir constantly over reduced heat, to prevent sticking and scorching, till the *dal* turns a light brown. Add the sugar and stir till the sugar melts.

2. Mix the milk powder and *ghee* well in a bowl and pour into a separate pan, stirring for few seconds over medium heat. Add this to the *dal*, stirring constantly over reduced heat. Add milk and stir (if required, gradually add 1 tsp *ghee*).

3. Add the *anjeer* and stir. Add the dry fruits and stir. Sprinkle in the poppy seeds and stir again. Finally add the salt and mix well.

4. Remove onto a greased *thali* or flat dish. Smoothen the surface by rolling into a diameter of 6" and ½"thickness. Decorate with silver foil and cool for 15-20 minutes. Cut into 12 pieces (if you find it to be greasy, place on kitchen paper). Store in a tin lined with wax paper and use as required.

DAL - Foods Of India
Dal Mithais

MOONG DAL PYASAM
Mung Beans Dessert

This popular dish in south India is a semi-liquid dessert like *kheer*.

INGREDIENTS
Makes: 2 cups (approx. ½ kg.)
125 gms (½ cup) mung beans *(moong dal)*,
  pick and roast for 10 minutes and remove
4 cups water
½ cup grated fresh coconut, ground with ¼ cup water
  and squeezed in a muslin cloth to strain the milk
¼ cup brown sugar
¼ cup milk
½ tsp green cardamom powder

282

METHOD
1. Place a thick heavy-bottomed pan on fire, add *dal* and water to it. Boil well for 6-8 minutes on medium heat till the *dal* is very soft and water is almost dried up.
2. Add coconut milk and brown sugar to the boiled *dal*. Cook covered for 8-10 minutes stirring occasionally on medium heat.
3. Add milk, stir and cook covered for 6-8 minutes on medium heat stirring occasionally.
4. Add cardamom powder, mix well and cook for few minutes.
5. Remove in a serving bowl and serve hot. It also tastes good when chilled.

PURAN POLI
Sweet Lentil filled Pancakes

This is a typical festival dish from Maharashta and southern Gujarat.

INGREDIENTS
Makes: 12
For the *Puran*
125 gms (½ cup) Bengal gram (*chana dal*)
125 gms (½ cup) pigeon peas (*tuvar dal*)
½ tsp oil
4 cups water
125 gms jaggery (*gur*), pounded coarsely
½ tsp dry ginger powder (*saunth*)
½ tsp green cardamom powder

For the *Poli*
1 cup flour (*maida*), sifted
½ cup wheat flour (*atta*), sifted
A pinch of salt
1 cup water
1 tsp oil
12 tsp clarified butter (*ghee*), 1 tsp for each *poli*

METHOD
1. Place a heavy-bottomed pan on the stove and boil water with the oil in it. Add the *dal*s and cook covered till well boiled but not over-cooked or mushy.
2. Add the jaggery and cook, stirring occasionally. Scrape the sides and bottom of the pan to prevent sticking and scorching. Cook for a few minutes till the jaggery and *dal*s are well blended and no liquid oozes out of it.

3. Remove and add the cardamom and dry ginger powders and mix well.
4. Grind into a smooth lump (in case the *dal* sticks scrape with a spatula).

OR

Use a grinding stone to make the *dal* filling (*puran*) into a smooth paste.
5. Combine both the flours, salt and water and knead well to form a smooth dough.
6. Place the dough in a grinding stone and pound till a soft elastic texture is achieved (the dough should stretch into long unbroken strings).
7. Pour in 1 tsp oil while pounding the dough if it sticks to the stone. Remove.
8. Take a lime-shaped lump of flour dough between greased palms and smoothen into a round flat cake. Pat with fingers dipped in oil, to make a diameter of 3½".
9. Pressing and pulling the edges upwards with your fingers, deepen to make a pot shaped depression.

10. Take a portion of *puran* and fill the depression made in the portion of dough.
11. Gather the edges of the dough to the centre. Join and seal. With greased fingers, bend and press the sealed, pointed portion on the top.
12. Now roll the *puran poli* on a rolling board. Using light pressure on a rolling pin dredged with flour, make a diameter of 5".
13. Heat a griddle and grease it all over using a muslin cloth dipped in oil.
14. Take a *poli* in your hand and invert onto the greased griddle. When the *poli* turns firm, pour ½ tsp melted *ghee* around the edges and over the surface. Turn over and pour the remaining ½ tsp *ghee* on the surface.
15. When cooked on both sides, remove onto a dry plate and repeat the process for the remaining *puran* and dough. Keep each *poli* separate after it is cooked.
16. Place a napkin in a tin and layer with wax paper. Pile up all the cooked and cooled *poli*s. Cover the *poli*s with wax paper. Lid the tin and store.

Note You can store the *puran poli*s for a week and use as required.

TRIDALI MITHAI
Three Lentil Sweet

INGREDIENTS
Makes: ½ kg

250 gms (1 cup) mixed *dals* eg. Bengal gram *(chana dal)*, black
 beans *(urad dal)*, and mung beans *(moong dal)*, roasted in a
 heavy- bottomed dry pan till brown & cooled & ground into a thick powder)
2 tbsp *ghee*
1½ cup water
¾ cup sugar
100 gms *khoa*/readily available *khoa burfi*
50 gms mixed fruits (egg. Almonds, pistachios, cashew nuts, shredded)
1 tsp green cardamom powder
2 tsp chironjia nut *(charoli)*
1 tbsp *ghee*
2 tbsp milk
2 edible silver foil *(warq)*

METHOD
1. Put *ghee* into a heavy-bottomed pan. Add the ground *dal* flour and stir constantly to prevent sticking and scorching till brown.
2. Place water and sugar in a pan and stir constantly over reduced heat till a one-thread consistency has been achieved. Cool the sugar syrup till lukewarm.
3. Add half the shredded dry fruits to the flour and mix well. Add the *khoa/khoa burfi* and mix well. Add the *charoli*, cardamom powder and mix well. Add the sugar syrup and stir vigorously. Add *ghee* and milk and stir.
4. Remove onto a greased board/ tray. Sprinkle with the nuts and decorate with silver foils. Cool for 12-15 minutes and cut into 16 square pieces. Wipe off excess *ghee* with kitchen paper. Store in a tin lined with wax paper. Use as required.

NON-VEGETARIAN DAL DISHES

- Chana Dal Aur Gosth Ke Tukde
- Cocktail Kabab
- Dal Ande Aur Palak Ki Cutlet
- Dal Aur Ande Ke Rolls
- Dal Aur Macchi Ki Cutlet
- Dal Jhinga Cutlet
- Jhinga Aur Masoor Dal
- Masoor Dal Mutton
- Moong Dal Aur Macchi Ka Sirr
- Mutton Dalwala
- Shammi Kabab

CHANA DAL AUR GOSTH KE TUKDE
Bengal Gram with Mutton Cubes

INGREDIENTS
Serves: 4

250 gms lamb meat *(gosht)*, boneless & cubed
¾ cup Bengal gram *(chana dal)*, washed &
  soaked for 2 hrs. & drained
2 tbsp clarified butter *(ghee)*
¼ tsp asafoetida *(hing)*
1 large onion, finely chopped
2 tsp minced ginger
6 garlic cloves, minced
2 bay leaves
1 tsp coriander powder
1 tsp curry powder
1 tsp red chilli powder
¼ tsp turmeric powder
1 tsp salt
1 medium-sized tomato, finely chopped
1 tsp dry fenugreek leaves *(kasuri methi)*
1 tbsp finely chopped coriander leaves

METHOD
1. Heat the *ghee* in a pan and add the asafoetida, onion, ginger, garlic and bay leaves. Stir fry for few minutes.
2. Add *gosht*, coriander, curry, red chilli and turmeric powders. Cook for a few minutes. Add the salt, dry fenugreek leaves and tomato. Stir till fat oozes.
3. Transfer *gosht* into a pressure cooker and cook under pressure for about 8-10 minutes till ¾ done.

4. Add the *dal* and stir, mixing well. Cook under pressure for another 6-8 minutes. Allow the pressure to fall before opening the cooker.
5. Remove into a serving bowl and garnish with coriander leaves. Serve hot with *roti*s and onion salad.

COCKTAIL KABABS

INGREDIENTS

Makes: 30

500 gms minced meat *(kheema)*, cleaned & washed
125 gms (½ cup) Bengal gram *(chana dal)*, washed
  & soaked for 25-30 mins & drained

3 cloves
1" cinnamon stick
2 bay leaves
2 large cardamoms
½ cup water
1 tbsp chopped mint leaves
2" piece ginger
15 garlic flakes
(Mint, ginger & garlic to be ground into a fine paste)
¼ tsp black pepper powder
½ tsp salt
2 slices bread, soaked in water & squeezed tightly in a cloth
½ cup finely chopped coriander leaves
2 eggs
1 tbsp water
1 cup breadcrumbs
Oil for deep frying

METHOD

1. Place the *kheema*, *dal*, cloves, cinnamon, bay leaves, cardamoms, salt and water into a pressure cooker and cook under pressure for about 15-20 minutes. Allow the pressure to fall before opening the cooker. Remove, cool and drain. Discard the whole spices. Lightly squeeze and pound the meat.
2. Combine the mint-ginger-garlic paste, black pepper powder, salt, bread, coriander leaves and meat. Mix well.
3. Divide the *kabab* mixture into 30 equal portions and shape each into an oval or round.
4. Mix the egg and water and beat well to prepare egg dip.
5. Heat oil in a frying pan and dip each *kabab* into the egg dip. Coat with breadcrumbs and dust off excess crumbs.
6. Slide 3-4 *kababs* at a time into the oil. Fry basting with oil till brown and crisp.
7. Remove the *kababs* onto kitchen paper and repeat the process for the rest.
8. Place on a serving platter and serve hot with chutney or tomato ketchup.

DAL ANDE AUR PALAK KI CUTLET
Lentil, Egg & Spinach Cutlets

INGREDIENTS
Makes: 12
¼ cup Bengal gram (*chana dal*)
¼ cup mung beans (*moong dal*)
(Washed & soaked separately for 3-4 hrs. Drained & ground into a paste together with 2-3 tbsp water
1 tbsp butter
1 tsp minced ginger

DAL ANDE AUR PALAK KI CUTLET

4 garlic cloves, minced
¾ tsp minced green chillies
1 small onion, finely chopped
1 tbsp maida (*flour*)
1 tsp salt
50 gms (½ cup) spinach (*palak*), cleaned, washed & finely chopped
3 eggs (*ande*), boiled & cubed
1 tbsp finely chopped coriander leaves
1 egg, beaten & mixed with 2 tsp water.
3 tbsp breadcrumbs

METHOD

1. Place a heavy-bottomed pan on the stove and add butter. When melted, add the *dal* paste and stir constantly for a few minutes, scraping the sides and bottom of the pan to prevent sticking and scorching. Remove.
2. Place a heavy-bottomed pan on the stove and add butter. When it melts, add the ginger, garlic and green chillies. Stir fry for 1-2 minutes.
3. Add the onions and stir till light brown.
4. Add flour and stir fry till light brown.
5. Add the salt, spinach and buttered *dal* paste. Stir for a few minutes.
6. Add the eggs and coriander leaves. Mix well and stir for 1-2 minutes.
7. Remove and divide into 12 portions. Shape into small squares or shape with small cutlet moulds.
8. Dip the cutlets in the egg and coat with breadcrumbs.
9. Heat oil in a frying pan and fry 2-3 cutlets at a time till light brown.
10. Remove the cutlets onto kitchen paper and repeat the process with the remaining cutlets.
11. Place the cutlets on a serving platter and serve hot with any sauce and salad of your choice.

DAL AUR ANDE KE ROLL
Lentil & Egg Rolls

INGREDIENTS

Makes: 6

125 gms (½ cup) mixed *dals*, eg. 25 gms each of :

    Mung beans (*moong dal*)

    Pigeon peas (*tuvar dal*)

    Bengal gram (*chana dal*)

    Black beans (*urad dal*)

    Red lentil (*masoor dal*)

Washed & soaked separately for 2 hrs. & drained

¾ cup water

1 tbsp clarified butter (*ghee*)

Oil or clarified butter (*ghee*), for shallow frying

1 small onion, finely chopped

1 tsp minced ginger

4 garlic cloves, minced

1 tsp minced green chillies

1 small carrot, grated

50 gms (1 small piece) cabbage, shredded

5 French beans, finely chopped

2 tsp salt

1 tbsp finely chopped coriander leaves

1 small potato, boiled, peeled & mashed

25 gms (1 cube) cheese, grated

½ tsp black pepper powder

1 cup flour (*maida*)

2 eggs, beaten

1/8 tsp baking powder

½ - ¾ cup water

292

1 tbsp cornflour
2 tbsp water

METHOD

1. Place a heavy-bottomed saucepan on the stove and add the *dal*s and water and cook for 6-8 minutes till the *dal* becomes tender.
2. Heat *ghee* in a pan and add the onion. Stir fry till light brown.
3. Add the ginger, garlic and green chillies. Stir fry for a minute or two.
4. Add the carrot, cabbage, beans and salt.
5. Add the *dal*s, coriander leaves, potato, cheese and black pepper powder. Stir constantly, scraping the sides and bottom of the pan to prevent sticking and scorching. Cook for a few minutes till well mixed. Remove.
6. Divide the filling into 6 portions and make rolls of 6" length.
7. Place the flour, eggs, baking powder, salt and water in a bowl and beat well till well mixed into a thin batter.
8. Heat a griddle and grease it with butter. Spread a ladleful of batter to form a thin round disc of 6-7" diameter.
9. Cook on reduced heat, turning once. Smear butter around the edges and on the surface. When cooked, remove. Repeat the process with the remaining batter.
10. Place the cooked side of the pancake on top on a wooden board and smear the paste lightly.
11. Place a roll on the pancake and turn over the pancake into a roll. Roll tightly by pressing the edges inwards and sealing all the sides with the paste.
12. Repeat the process with the remaining pancakes and *dal* rolls.
13. Heat oil in a frying pan and fry 2-3 rolls at a time till light brown. (If desired, you can shallow fry in *ghee*/butter on a non stick pan.)
14. Remove onto a serving dish and serve hot.

DAL AUR MACHHI KI CUTLET
Lentil & Fish Cutlets

INGREDIENTS

Makes: 16

250 gms (4 pieces) fish fillets (*rawas*/salmon), washed,
  steamed for 5 mins, cooled & mashed

3 tbsp mixed *dals*, eg. 1 tbsp each of:

Pigeon peas (*tuvar dal*)

Red lentil (*masoor dal*)

Bengal gram (*chana dal*)

(Soaked for 2 hrs. & drained & ground into a smooth paste)

1 tbsp clarified butter (*ghee)*

1 small onion, finely chopped

1 tsp minced ginger

4 garlic cloves, minced

1 tbsp grated dry coconut

4 whole red chillies

1 tsp poppy seeds (*khus-khus*)

(Coconut, chillies & poppy seeds ground to a powder)

1 tsp curry powder (refer Contents)

1 tsp salt

2 tbsp finely chopped coriander leaves

2 eggs, beaten

6 tbsp breadcrumbs

Oil for frying

294

METHOD

1. Heat *ghee* in a pan and add the onion. Fry till translucent.
2. Add the ginger and garlic and stir till the onion is light brown.
3. Add the ground powder and stir for a minute or two.
4. Add the ground *dal paste*, curry powder and salt. Stir, constantly scraping the sides and bottom of the pan to prevent sticking and scorching.
5. Add the mashed fish and coriander leaves. Stir gently for a minute or two, then remove.
6. Add 2-3 tbsp beaten egg to the fish mixture and mix well.
7. Divide into 16 portions. Make round balls and dip them in the remaining beaten egg. Coat with breadcrumbs and shape into ovals. Dust off excess breadcrumbs.
8. Heat oil in a frying pan and fry 2-3 cutlets at a time till golden brown.
9. Remove the cutlets onto kitchen paper.
10. Place the cutlets on a serving platter and serve hot with salad and/or French fries.

DAL JHINGA CUTLET
Lentil & Prawn Cutlets

INGREDIENTS

Makes: 12

4 tbsp mixed *dals*, 1 tbsp each of:
   Pigeon peas (*tuvar dal*)
   Mung beans (*moong dal*)
   Red lentil (*masoor dal*)
   Bengal gram (*chana dal*)
(Washed & soaked separately for 2 hrs. & drained & ground into a coarse paste)
150 gms prawns (*jhinga*), shelled, washed, slit, deveined & washed again
A pinch of turmeric powder
1 tsp salt
4 tbsp oil & for deep frying
1 medium-sized onion, finely chopped
1 tsp minced ginger
4 garlic cloves, minced
4 whole red chillies, boiled in ¼ cup water till the water dries, then coarsely pounded
2 tbsp grated fresh coconut
2 tbsp finely chopped coriander leaves
4 tbsp cornflour
4 tbsp *maida* (flour)
¼ tsp baking powder
6 tbsp water
6 tbsp breadcrumbs

METHOD

1. Heat oil in a pan and add the prawns, salt, turmeric powder. Sauté for 1-2 minutes. Remove, squeeze and pound flat.
2. Place a heavy-bottomed pan on the stove and add oil and the onions. Stir fry till the onion turns translucent. Add the ginger and garlic and stir for a minute.
3. Add the *dal* paste, red chillies, coconut, coriander leaves and salt. Stir constantly, scraping the sides and bottom of the pan to prevent sticking and scorching, till cooked through.
4. Add the prawns and mix well. Remove and divide into 12 portions.
5. Combine both the flours, salt, baking powder and water in a bowl and mix well the batter.
6. Heat oil in a frying pan. Shape each portion into a round or oval but slightly flattened shape and dip in the batter. Coat with breadcrumbs. Dust off excess breadcrumbs.
7. Slide 2-3 cutlets at a time into the oil and fry, basting with the oil, till the cutlets turn golden brown.
8. Remove the cutlets onto kitchen paper.
9. Place the cutlets on a serving platter and serve hot with any salad.

JHINGA AUR MASOOR DAL.
Prawns with Red Lentil

INGREDIENTS
Serves: 6

125 gms (1/2 cup) *masoor dal* (red lentil), picked, washed,
  soaked in sufficient water for ½ an hr. drained
1 tbsp oil
250 gms medium prawns, shelled, slitted, deveined, washed, rubbed
  with ¼ tsp turmeric powder and 1 tsp coarse salt and kept for 8-10 mins.
4 tbsp oil
1 medium potato, boiled, peeled, cubed and fried
1 medium onion, finely chopped
1 tsp minced ginger
4 garlic cloves, minced
½ tsp minced green chillies
4 whole red chillies, boiled in ¼ cup water till water dries and coarsely
pounded
¼ tsp turmeric powder
1 tsp salt
1 tsp lime juice
1 cup coconut milk (recipe given)
1 cup water

METHOD
1. Heat oil in a pan, squeeze the prawns lightly and sauté for 1-2 minutes.
    Remove.
2. Place a heavy-bottomed pan on the stove and add oil and the onions. Stir
    fry till light brown.
3. Add the ginger, garlic and green chillies. Stir fry for a minute.
4. Add the whole red chillies, turmeric powder and *dal*. Stir and mix well for
    3-4 minutes.

5. Add the potatoes and stir for 1-2 minutes.
6. Add the prawns and stir for 2-3 minutes.
7. Add the salt, lime juice and coconut milk. Mix well.
8. Gradually add water, stirring continuously. Simmer covered on reduced heat for 6-8 minutes.
9. Remove into a serving bowl and serve hot with *roti*s or rice.

MASOOR DAL MUTTON
Red Lentil & Mutton

INGREDIENTS
Serves: 6
½ kg mutton (lamb meat or *gosht)* cut into 2" pieces
200 gms red lentil (*masoor dal*), washed
2 tbsp clarified butter (*ghee*)
3 medium-sized onions, finely chopped
2 tsp ginger paste
2 tsp garlic paste

For the *Masala*
6 tbsp grated fresh coconut
1 tsp poppy seeds (*khus-khus*)
6 whole red chillies
(Ground to a fine paste)
3 tbsp peanuts
4 tbsp curd, whisked
2 medium-sized tomatoes, blanched
1½ tsp salt
¼ tsp turmeric powder

2 tsp curry powder (refer Contents)
2 cups water
2 tbsp finely chopped coriander leaves

METHOD

1. Heat *ghee* in a saucepan and add the onions. Stir till half-cooked.
2. Add the ginger and garlic. Stir till the onions turn light brown.
3. Add the ground *masala* and stir for 1-2 minutes.
4. Add the meat pieces and stir for 4-5 minutes.
5. Add the curd and tomatoes and stir for a few minutes.
6. Add salt and the turmeric and curry powders. Stir.
7. Gradually add water and coriander leaves and cook covered, stirring occasionally, for 20-25 minutes on reduced heat till the *ghee* oozes out and the mutton is coated with the *masala*.
8. When the mutton is ¾th done and gravy has become thick, add the *dal*. Mix well.
9. Cook covered on reduced heat, stirring occasionally, till the meat and *dal* are both tender, well mixed and have a semi-liquid consistency.
10. Remove and serve hot with *chapatis* or plain boiled rice.

MOONG DAL AUR MACHHI KA SIRR
Mung Beans & Fish Head Curry

INGREDIENTS
Serves: 4

125 gms (½ cup) mung beans (*moong dal*),
  washed & soaked for ½ hr. & drained. Preserve the water.
300 gms (6 pieces) fish head (preferably *Rohu* or *Katla*), washed,
cleaned & marinated with 2 tsp coarse salt and ½ tsp turmeric
  powder rubbed in well & left for 25-30 mins.
6 tbsp oil, preferably mustard oil *(sarson ka tel)*
3 cloves
4 bay leaves
1" cinnamon stick
1 large onion, finely chopped
1 large onion, ground to paste
1½ tsp minced ginger
6 garlic cloves, minced
1 tsp minced green chillies
1 tsp red chilli powder
1 tsp *garam masala* powder
1 tsp cumin powder
1/8 tsp turmeric powder
1 tsp salt
½ tsp sugar
1 tbsp finely chopped coriander leaves

METHOD

1. Place a heavy-bottomed pan on the stove and add oil, the cloves, cinnamon, bay leaves and onions (chopped and paste). Stir fry till the onion is translucent.
2. Add the ginger, garlic and green chillies. Stir fry for a few seconds.
3. Add the fish head pieces, red chilli, *garam masala*, cumin and turmeric powders, salt and sugar. Mix well and stir for 4-5 minutes.
4. Add the *dal* and coriander leaves and stir for 1-2 minutes.
5. Add the preserved *dal* water and simmer covered for 5-6 minutes on reduced heat till a semi-liquid consistency has been achieved.
6. Remove into a serving bowl and serve hot with rice.

302

MUTTON DALWALA
Lentil with Mutton

INGREDIENTS
Serves: 6
For the *Dal*
250 gms (1 cup) Bengal gram (*chana dal)*, washed
  & soaked for 20-25 mins & drained
¼ tsp turmeric powder
½ tsp salt
1 cup water

For the Mutton
1 kg mutton (Lamb meat or *gosht)*, cleaned & washed
8 tbsp oil
2 bay leaves
6 cloves

2" cinnamon stick
6 green cardamoms, bruised
4 black cardamoms, bruised
3 medium-sized onions
2" piece ginger
25 garlic flakes
(Onions, ginger and garlic to be ground into a fine paste)
2 medium-sized tomatoes, blanched and puréed
½ cup curd, whisked
4 whole red chillies, roasted
1 tbsp coriander seeds, roasted
(Whole red chillies, coriander seeds & 2 tbsp water, ground into a smooth paste)
½ tsp *garam masala* powder
1½ tsp salt
3 cups water

For the Garnish
2 tbsp finely chopped coriander leaves
½ tsp Cinnamon powder
½ tsp black pepper powder

METHOD
1. Boil *dal* with salt and turmeric powder with 1 cup water. When done, remove from fire, drain and set aside.
2. Heat oil in a pan and add the bay leaves, cloves, cinnamon stick and both the cardamoms. Stir for 1-2 minutes.
3. Add the onion-ginger-garlic paste. Stir fry for 2-4 minutes.
4. Add the tomato purée and curd. Stir for a few minutes.
5. Add the mutton and stir for a few minutes.
6. Add the red chilli-coriander paste and stir.

7. Add the *garam masala* powder and salt and stir.
8. Gradually add water and cook covered, stirring occasionally, for 25-30 minutes on reduced heat, till oil oozes and the mutton is coated with *masala*.
9. When the water reduces and the mutton is half-cooked, gradually add 1 cup more hot water, if required, stirring continuously. Cook covered on reduced heat till the mutton is tender and done.

OR

Transfer the mutton into a pressure cooker and cook under pressure for 15-20 minutes on medium heat and for 10 minutes on reduced heat. Cool, open lid and cook uncovered on medium heat for 8-10 minutes till the gravy becomes thick and the water is absorbed.

10. Add half the boiled *dal.* Stir for 1 – 2 minutes.
11. Remove into a serving bowl and garnish with the remaining boiled *dal* and coriander leaves.
12. Sprinkle cinnamon and black pepper powders and serve hot with *chapatis.*

SHAMMI KABAB
Minced Mutton Kababs

INGREDIENTS
Makes: 24
1 kg minced meat *(kheema)*, cleaned and washed
250 gms (1 cup) Bengal gram *(chana dal)*, washed
  & soaked for 1 hr. & drained
1 tsp salt
½ cup water

For the *Masala*
¾ tsp black cardamom powder
1 tsp cloves
1 tsp cinnamon powder
2″ piece ginger
30 garlic flakes
8 green chillies
(Ginger, garlic & green chillies ground into a fine paste)
½ tsp black cumin seeds (*shahjeera*)
½ tsp salt
1 egg yolk, whisked

For the Filling
1 tbsp oil
2 medium-sized onions, finely chopped
2 tsp shredded ginger
1 tbsp raisins
¾ tbsp blanched & shredded almonds
¼ tsp *garam masala* powder
¼ tsp salt
2 tsp lime juice
½ tbsp finely chopped mint leaves
2 tbsp finely chopped coriander leaves
Clarified butter (*ghee*)/oil for shallow frying

METHOD
1. Combine the *kheema*, *dal*, salt and water in a pressure cooker and cook under pressure for about 15-20 minutes. Allow the pressure to fall before opening the cooker. Remove, drain and lightly pound the *kheema* and *dal*.
2. Combine all the *masala* ingredients and mix well.
3. Add the *kheema & dal mixture* to *masala* and mix thoroughly. Divide the mixture into 24 portions. Set aside.

4. Heat oil in a pan and add all the Filling ingredients.
5. Sauté for few minutes and remove. Divide into 24 portions.
6. Flatten each portion of *kheema dal masala* mixture on your palm and place a portion of filling in the centre. Cover the filling on all sides. Then seal and shape into round *kabab*s. Press the round *kabab* in between the palms to flatten to a telescopic round.
7. Heat *ghee*/oil in a frying pan and shallow fry 3-4 *kabab*s at a time on both sides, till light brown.
8. Remove onto a serving dish and serve hot with a chutney of your choice.

306

GLOSSARY OF TERMS
HINDI TO ENGLISH

Aam	: Mango
Adrak	: Ginger
Ajwain	: Carum Seeds
Aloo	: Potato
Amchur	: Mango Powder
Anardana	: Pomegranate Seed
Anda	: Egg
Anjeer	: Fig
Arbi	: Colocasia
Badam	: Almonds
Badi Ilaichi	: Big Cardamom
Baigan	: Aubergine
Bajri Ka Atta	: Millet Flour
Besan	: Bengal Gram Flour
Bhindi	: Ladies Finger
Bhopla	: Pumpkin
Bhura Chana	: Black Chickpeas
Bhutta	: Corn Cobb
Chana	: Roasted Bengal Gram
Chana Dal	: Bengal Gram
Chana Chor Garam	: Pressed Bengal Gram
Charoli	: Chironji Nut
Chavli /Lobia	: Cow Peas
Chawal	: Rice
Char Magaz	: Kernel Seeds
Chingri	: Prawns
Churi Varially	: Sweet Aniseed
Dahi	: Curd
Daalia	: Split, husked, roasted Bengal Gram
Dalia	: Coarse Wheat Flour
Dalchini	: Cinnamon

Dhania Dal	: Coriander Seeds
Dhania Patta	: Coriander Leaf
Dhania Powder	: Coriander Powder
Dhingri /Khumb	: Mushroom
Farsan	: Mix of Salted & Fried Items of Bengal Gram
Fransbean	: French Beans
Gajar	: Carrot
Gaund	: Edible Gum
Ghee	: Clarified butter
Gosht	: Lamb / Mutton
Gur	: Jaggery
Hara Pyaaz	: Spring Onion
Hari Ilaichi	: Green Cardamom
Hari Mirch	: Green Chilli
Hing	: Asafoetida
Imli	: Tamarind
Jaifal	: Nutmeg
Javitri	: Mace
Jawari Atta	: Milo Flour
Jeera	: Cumin Seeds
Jhinga	: Prawns
Kabuli Chana	: White Chickpeas
Kadi Patta	: Curry Leaves
Kaju	: Cashewnuts
Kakdi	: Cucumber
Kala Chana Chor Garam	: Pressed Black Chickpeas
Kala Jeera / Shahjeera	: Black Cumin Seeds
Kala Namak	: Black Salt
Kalaunji	: Black Onion Seeds
Kali Mirch	: Black Pepper

Hindi	English	Hindi	English
Kamal Kakdi	: Lotus Stem	*Phool Gobi*	: Cauliflower
Karela	: Bitter Gourd	*Pista*	: Pistachio
Kasuri Methi	: Dried Fenugreek Leaves	*Pudina*	: Mint
		Pyaaz	: Onion
Khajur	: Date	*Rai*	: Mustard Seeds
Kheema	: Mince (Meat, Eggs, etc)	*Rajma*	: Red Kidney Beans
Khoa	: Dried Milk, unsweetened	*Rawa*	: Semolina
Khuskhus	: Poppy Seeds	*Roti*	: Flat-rolled Indian Bread
Kishmish	: Raisin	*Sabut Hing*	: Whole Asafoetida
Kokum	: Garciana Indica	*Sabut Kali Mirch*	: Peppercorn
Lasun	: Garlic	*Sabut Masoor*	: Whole Black Lentils
Lauki / Dudhi	: Bottle Gourd	*Sabut Moong*	: Whole Mung Beans
Laung	: Clove	*Sabut Urad*	: Whole Black Beans
Machhi	: Fish	*Salad Patta*	: Lettuce Leaves
Maida	: Refined Wheat Flour	*Sali*	: Fried Potato Juliennes
Makai Ka Atta	: Corn Flour	*Sarson Ka Tel*	: Mustard Oil
Makhana	: Fox Nuts	*Saunf*	: Aniseed / Fennel
Makhkhan	: White Butter, unsalted	*Saunth*	: Ginger Powder
Masoor Dal	: Red Lentils	*Sev*	: Fried Gram Flour Strings
Matar	: Green Peas		
Matki	: Moth Beans	*Shakarkand*	: Sweet Potato
Methi	: Fresh Fenugreek Leaves	*Shakkar*	: Sugar
		Simla Mirch	: Capsicum
Methi Dana	: Fenugreek Seeds	*Sukha Dhania Dana*	: Coriander Seeds
Mooli	: Radish	*Sukhi Lal Mirch*	: Sundried Red Chilli
Moong Dal	: Mung Bean Lentil	*Suran*	: Yam
Moong Dal Chhilka	: Split Mung Beans	*Tamatar*	: Tomato
Munga/ Sengue/Senghi	: Drumstick	*Tawa*	: Griddle
Mungfalli	: Peanuts /Groundnuts	*Tej Patta*	: Bay Leaf
Murmura	: Puffed Rice	*Til*	: Sesame Seeds
Namak	: Salt	*Turi*	: Ridge Gourd
Nariyal	: Coconut	*Turmeric*	: Haldi
Neebu	: Lime / Lemon	*Tuvar Dal*	: Pigeon Peas
Palak	: Spinach	*Ukhada Chawal*	: Boiled Rice
Paneer	: Cottage Cheese	*Urad Dal*	: Black Beans
Pao	: Buns	*Urad Dal Chhilka*	: Split Black Beans
Patta Gobi	: Cabbage	*Val*	: Field Beans
Poha	: Pressed Rice	*Varq*	: Edible Silver Leaf

308

GLOSSARY OF TERMS
ENGLISH TO HINDI

Almonds	: Badam	Coriander Powder	: Dhania Powder
Aniseed / Fennel	: Saunf	Coriander Seed	: Sukha Dhania Dana
Asafoetida	: Hing	Coriander Seeds	: Dhania Dal
Aubergine	: Baigan	Corn Cobb	: Bhutta
Bay Leaf	: Tej Patta	Corn Flour	: Makai Ka Atta
Bengal Gram	: Chana Dal	Cottage Cheese	: Paneer
Bengal Gram Flour	: Besan	Cow Peas	: Chavli /Lobia
Bitter Gourd	: Karela	Cucumber	: Kakdi
Black Beans	: Urad Dal	Cumin Seeds	Jeera
Black Cardamom	: Badi Ilaichi	Curd	: Dahi
Black Chickpeas	: Bhura Chana	Curry Leaves	: Kadi Patta
Black Cumin	: Kala Jeera/Shahjeera	Date	: Khajur
Black Onion Seeds	: Kalonji	Dried Fenugreek Leaves	: Kasuri Methi
Black Pepper	: Kali Mirch	Dried Peas, Green/White	: Vatana
Black Salt	: Kala/Sendhya Namak	Drumstick	: Munga /Senghi/Sengue
Boiled Rice	: Ukhada Chawal	Edible Gum	: Gaund
Bottle Gourd	: Dudhi / Lauki	Edible Silver Leaf	: Varq
Bread Rolls/Buns	: Pao	Egg	: Anda
Butter	: Namkeen Makhkhan	Fenugreek Seeds	: Methi Dana
Cabbage	: Patta Gobi	Field Beans	: Val
Capsicum	: Simla Mirch	Fig	: Anjeer
Carrot	: Gajar	Fish	: Machchi
Carum Seeds	: Ajwain	Fox Nuts	: Makhana
Cashewnuts	: Kaju	French Beans	: Fransbean
Cauliflower	: Phool Gobi	Fresh Fenugreek Leaves	: Methi
Chironji Nuts	: Charoli	Garciana Indica	: Kokum
Cinnamon	: Dalchini	Garlic	: Lasun/Lassan
Clarified Butter	: Ghee	Ginger	: Adrak
Clove	: Laung	Ginger Powder	: Saunth
Coarse Broken Wheat	: Dalia	Green Cardamom	: Hari/Chhoti Ilaichi
Coconut	: Nariyal	Green Chilli	: Hari Mirch
Colocassia	: Arbi	Green Peas	: Matar
Coriander Leaves	: Dhania Patta		

Griddle	: Tawa	Raisin	: Kishmish
Groundnuts/Peanuts	: Mungfalli	Red Kidney Beans	: Rajma
Jaggery	: Gur	Red Lentil	: Masoor Dal
Kernel Seeds	: Char Magaz	Refined Wheat Flour	: Maida
Lady Fingers	: Bhindi	Rice	: Chawal
Lamb Meat/Mutton	: Gosht	Ridge Gourd	: Turi
Lettuce	: Salad Patta	Roasted Bengal Gram	: Chana
Lime/Lemon	: Neebu	Salt	: Namak
Lotus Stem	: Kamal Kakdi	Semolina	: Rawa
Mace	: Javitri	Sesame Seeds	: Til
Mango	: Aam	Spinach	: Palak
Mango Powder	: Amchur	Split Black Beans	: Urad Dal Chhilka
Millet Flour	: Bajri Ka Atta	Split-Husked-Roasted	
Milo Flour	: Jawari Ka Atta	Bengal Gram	: Daalia
Minced Meat	: Kheema	Split Mung Beans	: Mung Dal Chhilka
Mint	: Pudina	Spring Onion	: Hara Pyaaz
Moth Beans	: Matki	Sugar	: Shakkar
Mung Bean Lentil	: Moong Dal	Sweet Aniseed	: Churi Varially
Mushroom	: Dhingri/Khumb	Sweet Potato	: Shakarkand
Mustard Seeds	: Rai	Tamarind	: Imli
Mustard Oil	: Sarson Ka Tel	Tomato	: Tamatar/Tamater
Nutmeg	: Jaifal	Tamarind	: Imli
Onion	: Pyaaz	Turmeric	: Haldi
Pressed Bengal Gram	: Chana Chor Garam	White Butter	: Makhkhan
Pressed Black Chickpeas	: Kala Chana Chor Garam	White Chickpeas	: Kabuli Chana
		Whole Asafoetida	: Sabut Hing
Pigeon Peas	: Tuval Dal	Whole Black Beans	: Sabut Urad
Pistachio	: Pista	Whole Black Lentils	: Saboot Masoor
Pomegranate Seeds	: Anardana	Whole Mung Beans	: Sabut Moong
Poppy Seeds	: Khuskhus	Whole Red Chilli	: Sukhi Lal Mirch
Potato	: Aloo	Yam	: Suran
Pressed Rice	: Poha		
Puffed Rice	: Murmura		
Prawns	: Jhinga /Chingri		
Pumpkin	: Bhopla		
Radish	: Mooli		

310

Sizes & Measures

Sizes of vegetables

Small   : 50 gms. approx.

Medium   : 100 gms. approx.

Large   : 150 gms. approx.

Water 1 cup   : 225 ml.

Measures

- 1 tsp (teaspoon)   = 5 ml
- 1tbsp (tablespoon)   = 3 tsp
- A Pinch = 1/8 tsp (literally a pinch)
- A dash = 1 – 2 drops
- The cup measure in this book is of 8 oz. cup (225 ml)
- All spoon and cup measures are level unless and otherwise indicated
- Size of all the vegetables is medium unless and otherwise indicated

ACKNOWLEDGEMENTS

I must thank Leadstart Publishing for reposing faith in me as an author for such an uncommon subject as *Dal*. When I ventured into writing this book, I realised that despite my many years of cooking and teaching, that this subject is both and challenging.

Vanita and Jimmy took painstaking notes of my experiments and helped to convert them into recipes and then prepared the final manuscript on my computer. Thank you both.

My maid Jeeja, was as excited as I and was part of my kitchen team. Without her support in organising the equipment, I could not have finished my experiments in the record time that I did. I thank Jeeja for her efforts.

Aman, my young neighbour in Mumbai, barely in his 20s, was an excellent critic of my dishes as they were made again and again till they turned out just right. Thank you Amandeep Singh.

My thanks to Chandralekha Maitra of Leadstart Publishing, for editing the manuscript so skilfully and making it presentable and to Suhita Mitra, for the wonderful illustrations and attractive cover.

Finally, my deepest gratitude goes to my husband, Asoka, without whose continuous encouragement and back-office support, this book would not have been possible.

Printed in Great Britain
by Amazon